bOHEMIAN hEART

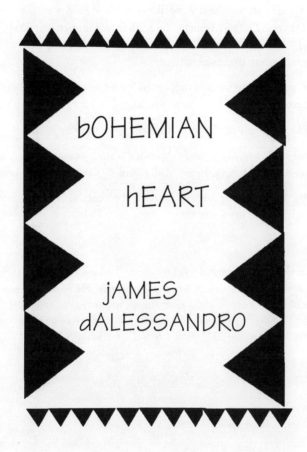

bOHEMIAN

hEART

jAMES dALESSANDRO

ST. MARTIN'S PRESS

ACKNOWLEDGMENTS

To Jan Golab and Maitland Zane, for their great help with my story; to Tracy Dewey, Thomas Cahal, Meredith and Maurice Bar-David, Pat and Bud Cochran, and Michael Pariser, all of whom helped with the preparation of my manuscript.

Thanks for two decades of support to Neal Coonerty of the Bookshop Santa Cruz.

Thanks to John Paul DeJoria for more help than he knows.

Special thanks to my great St. Martin's editor, Reagan Arthur, and to dear friend and manager, Peter Miller, and to the great Paul Aratow.

Finally, to Pamela and Rudy Durand, for years of love and support, and for giving me my great title.

Design by Basha Zapatka

Library of Congress Cataloging-in-Publication Data

Dalessandro, James.
    Bohemian heart/James Dalessandro.
        p. cm.
    "A Thomas Dunne book."
    ISBN 0-312-09756-5
    1. Private investigators—California—San Francisco—Fiction.
2. San Francisco (Calif.)—Fiction. I. Title.
PS3544.A4164B6   1993
813' .54—dc20   93-25499
                                                  CIP

First edition: September 1993
10 9 8 7 6 5 4 3 2

To my wife, Katie, my friend, my believer, my personal coach and editor, and the best person I know. I'm just thrilled to be married to you.

1

San Francisco had been a month without fog. From the picture window of my house just below Coit Tower, I could see across Cow Hollow, the Marina, the Presidio, all the way to the Golden Gate. No fog, not even a dirty rumor.

I lived in the third-oldest Victorian on Telegraph Hill, built by my great-grandfather, bequeathed to me by my parents. In my forty years of bridge watching, I couldn't remember an entire May without the afternoon fog.

Pulling on my leather jacket and gloves, I grabbed my motorcycle helmet, slipped a 9mm Walther and a spare clip into a special pocket sewn inside my jacket, bounded down a hidden stairway from my bedroom loft on the fourth floor, emerging in the office at ground level. As I exited to the street, I flipped over the sign saying BE BACK, I HOPE beneath the gold-stenciled CITY LIGHTS DETECTIVE AGENCY.

Standing on the pegs of my antediluvian Norton Commando 750 as I descended Lombard Street, I double-checked the bridge. No fog. A bad omen.

I charged up Lombard on the other side of Columbus until it became one way, "the world's crookedest street," zigged through a dozen camera-wielding tourists, turned left, crossed Union Street and passed Grace Cathedral on Nob Hill. Then I leaned back in the saddle as I dropped down one of the steepest descents in the city, Jones Street into the Tenderloin.

The Tenderloin may be the only neighborhood in the world named for police corruption. During the time my great-grandfather and grandfather walked this beat, after the Great Earthquake, the thirty square blocks between City Hall and Union Square were the center cut, the sweet meat for bribes and grafts for the old SFPD. The Tenderloin.

I made Turk Street in three minutes flat, parked the Norton in a lot where I knew the attendant, Enrique, a Guatemalan refugee. I tipped him to keep an eye on it. The bike wasn't so great, but neither was the neighborhood; they'd steal your gold teeth if you yawned too long.

On one corner stood a fine specimen of Tenderloin manhood: curly blond hair, pork chop sideburns, one-piece dirty white jumpsuit with two-foot elephant bell-bottoms, huge red flame patterns up the inside of each thigh pointing toward a knockwurst stuffed in the bikini briefs outlined underneath. He trolled discolike for passing females and looked genuinely surprised when they sped up or crossed the street.

A taxi stopped in front of the Turk Street a.k.a. Jerk Street Showcase, and a gray-suited businessman rushed inside to catch the patriotic double bill, *Fox Hole Boys* and *Rear Admiral.* Between screenings, some mother's son would bump and grind his way through a live display of the family heirlooms as the distinguished audience cheered, drawers to their knees, choking each other's chickens.

Even sin ain't what it used to be.

I reached the corner of Mason and Eddy streets where my newest client, Sergei Kostonoviev, senior attaché to the Russian consulate, had last seen his burgundy limousine. Five feet away was a sign that said NO PARKING—TOW AWAY ZONE.

I'm in the stupidity business. If it wasn't for stupidity, guys like me would be out of work; stupidity and bad luck, the latter usually the excuse for the former.

Directly across the street was an all-night coffee shop named the Tide-E Diner, which it wasn't. I jaywalked and entered. A tinkling bell announced my arrival.

Immediately the heavy, repressive air engulfed me, the ether of bad food and sadder stories. A chef who might have cooked the Last Supper chain-smoked over a pile of plastic eggs, refried flounder, frozen potatoes in 40-weight.

I scanned the place quickly. Three whores of indeterminate age and origin, dressed in last year's Christmas wrappings. One female mumbler, serious enough in muted discourse to be lecturing Napoleon. One flaxen-haired man with the shape and texture of a crouton left floating in onion soup too long, the crust a cheap blue suit.

In the corner a dozen feet away was a Samoan drag queen, big enough to have played linebacker in the NFL, missing a left eye, which was now held shut by a Band-Aid. The drag queen tilted faded black-leather pumps, opening up his/her legs, hiked a rainbow-colored muumuu, and offered me a glimpse of stretch-marked brown thigh. He/she smiled an invitation. I smiled a polite decline.

They all stared as I headed to the counter.

The waitress wore the kind of stiff white uniform most often found on emergency room nurses, a dime-store wedding ring to keep the hustlers away, and a name tag that said VIVIAN. I should have guessed.

"Excuse me, ma'am, but were you working yesterday afternoon about four o'clock?" I asked.

"Every afternoon for the last sixteen years." She looked me up and down. "Cop?"

"Private investigator." When she didn't bite, I pulled out my ID and handed it over. The rest of the room was now either very interested or very nervous.

" 'Francis Fagen, private investigator,' " she read aloud. "What can I do for you, Francis?"

"Frankie. Did you happen to notice a burgundy limousine parked outside yesterday afternoon at about four?"

That brought a smile to Vivian's face. "Yeah, I seen it." She turned to the three whores and said, "This guy's a private detective; he wants to know if we seen that burgundy limousine."

They practically tripped over their tongues getting the story out.

"You talking about Uncle Boris, that guy from the Russian embassy?" Russian consulate, but I wasn't about to stop them when they were on a roll.

"Dude's here every *day*, girls damn near bust an ankle gettin' to that sucker. No wonder them people over there ain't got no food, the money that dude spends on pussy."

While they treated themselves to a forced laughing fit, a tow truck pulled up directly across the street and hooked a 1976 Buick Le Sabre.

"Did you see the limousine get towed yesterday?" I asked Vivian.

"I sure did. He parked it outside there about ten to four. Him and his chauffeur talked to two girls, then they got out and went to the Argonaut Hotel a coupla doors up. I know, 'cause I said to a customer, you think that fool would know by now that this street is a towing zone from four to six. That's the first one they grabbed."

"You didn't happen to notice the name of the towing company, did you?"

"Sure did," said Vivian, proud of her amateur detective work. "Truck said San Andreas Towing right on the side."

I thanked her and laid a ten-dollar bill on the table. She took it, squinting as she stared at me.

"Were you that cop they called Peekaboo Frankie Fagen?"

"Different Frankie Fagen," I lied, "little shorter, better-looking." Vivian smiled and knew better. I nodded at the still cackling streetwalkers and left.

After three attempts I found a pay phone that hadn't been vandalized and called my cousin Jimmy, the owner of a car dealership on Van Ness, and made arrangements to borrow a customized van for a few hours. Then I called Henry Borowski, one of the three detectives who worked for me. I asked him to pick up the van and meet me at my garage.

I was there and waiting only five minutes when he arrived. I told him Kostonoviev's limo had disappeared the previous afternoon, and that the towing company denied they had ever seen it. A check of police files over the past six months revealed eighteen complaints against the company for stripped or missing vehicles.

"What vas Russki bastard do-hink on Eddy Street ven consulate is vay hover in Pacific Heights?" He said *Heights* like he was coughing up a fur ball.

"Doing research on Western culture." We both laughed.

I checked my list: flashlight, blanket, water, camera, plastic pot to piss in if necessary—the life of a private detective is very exotic, very exciting—portable phone, half a Genoa salami sandwich from Molinari's deli and a copy of Henry Miller's *Time of the Assassins*.

I decided not to change my .32 Walther for the nickle-plated .45, but just for good measure I strapped my backup .380 to my left ankle. Henry climbed behind the wheel as we headed back to Eddy Street.

Henry is my bulldog, the kind of detective every agency needs: tough, unshakable. At twenty, a member of the Hungarian weight lifting team, he supported his Czech neighbors during the 1968 Prague Spring Revolt. The Russians decided to make an example of him and hung him from a makeshift gallows in a Budapest square.

But Henry's neck was so strong he wouldn't die. He hung from the noose for five minutes before the unnerved Russian commandant cut him down. For rehabilitation, they made him a police officer. After sixteen years on the Prague police force, he defected to the U.S. and had worked for me ever since.

Henry turned his head as we made the left onto Eddy Street, and I could see the cruel necklace the rope had left around his throat above the collar he always kept buttoned. He parked the van in the tow-away zone, pulled his camera out of his pocket, and said, "I vait at home till you call if need me."

As he climbed out, he added, "Russian hattaché's is all KGB stooge. You find lhimo you find himportant papers meh-hebe you ghet Congress Medal Honor." Only death would end the Cold War for Henry.

As Henry found a discreet place from which to photograph the van and the tow truck when it arrived, I quickly climbed in back and crawled under the fold-down seat. Switching on my flashlight, I stuck screwdrivers in the seat's hinges and between the two back doors so they couldn't be opened from the outside. At 5:47 I heard the tow truck pull up. The door slammed, and the driver started to snake out the cable and hook up the van. The front tilted up, and we lurched forward.

I've sailed a lot on San Francisco Bay, often in rough seas, but nothing compared with being slammed from side to side as the van took a half dozen curves on one wheel. At 5:56, after ascending a steep ramp, we screeched to a halt and the driver dropped the van, which landed with brain-damaging impact. I had no idea where I was—or what I was doing. That, I figured, was the epitome of what being a private detective is all about.

In fiction, a balding potbellied PI walks into a room wearing a suit from the George Raft/JC Penney collection and women with the bodies of Daisy Mae instantly start taking their clothes off. Or a Holmes-like character looks at the stain on a suspect's shirt and immediately knows thirteen crucial facts the cops missed in two months of hard work.

Me, I was fit, forty, and handsome as vacation pay. All that had gotten me recently was a come-on from a Samoan drag queen and The Case of the Missing Limo.

To me, being a private detective is somewhere between a garbage collector, a spear catcher, and a Peeping Tom. If the boredom doesn't kill you, one of the bad guys might.

I lifted the back seat above my head and eased my way out. The heavy, muted blast of a cargo vessel came from outside the wall to my right. When the main towing garage filled during afternoon rush hour, they took the overflow to some of the Embarcadero warehouses that stand on pilings over the Bay. At least I knew where I was.

I slid the van door open, jumped out, and stood for a minute, looking and listening. There was nothing but long rows of cars on the floor I was on, so I dashed down the steps to the first floor.

Up front was the check-in area where an endless stream of the world's most disgruntled people came to pay the seventy-eight-dollar towing fees, receive their sixty-dollar traffic ticket, and get less respect than your average serial killer. In the back was another cavernous area, nearly a city block long, where two or three hundred more vehicles were parked. At the end there were two enormous steel doors.

I ducked around the end of a row of cars, narrowly missing being seen by an employee who'd come to fetch one that someone had claimed up front. As soon as he disappeared, I sprinted toward the steel doors. I'd done this kind of thing a thousand times, and as stupid as this escapade seemed, my heart still pounded.

The doors were held fast by double padlocks. I snuck back down the aisle, up the stairs, and back into the van. Once safely under the seat, I called Henry on the cellular to let him know I was inside.

My whole scheme was based on the attractiveness of the bait: a gaudy, tricked-out van with both CB and car phone antennas.

Exactly two hours after entering the garage, it was showtime.

I heard the tow truck skid to a stop in front of the van, the driver climb out, lower the winch cable, and hook up the van. I was going for another ride.

This one was extremely short. After hurtling down the steep ramp, we banked a hard right, then squealed to a halt. The driver got out and I could hear him and another man talking. There was the sound of large metal doors being opened.

The van was dropped. Someone put a slim-jim through the

driver's side door and popped the locks, and the two of them pushed the van inside. The doors banged shut behind us.

People who make a living ripping people off think it's some God-given right and when you confront them, you're the asshole.

I checked the screwdrivers I'd used to secure the underside of the back seat and the rear doors. Then I reached into my coat and pulled out my Walther, flipping the safety off with my thumb.

"Hot shit, Jackie, leather captain's seats. Ernie'll give us three hundred for the set."

"Alpine CD; buck and a half. Speakers—how many speakers . . . eight. 'Nother buck and a half."

I got sick listening to the cacophony of capital gains, whirring tools, and Headbanger Greatest Hits cranked up to top volume. It killed me to let them dismantle my cousin's van, but I wanted to get them for more than just intent.

The whole job took them less than thirty minutes. I wiped the sweat from my hands and fingered the trigger of the Walther.

"Whatta ya wanna do?" one asked the other. "You wanna go for the engine and tranny?"

"We ain't got rid of the last six, what the fuck we gonna do with another one? Let's just roll the fucker."

Roll the fucker. Did that mean what I thought it did?

I heard a second set of doors being opened in front of us and felt the van start to roll as one of them let off the emergency brake and started to push. When the second one opened the passenger door to help, the van picked up speed.

In that one frozen moment of supreme clarity common to the rudely awakened, I realized what was happening, just as the van fell through a hole in the dock and plummeted toward the San Francisco Bay a dozen feet below.

I had no time to even brace myself as the nose smacked into the water, followed by the rear end. It felt like the van had landed on pavement.

My head bounced off the underside of the wooden seat. I bit my lip and crashed back down.

I was in big trouble.

I jerked the screwdriver out from under the seat and scrambled out just as the van tipped forward in the cold, dark Bay.

Bracing one foot in front of me, I tried to steady myself as the tilt of the van increased and I fought to slide open the side door. It wouldn't budge.

I could see the lights of Richmond and Oakland off to the right, Alcatraz and Marin County to the left. One muffled boat horn sounded.

With the front end being pulled down by the weight of the engine and transmission, the van was sinking by the second. I knew the front doors wouldn't open against the water pressure outside, and with the engine off, the power windows wouldn't work.

I leapt over the back seat and tried to reach the screwdriver securing the back doors at the bottom. It was inches from my grasp. As I tore at the back seat, I lost my grip and fell to the front, cracking my back across the engine cover, landing against the dash near the steering wheel. I knew my weight would start the front sinking even faster.

The water was a foot below the driver's window, still impossible to open the door. Then I noticed that the windows had hand cranks and not buttons. I felt stupid, embarrassed, but not as much as I felt thankful and relieved. Furiously, I rolled down the window and swam to safety.

It was only a few icy strokes to the pilings beneath the dock. I climbed the cross-braces and clambered up onto the dock platform outside the chop shop. Shivering, I stood watching as the van sank below the surface of the water. The area was dark, remote from the restaurants a few blocks away, with no boats passing nearby. I could have drowned without anyone knowing.

I was dripping wet and furious, not because my life had been endangered but because I'd been made to feel so foolish and helpless. Light shone through a crack in the outer doors of the chop shop. Peering in, I could see that the steel inside doors were closed. Only a hook held the outer doors shut, so I fished out my pocket knife, slipped the blade inside, worked it a moment until it popped.

Paramount in my mind was putting 9mm slugs in the kneecaps of the two clowns who'd shoved me in the freezing Bay. Fortunately there was no one inside.

It was a beauty of a chop shop, acetylene torches, refrigerator-sized toolboxes, hoists, a hydraulic lift, enough parts and accessories to open your own Pep Boys.

I found a bathroom, flipped on the light. There, taped to the walls, were the "secret papers" that had the attaché on the edge of a coronary. I dried my hands and face on paper towels, then carefully removed the tape and called Henry from a pay phone on the bathroom wall. Within an hour the SFPD had arrived, arrested everyone in the place, and gotten a nearby diver who'd been replacing dock pilings to have a look below. He found another dozen vehicles rusting on the bottom of the Bay.

I gave my report to Inspector Manny Torres, an old friend, and climbed into Henry's Rambler for the ride back to the office. As we drove away, I saw the garage clowns being led away in handcuffs beneath a sign that read SAN ANDREAS TOWING—IT'S NOT OUR FAULT.

My shoes squeaked and water ran down my neck as I walked into the office with Henry. Arnie Nuckles and Martha Walley were reading files for an upcoming insurance fraud case. Arnie was my best friend, a walking charm factory; tall, black, and handsome. A former Golden Gloves champion, he worked for me days and spent his nights as a stand-up comic in local clubs, waiting for fame to call. He was a natural actor, master of a thousand characters and voices, the only one in the agency who'd never been a cop.

Martha Walley was a superb athlete, blonde, blue-eyed, even brighter than she was beautiful. She'd been with the San Jose Police Department until she got tired of the ass pinching and harassment. When she dressed up and smiled, strong men would tell her anything.

They both looked me up and down, raised their brows, and waited silently until I explained.

"I went for a swim in the Bay."

"With your favorite jacket on," Martha said.

"I found some top-secret Russian documents my client had in his limousine when it was towed."

Martha held her hand out, as did Arnie. "You sure you want to see these?" I asked Martha, unable to keep a straight face. She grabbed a few out of my hand.

"Jeez," Martha said, "the attaché is pretty limber for an old guy." She was looking at the one where Kostonoviev was bent backwards over a chair with a woman straddling his Johnson and another one sitting on his face.

"I heard he was a gymnast," I answered.

"I don't recall any of these events at the competition," Arnie added, examining a Western tableau with the naked attaché being ridden by a pasty white whore sporting pink hair, cowboy boots, and a ten-gallon hat.

"Commie bastards," said Henry. "But Frankie iz not only find limo, he iz fix crooks good at tow-hink garage. Kill two bird viz vone rock!" Henry had once made the Malaprop Hall of Fame by telling the female director of an erotic art exhibition that "booty was in the eye of the beholder."

It'd been a slow day, a slow week, and the pictures were a cheap thrill. As they were passed around, Martha handed me a square envelope, the kind greeting cards come in. It was addressed by hand: *Mr. Francis Fagen Only.*

"A Hispanic woman brought it by at five forty," Martha added. "She rang the bell, handed it to me, and left."

I got another round of shivers and noticed that my prized black leather jacket was turning chalky gray from the salt water. Putting the hand-delivered letter atop the rest of my mail, I dragged myself upstairs, feeling so low I'd need a stepladder to bite myself on the ass. My secret Russian documents were nothing but bad porno pictures. My cellular phone and best camera were at the bottom of the Bay, and tomorrow I'd have to tell my cousin Jimmy his custom van was now a fish tank.

Going into the kitchen I switched the light on, dropped the mail on the table, and began peeling off my jacket, shirt, boots, and denims. Then I found a clean towel and stood shaking as I stared out across the rooftops of the city at the crystal-clear skyline and the bridge. It was hard to be miserable in front of a sight like that, but I managed just fine. I had a good bummer going and I wasn't about to let anything ruin it.

I looked down at the hand-delivered letter, trying to figure what it could be as I dried my hair. Putting the towel around my neck, I ripped open the envelope.

The first thing I found was a single ticket to that night's performance of the San Francisco Opera, where José Carreras was scheduled to sing the part of Don José in *Carmen*. So far so great. The second was a note written in a woman's hand, strong, elegant, not flowery or pretentious. The linen paper was expensive.

Dear Mr. Fagen
Sorry for this unusual approach to a meeting, but you'll understand when we speak. I wish to employ your services on a matter that is most certainly one of life or death—mine. Please come. When you arrive at the opera house, do not ask any of the ushers for help but take the small stairs on the north side of the auditorium and find your own way to my box.

Box, it said. I checked the ticket and noticed there was no seat number, just the box letter, which I reckoned was to the right of the stage, second level. You needed more money than a creative savings and loan executive and better connections than the Pope to get one of those, especially on opening night. "My box" probably meant she'd had it for some time.

It was signed with the initial *C*.

I didn't know who I was meeting or what it would lead to, but this was the panacea my old heart needed. Carreras. *Carmen*. A matter of life or death. A woman with money and good handwriting.

Then I checked the clock. The curtain would rise in thirteen minutes and I was filthy, unshaven, and starving.

I leapt for the shower and managed a comprehensive cleanup and shave in less than five minutes without cutting my throat.

In three and a half minutes more I was dressed and flying down my stairs.

2

I SHOULD HAVE driven my '63 Corvette convertible, the proper ride for such an occasion, but tardiness prohibited. Besides, it would have deprived the city of a chance to see a six-foot-three-inch PI on a Norton Commando, dressed in satin tuxedo pants, a full set of leather tails tied carefully around his waist to avoid an Isadora Duncan, a snow-white Guatemalan wedding shirt, and a Mississippi string tie fastened by a chunk of polished Carrara marble bearing a perfectly engraved bas-relief portrait of Trigger.

I was a sight, even in San Francisco.

Although I was a big hit with the multinational parking crew when I arrived, I chained the bike to a lamppost in front and sprinted inside.

A handful of people were scurrying toward their seats, the curtain delayed a few minutes to accommodate them. I reached the staircase at the north end, took the steps two at a time, and jerked open the door to the box just as the conductor stepped to the podium and received a wave of applause.

The box was empty. I checked the ticket, checked the door, shrugged. An empty box on the busiest night of the opera season. I settled into a seat away from the door.

A paranoid, I believe, is someone who has been given all the facts. The facts are, I'd been a cop and a PI long enough that anonymous meetings under strange circumstances always made me a little uneasy, especially when the other party didn't show. Uneasy enough to sit to the backside of the door and check in my pocket to make sure I could get my gun out in a hurry if I had to. As always, I felt ridiculous doing it, but I'd rather be silly and alive than the other way.

As the music started, I scooted up to the edge of my seat and peered at the audience below—at the San Francisco Opera, the audience is half the show. Most of the crowd was standard issue: gray-haired gents with patent leather shoes and all the answers; old women swimming in a sea of blue hair, shellacked to bulletproof perfection, sporting enough diamonds to end poverty in Haiti. Occasionally one of the old geezers would trade down the food chain for a culture-proof blonde with a low-cut display of the latest in elective surgery. He would, on such occasion, parade his catch around hammerlocked to her waist, eyeball to saline bosom, the way Hemingway might have posed with a giant blue tuna.

Then there were the other, more colorful coteries. Young radicals in granny dresses and earth shoes, men in leather jeans and rainbow-colored Indian shirts, a half dozen drag queens, an occasional biker in full-dress leathers.

As I peered along the row of boxes, I noticed something out of whack: few in the high-priced seats were watching the stage.

Most were staring at me.

Some of them were craning their necks, some had their opera glasses to their faces, but everywhere there was someone staring intently in my direction.

Easing back into the shadows, I wondered whose box I was in. It was obviously someone of great interest to the Chablis-and-fondue set.

Carreras took the stage, found his cue, and instantly transported the audience to a public square in Seville. I relaxed and went with them, not knowing what was ahead except that one of the masters had come to sing. I did laugh, however, remembering that it was the same role, Don José in *Carmen*, that Caruso had sung here the night before the 1906 earthquake. The thought brought on a bad case of omen-itis.

As intermission approached I was still alone and almost didn't care. When I pushed the black button I found a waiter appeared. I ordered an abalone steak and two Heinekens. As the music ended and the curtain began to fall, we all leapt to our feet, rocking the place with applause.

That's why I didn't hear her enter. I jumped when she said, "Mr. Fagen?"

I turned, totally unprepared for what I saw. Her face was a foot away, and her eyes were almost on a level with mine. Jade green eyes, heart-stopping eyes. She had flawless alabaster skin and dark hair with one thin, natural gray streak in it, the kind you will occasionally find with a true Irish girl.

I have seen some beautiful women in my life but this one sucked the breath right out of me. She fixed her gaze on me for a second, looked right through me, smiled, then gazed down at my mouth intently.

"The first act must have been pretty exciting. Your lower lip is bleeding." She reached in her purse and pulled out a tissue and touched it to my lip. I didn't tell her I'd bitten myself performing the Amazing Flying Van feat. I didn't move or say anything.

As she dabbed away, she noticed the polished marble clasp on my Mississippi string tie. She made a feeble attempt not to smile, then looked at me questioningly.

"Trigger?" she asked, pressing the tissue against my lip. I nodded.

"I apologize for being so late. I was at my lawyer's office going over some last-minute depositions for the trial tomorrow." She took the tissue away from my mouth.

It was then and only then that I realized who she was, despite having seen her in the papers and on the news without stop for a year and a half.

"I'm Colleen Farragut," she said. "I guess you must have heard about my legal problems."

Only a head trauma victim could have missed them. I felt a strange rush in my ears, the noise of the audience suddenly disappearing. A painful and half-dead part of my past welled up inside of me: I could feel sweat break out on my forehead.

The Farragut murder case. That's why everyone in the surrounding boxes had been staring, to catch a glimpse of Colleen Farragut if she appeared.

The trial, scheduled to begin the next morning, was the most sensational murder case since the trial of Warren Dillon for the murder of San Francisco mayor Alan DiMarco. And not since Patricia Hearst or the Reverend Jim Jones and the Jonestown massacre had a San Francisco story received such national attention. The defendant, the woman accused of murdering one of San Francisco's most powerful men—her husband—was standing in front of me.

"I've heard," I said, as softly as I could.

"I need your help, Mr. Fagen. My situation is desperate." From what I knew of her situation, desperate was an accurate assessment.

"I'm sorry to ask you here like this, but it seemed . . . I don't know what it seemed."

I came out of my coma and tried to help her out. "This seemed the easiest place, in the shadows, away from all the scandalmongers. You sent me the handwritten note because you're even afraid your phone is tapped."

She seemed impressed by my deduction, as most people will be if you talk fast enough. I'm not the world's greatest detective, but I am hell on the obvious.

She looked around the opera house, regained her composure quickly, secure in the fact that we were out of sight at the rear of the box.

"I also wanted to come here to hear Carreras sing," she said quietly. "One of the great joys of my life has been coming to this beautiful place, listening to this wonderful music. I'm afraid that, after tomorrow . . ."

After tomorrow her life looked like a short walk to the gas chamber or a long stay in a living hell.

"Mr. Fagen," she said, her eyes growing slightly moist, making her even more beautiful, "I don't want to talk here. I just wanted to meet you on neutral ground. Please come to my house after midnight so I can tell you everything. If you have another engagement, I'm asking you to break it. Please."

I just nodded my head.

"I assume you know where the house is?"

"Yes." Of all the houses I knew in San Francisco, hers was preeminent in my memory, but for all the wrong reasons. "I have a van I use for surveillance, painted with Firenze Plumbing on the side. I'll go to the back entrance of your house and press the buzzer."

She nodded. "Consuela will let you in."

Her voice was seductive, disarming. She stared at me for a second, managed a smile and turned to leave. Near the door she stopped and looked back. "Did you know Caruso sang the part of Don José the night before the 1906 earthquake?"

"Yes, and when it hit he stormed through the lobby of the Palace Hotel bellowing *'Non ancora cantero qui!'*"

"Never again will I sing here," she translated perfectly.

I nodded good-bye and watched her exit, silhouetted by the hall lights outside. Six feet in her heels, she must be five foot nine barefoot.

Her every movement was graceful, feline, erotic. She wore her tight black dress above the knee, the way a panther wears her hide. Her back, visible through an oval opening, was lean, muscled, V-shaped—all flowing into a set of fluid-motion hips.

It was the legs, though, that really did it: a Pacific Coast Highway of endless beauty. Shaded in black stockings, her calves swept in graceful lines from perfect knees, melted into thin, perfect ankles, then disappeared into patent leather pumps. It was moments like this that reminded me of God's innate glory and cruelty.

Why would He create such a woman as this, then tell a few hundred million men they couldn't have her?

The waiter came. I tried to eat and couldn't. A great meal was wasted by the goulash of emotions that swirled inside of me. I was overwhelmed by her beauty and by that dizzying hope that beats in the heart of any male when he meets such a woman. That was replaced by guilt for having stared into the face of a desperate woman and thinking first of her beauty.

Worst of all was a crushing dread evoked by memories of her late husband, William Farragut IV, a real estate developer, a fiscal Einstein with the morals of a hired killer, the pursuit of whom had cost me my job when I was a young SFPD inspector in charge of the white-collar-crime division.

I couldn't figure what she wanted with me. Her lawyer was Calvin Sherenian, who'd once told the graduating class at Hastings Law that he could get the Devil's loss to Daniel Webster overturned on appeal. In the hierarchy of great American trial lawyers, Edward Bennett Williams, Gerry Spence, "Race Horse" Haynes, et al., Sherenian was chauffeur to none of them. He had personally tried eleven capital murder cases in the past twenty-five years, winning acquittal in every one.

Sherenian had been the attorney, confidant, and occasional business partner of the late Mr. Farragut, and now that Farragut's wife was charged with her husband's murder, Sherenian was defending her. Normally tight-lipped when trying a case, he had been ferocious in his public declarations of Colleen's innocence. The biggest show in town, it was tailor-made for Calvin.

Calvin also had access to every imaginable resource, including an army of private investigators. So why was she coming to me, the night before the trial?

I tried to watch the final act, but I wouldn't have known if poor Carmen turned the tables this time and stabbed Don José. I kept running Colleen's story through my mind, trying to access random information so I'd seem like the genius I liked to imagine myself.

When the last note was sung—and I'm not sure by whom—and

the audience jumped to its feet, I took advantage of the opportunity and made a hurried exit. I flew down the steps, leather tails streaming behind me, looking, I'm sure, like the Phantom himself.

I hopped on the Norton, roared down Franklin to Union and back to my digs on Telegraph. As I peeled off the penguin suit and slipped into overalls, I ran through the rest of Colleen Farragut's story. My heart pounded with anticipation of the unknown.

My long-time friend, Zane Neidlinger, senior reporter on the *Clarion*, had been the first to dig up her story, long before the murder of Farragut at their mansion. He'd told me Colleen's tale over dinner at the Washington Square Bar & Grill in North Beach, years before the national media had picked it up.

Colleen had been raised in some hellhole nontown outside of Modesto in the San Joaquin Valley. When she was fifteen, her stepfather, an alcoholic who drove a "honey bucket," a big truck that pumps out septic tanks, tried to introduce her to the joys of posing for home Polaroids in the barn. She bit off a piece of his ear and ran away to San Francisco, where, as Zane told it, she arrived with one dress, one pair of shoes, and less than a hundred bucks, which she'd earned baby-sitting.

She looked up the girlfriend of her oldest sister, who got her a fake ID and a job waiting tables at one of the Broadway strip joints near Carol Doda's infamous Condor. A now famous picture of Colleen had appeared on the cover of the *National Enquirer* two weeks after Farragut's murder. Dressed in a black lace corselette and fishnet stockings and sitting on the lap of some fat old fart, she looked older than thirty and younger than fifteen. The guy had paid her five dollars to pose with him, and he probably sold the photo to the *Enquirer* for five thousand.

According to Zane, she had a wizard IQ and had been determined to make something of her life. She kept her nose squeaky clean, passed her GED exams with flying colors, and after two years at City College, got accepted to UC Berkeley. Working nights as a waitress on Union Street by then, she managed a double major in art history and foreign languages, graduating summa cum laude. She followed that with a master's degree in fine art.

She was working in a Battery Street art gallery at the age of twenty-five when William Farragut IV came to see a Modigliani collection they were selling. He was thirty-eight at the time. They married nine months later.

Farragut was the exact opposite of Colleen. Like me, he was a fourth-generation San Franciscan. Our great-grandfathers had emigrated within a few months of each other in 1851.

But while I was a fourth-generation cop, Farragut was a fourth-generation builder and real estate speculator. There were two schools of thought on the late Willy IV: according to one, that of his friends and cronies, he was a great "architect" of the city, a master facilitator able to cut through red tape, responsible for renovating and rebuilding slums and modernizing the city's sky-line; the second school, of which I was a die-hard member, be-lieved that he cared nothing for the city beyond the profits he could take from her, that his methods were bribery, extortion, intimidation, and worse.

The Farragut haters, and they were legion, saw his "urban renewal" as an excuse to drive poor and blue-collar people out of the city by building high rises and "Manhattanizing" San Fran-cisco until a tiny one-bedroom apartment that rented fifteen years before for one fifty a month now sold for three hundred thousand as a condominium.

The real losers were the families, the working class, the artists and assorted characters that had made San Francisco a comfortable and magic place. What was once a home for the Beat generation and Emperor Norton, for merchant marines and mom-and-pop groceries was now an open-air shopping mall for a million camera-toting tourists.

Soon after they married, Colleen built a sizable reputation as San Francisco's premier patron of the arts and supporter of chari-table causes. There were a number of jokes over the years that

Willy IV was having trouble stealing fast enough to keep up with his wife's humanitarian endeavors.

Then it got ugly in the Farragut home, or so the newshounds claimed. Colleen and William grew distant, preoccupied with their Simon Legree and Florence Nightingale roles, and found recreational outlets elsewhere. It had been rumored, but not proven, that Farragut had one or more two-thousand-dollar-a-night sweeties to whom he'd play Evil Uncle Ernie, paddling their high-priced behinds with a variety of leather instruments not found at Macy's, unless they have recently opened an equestrian department.

Colleen had been the principal financial supporter of SOHO, an innovative urban renewal project, and eventually became the principal horizontal supporter of its director, Tommy Rivera, a strapping ex–street hoodlum with the looks of a Latin matinee idol.

In the annals of juicy scandals, this was a world-class beauty, and the gossip rags had been writhing in orgasmic delight. The "legitimate press," however, fraught with moral indignity over a woman who had apparently murdered her husband to inherit his estate, were practically screaming for her head behind the Equal Justice for the Rich banner.

District Attorney Ian Jeffries, a rat-faced pornography fighter seeking election to the state attorney general's office on the Idi Amin–Benito Mussolini ticket, was asking for the death penalty and promising no less than life without possibility of parole.

Except for her attorney, Calvin Sherenian, Colleen didn't seem to have a friend in the state of California.

I checked the clock for the fifteenth or twentieth time. When it had finally crept to 11:50, I donned my plumber's cap and went down the front steps to the garage.

As I stuck my key into the automatic door opener, I checked in every direction. No one was reading a newspaper in a doorway or sitting in a parked car, so I climbed into the plumber's van and drove off.

I liked to take it easy on the old van, so I avoided the Union Street hills, making a right on Columbus and a left on Bay Street near Ghiradelli Square. I passed Galileo High where DiMaggio, O. J. Simpson, and I had all gone to school, with different results. At Steiner I cut up to Filbert and made my way into the Presidio.

Arriving in Presidio Heights, I cruised the neighborhood looking for reporters or news crews. When I saw the Farragut mansion was dark and without unwanted visitors, I drove to the rear gate, leaned out, and pushed the buzzer.

Several reporters and photographers suddenly appeared from the bushes across the street and made a mad dash toward the van.

Within seconds a tinny voice asked who it was. I barked, "Firenze Plumbing," and was immediately buzzed in. I escaped the fastest of the reporters by less than ten feet. Several frustrated looks appeared in my rearview as the gate closed and I swung around the back of the house.

3

*A*s I ROUNDED the carriage entrance at the rear a white garage door, one of eight, opened magically and admitted me to the dark interior. I'd now gone farther into the Farragut sanctuary than I had in my catastrophic two-year pursuit of William IV.

As the door closed and the darkness grabbed me, a light came on, and Consuela entered from a side door. A plain-looking woman in her early forties, short, heavyset, and seeming very shy, she kept her head down as she smiled and nodded for me to follow her.

We walked past several dusty cars that were parked in the garage: a Stutz-Bearcat, a Deusenberg, a gull-wing Mercedes, a few others of equal vintage. Several million on wheels.

We went outside and down a lengthy covered walkway. The moon had just snuck over the trees of the Presidio to the right and was illuminating the house. It was big, the size of your basic airline terminal, and Tudor-style, my least favorite form of architecture, a cow barn with racing stripes. There was one minuscule light coming from a bedroom several stories up. It would have made a nice home for Norman Bates and his mother, had they been more successful in the motel business.

Consuela pulled open a hangar door and we entered through a vestibule into a "family room" big and cold enough to hang meat in. We walked through a dining room the size of the one at West Point, continuing through a kitchen and pantry to a private elevator, which Consuela operated. I had to smile at her as we slowly rose five floors to where the mistress of the castle was waiting. I wished I still had my tuxedo on.

Consuela led me down a series of hallways to the room from which the faint light had emanated. I'd been on shorter hikes in the Boy Scouts. Consuela knocked softly before admitting me.

The room was as warm and comfortable as the rest of the house was cold and intimidating. A fire was burning in the huge stone fireplace. From the giant windows at the far end of the huge bedroom, I could see over the trees to what the Pacific Ocean saw when it looked up at the bridge. Lights from Belvedere Island, Alcatraz, and the East Bay sparkled behind it.

Colleen was on the phone when I entered. After a moment she said something into the phone, hung up, and came toward me. She was wearing tight Levi's and red boots with heels, and a V-necked sweater that clung to small, perfect breasts. Her nipples poked upward through the weight of the heavy knit fabric. No mean feat, I thought. I should have run. I didn't.

"Thank you for coming, Mr. Fagen."

"Frank," I said. I saved Frankie for waitresses in doughnut shops. She told me to call her Colleen. I'm always glad when that part is over.

"I asked Consuela to make us some tea. Would you prefer something else?"

I shook my head, then followed her across the bedroom through open French doors into an enormous sitting room filled with gray leather furniture and more paintings than you are likely to see at the De Young Museum. I counted three Magrittes, two Dalís from his Soft Watches Period, a Matisse, several Modiglianis, a half dozen of Duchamp's best, and a liberal sprinkling of Man Ray's photographs, plus a handful of up-and-coming San Francisco painters. A tasteful and valuable collection, some of the best the twentieth century had to offer. We sat. Neither of us smoked. She was nervous. I was nervous. There was a lot of nervousness.

"I don't know where to start."

"Start anywhere."

"What do you think of my case?"

"I only know what I read in the papers."

"You're ducking the question."

She'd challenged, I accepted. "You're in a lot of trouble. The DA wants to hang you, the evidence is one-sided, and the newspapers think you're the Wicked Witch of Presidio Heights. The biggest thing in your favor is the sharpest mouthpiece in town, and the fact that he hasn't lost a big one since they discovered penicillin."

"And I'm terrified I'll be the first," she said.

She got a moment's reprieve as Consuela entered with a tray bearing a teapot, two cups, and an antique honey jar. Consuela poured and handed us cups. Colleen raised hers to her lips, hands trembling. She blew on the surface of the hot tea, took a sip, gathered her nerve as best she could.

I felt sorry for her, even if she had pulled the trigger. To be a murderer you have to kill something human, and there were a lot of people who felt the late Mr. Farragut didn't qualify. I was one of them.

"It wasn't just business between you and William, was it?" she asked me when Consuela had left.

"It was never just business with me, that was my problem. I despised every drunk driver, child molester, every white-collar crook I ever busted. I wasn't a cop, I was the graceless crusader. Well, here I am, living proof that no good deed goes unpunished."

I drained my teacup and wished I had accepted something stronger. She'd got me going, but I'd learned a little over the years; I reined it in. Now it was her turn.

"Come on," she said, "I want to show you something."

We walked through her bedroom and back into the Hallway Without End. We passed the elevator, two more bedrooms, another bathroom, a game room, and a library. An easy fifteen-dollar cab ride later, a marble and brass staircase brought us to the floor below.

The third floor was taken up almost completely by a bedroom the size of Pittsburgh. "I had just gone out into the hallway from my room above when I heard him get off the elevator. I came down to tell him his mother had called. He was pretty drunk."

"We had been arguing for weeks. He found out about my affair with Tommy Rivera and was saying he'd divorce me, take away everything, including what I'd earned myself."

I asked her how William had found out. She suspected he had hired a private detective. I made a mental note to find out who the detective was, and where and when he'd caught her.

"In the middle of the argument, he suddenly decided he needed another drink, so he went downstairs to the bar."

"Why did he do that?" I asked. "You have servants, and there must be a bar in here somewhere."

"The only servant who ever lived in was Consuela and she has Monday nights off. She takes BART, then a bus, to San Jose to stay with her brother and his kids. And the bottle of Glenlivet in the bar over there"—she pointed to an armoire in the adjacent sitting area that looked like it had once held Napoleon's favorite suits— "was empty. Glenlivet is the only thing that William drank."

She motioned for me to follow her. We trekked back down the hallway, descended the stairs again.

Within the hour we arrived at a den filled with overstuffed red leather furniture, the walls covered with college graduation certificates and awards for citizenship and humanitarian achievements given to William and his ancestors. I had my own opinion about these last but kept my tongue. A long marble-topped bar along one wall was better stocked than the ones I usually visit. Adjacent to that was a set of French doors where they let the Hindenburg in and out.

There were a few other things that made it different from the average den. The first was a yellow banner across the entrance reading DO NOT CROSS—POLICE LINES and a court order tacked to the wall. Then there was the chalk outline of a body in the middle of the thick gray carpet, and two large bloodstains that coincided with the account in the police report, which stated that Farragut had taken two slugs, one through the pumper and one through the right lung. Several drawers had been pulled open and dumped, trophies and knickknacks were scattered on the floor, along with some broken glass.

I looked at Colleen, waiting for her to continue. She took a deep breath. I could see her pulse beating beneath the almost translucent flesh of her neck.

"As soon as William went downstairs, I went back to my room and took a shower, to try to calm down. I never heard the shots: the walls of this house are as thick as a vault."

"How long was it before you went downstairs and found his body? It was you that found him, right?"

"It wasn't until the next morning. After I took my shower, I just figured he'd stayed downstairs because he was drinking and had lost interest in fighting. I was dead tired and I went to bed."

"You weren't sleeping together?"

"No. I was sleeping upstairs in the room we were just in. We hadn't slept together in months. Not since I'd found out about the S&M adventures with his high-priced girlfriend."

"Then what happened?" I asked.

"Next morning, before Consuela returned from San Jose, I went downstairs. It was real creepy. All the lights were on, and it was deathly silent. I could see the curtains blowing in the den at the end of the hallway; the French doors were open. I saw him lying on the floor. I thought he'd passed out, or fallen and hit his head, or maybe had a heart attack. When I got up closer . . . " She covered her face with her hands. "That's when I saw the blood on his clothes, two huge stains. I'll never forget his eyes, wide open, staring at the ceiling. I had this weird, creepy feeling that if I looked in his eyes I'd see the person who shot him, you know, like his eyes were a camera or something."

She shivered. I got an Indian blanket from the adjacent parlor and wrapped it around her shoulders. It gave her time to catch her breath and compose herself.

"The gun was lying there, where the *X* is." She pointed to the chalk mark on the carpet. "There was an officer here in less than three minutes. He was only a few blocks away when he got the call. I showed him the body, and he said William had been dead for hours. The blood had coagulated on his shirt and on the rug. Then the paramedics and a dozen cops showed up, the coroner, everybody."

"What made you think that the murderer, or murderers, was already gone and that you weren't in danger?"

"I didn't. I never thought about it. When I saw the gun on the floor, I figured whoever did it dropped it on the way out."

"And it was your gun?" I asked.

"It was William's. He kept it in a drawer by the bar, since he spent a lot of time in his den and always had the French doors open. He used the Jacuzzi almost every night and worried that someone might come over the wall behind the house. The other side is just woods. The land belongs to the Presidio."

"The papers said the gun had your fingerprints on it, as well as his."

"I'm a farm girl; my stepfather had guns all over the place. I'm not afraid of guns. But Consuela is. William had a habit of getting drunk, taking the gun out, and forgetting to put it away. Consuela wouldn't even go in the room unless I put it in the drawer."

Classy stuff. One of the country's wealthiest men, loaded on scotch and playing country club cowboy with a loaded revolver.

"How long before the shooting had you last handled the gun?" I asked her.

"About a week."

Fingerprints could last for months, even years. "And the only prints were yours and William's."

"Yes. Two hours after the police came, I submitted to a blood test for drugs and alcohol. Then they ran a test to see if I had fired a gun. There was no gunpowder residue on my hands or on my clothes."

"Was anything taken?"

She pointed to a display case nearest the door. "Do you know the Italian artist Ghiberti?"

"Yes. If you've ever been to Florence, it's impossible not to know him." Ghiberti sculpted the brass doors on the exterior of the Baptistry, the octagonal building constructed as a tribute to John the Baptist. It stands in front of the Church of Santa Maria del Fiore, third-largest church in the world, atop which rests Brunelleschi's Duomo. The dome is considered the greatest architectural achievement of the Renaissance.

Ghiberti's creation, dubbed "the Doors of Paradise," is divided into panels, each meticulously sculpted to depict a scene from the Bible, each in solid brass and weighing scores of tons. They are the most famous doors in all the world and took Ghiberti fifty-one years to complete. Only one of the doors has ever been reproduced. It stands at the main entrance to San Francisco's Grace Cathedral.

Colleen then explained to me that Ghiberti, ever the crafty and calculating artist, had begun his project by first working each design out in the form of a silver plate, knowing they would be immensely valuable when the project was finished. He abandoned the idea after making only four silver plates.

Two had allegedly been lost, the other two had been bought by William's father at the start of World War II. Colleen told me they were in the display case the night of the murder and must have been taken by William's assailant.

According to Colleen, the plates appeared on an insurance inventory and had been seen by dozens of witnesses in the spot from which they disappeared. Consuela had signed an affidavit that the plates were on the shelf the day of the shooting.

"Let's go outside, get some air for a moment. All right, Frank?"

I nodded and followed her past the yellow police ribbon and into another room, waiting patiently as she opened enough locks to make a New Yorker proud. The locks were new, untarnished, and didn't fit in with the decor of the room. Obviously added after the murder.

In back of the house the grass was overgrown, the trees un-trimmed. There was a large masonry wall surrounding an enormous gazebo that looked like an outdoor dance pavilion. To the right was a Jacuzzi-cabana area and a boarded-up wet bar. It was warmer outside than it was in the house.

I could tell by the height of the trees behind the wall that there was a long drop from the top of it to the ground inside the Presidio.

"Now what do you think, Frank?" she asked, turning to face me.

I hesitated.

"Tell me," she said impatiently. "I don't have much time. In about eight hours it's really going to get ugly." She was suffering, ready to crack at any moment.

I told her the truth as gently as I could. "It's a hard story to believe. First, it's difficult to imagine that anyone would burglarize this house, especially at night when they'd expect people to be home. Most residential burglaries in houses like this are in the daytime.

"His gun, your fingerprints, bad sign. No gunpowder on you or your clothes will be easy for the prosecutor to dismiss. Almost nine hours passed between the shooting and your call to the police. You could have taken five showers and washed the clothes you were wearing. And the jury might have a hard time believing someone gunned your husband down without you hearing the shots, that you slept the night away with the body downstairs. Although I'd suggest that Calvin Sherenian bring the jury out here to see the size of this place for themselves."

Again I hesitated, but she seemed to be holding up. "You were arguing, he was threatening to divorce you. If the papers are correct, your prenuptial agreement would give you nothing if he could prove you were doing horizontal aerobics with another man."

She nodded her head. I was kicking a dying horse. I didn't like it but did it anyway. I had a lot of practice.

"They got you on three of the primary pieces of evidence: motive, because of the divorce threat and prenuptial agreement; opportunity, because the two of you were home alone; and physical evidence, because of your prints on the murder weapon. But that still doesn't mean you're guilty. All that is just circumstantial. You have no criminal record, no history of violence, and your reputation for helping other people shows that you aren't one of those self-indulgent cretins that everyone hates. Calvin Sherenian has won acquittals with more evidence than that stacked against a defendant. The good thing is, no one says they saw you do it or saw you leaving the scene. Eyewitness accounts are the most damning kind of evidence. And no one has accused you of prior intent, of making a previous attempt on his life."

When I said "previous attempt" she looked up at me, then put her head down and sobbed almost imperceptibly. Her face was strained, but she didn't crack, as though by freezing her face she might freeze her emotions. But her nose was running, and a bubble of saliva slipped from between her lips. She gasped once, wiped her nose and mouth on a tissue she took from her pocket, then pulled herself back together.

I waited, and then it came.

"Yesterday, Tommy Rivera . . . " She looked at me, looked away again. "He said—he told the DA, he signed an affidavit and everything. He told them I'd tried to get him to get some of his ghetto buddies to . . . to kill William and that I promised to pay Tommy a lot of money once the estate was settled."

I'd figured it was going to be ugly, but not that ugly.

"He's going to testify against me," she gasped, shaking, and the brave face folded. Tears streamed down her cheeks and she made no attempt to stop them. She had a right to be terrified. That's why Ian Jeffries had taken murder one to murder one with special circumstances: premeditation, prior attempt, murder for financial gain.

It also elevated the circumstantial evidence to the level of corroborating evidence.

I waited a minute. "Why would he do that?" I asked. "Why would Tommy Rivera pull a stunt like that?"

"Money—and revenge I guess. He hated me because I dumped him, and a few months after the murder he came to me and said he'd tell this story to the police unless I gave him money. A lot of money."

"Did Calvin try to trap him, to prove he was extorting money from you?"

"Yes. Calvin had a tap on the phone when I spoke to Tommy several times afterward, but I could never get him to repeat anything incriminating. He was too smart. He told me when he threatened me that he would never mention it again, but that he'd be 'most grateful' if I offered him a palimony settlement. He just called from time to time and said, 'How 'ya doin', can I help?' When I changed my number he sent me cards that said 'Been thinking about you, let me know if there is anything you need or anything I can do. Love, Tommy.' The guy is scum. I really didn't think he would go through with it."

She was dead meat, I didn't care how good Calvin Sherenian was. My partner and I had busted Tommy once when he was an eighteen-year-old gang-banger. Even then he was glib, cocky, with a lightning-fast mind. I doubted if even Sherenian could rattle him on the witness stand.

There was a bench nearby. Colleen stumbled over and slumped down on it as if her knees had gone on strike. I paced forth and back, staring up at the moon, which was now higher in the sky out over the Pacific, bathing everything in cold, pale light. I offered her no comfort.

"Frank," she said. "My attorney has had a dozen private detectives looking for the burglar ever since the murder. They've found nothing, no burglar, no silver plates, nothing. The cops have been doing 'due diligence' and haven't found anything either. Unless someone finds the person who did this . . . " She was too scared to finish the sentence.

In my mind, I finished it for her. While the death penalty seemed unlikely—an educated woman with no criminal record was unlikely to be condemned—the mere possibility would reduce anyone's heart to jelly.

And the alternative was even worse. A lifetime at Frontera women's prison, growing old in a five-by-ten hellhole surrounded by a mix-'n'-match collection of the biggest fuck-ups and psychopaths society had to offer. Being raped and tortured for the rest of your life could make death seem like an enviable alternative.

If acquitted, she'd inherit three hundred million, the artwork, the opera seats, the car collection, and Castle Farragut. Skiing and aperitifs at Gstaad. Regattas on the Costa Brava, sunsets at Portofino. And the only way she could guarantee herself an acquittal was for someone to find the Invisible Burglar.

"My husband hated you, Frank. You know why? Because he couldn't buy you. Because you almost ended his little reign of terror over this city. He used to brag that you were the hotshot young detective in San Francisco, the most obsessive man hunter the department had. He gloated over beating you, because he said you were the best. How good are you, Frank? Can you find someone no one else can find?"

People usually tell you you're the best when they're trying to get you to work for free. Judging by the lack of heat and maintenance at the Castle, I figured that was next. I answered the question as quietly as egomania allows.

"I'm a good detective, I've always considered myself one of the best. But I'm not Merlin, I can't find someone who doesn't leave a trail, who hasn't made any mistakes. And I'm extra-bad at finding someone who doesn't exist."

She looked at me with a start, but I had to do it. I had to clue her in that I still had problems with her story.

Gritting her teeth, she went back on the offensive. "I want someone who will work for me, for me only. I don't trust anybody

34

right now, I'm just too scared. I got through life trusting my own instincts, relying on myself when things got rough. I don't have much money left; the court froze everything, the cars, the art, all but my personal property. I've sold my car, my jewelry, what little artwork I owned. I've used it all to make bail, pay Calvin's fees and expenses, and to pay for an army of private detectives—who found nothing.

"I have ten thousand dollars to my name. I need a little so I can eat and pay Consuela. She's my only friend now, I'd go nuts in this house without her. But I'll give you most of what I have for expenses. And, if you find whoever did this—who killed William, who stole those silver plates—if you save me from this nightmare, I'll give you one million dollars when the estate is released by the court."

The best I could do was stare. I stared a long time. She stared back, barely blinking. I'd been offered a lot of things in my PI life, from stud-fee shares in a blue-ribbon pig to a ménage à trois with a ballet dancer and her twin sister. One of which I accepted.

But never a million dollars. And never anything by anyone as sad and beautiful as Colleen Farragut.

"The trial should only last a month, Frank. It's a month out of your life, and if you're successful you will get your million dollars. I'll put it in writing. I need to know now. I've got no place to hide and nowhere else to go."

I gave myself another minute, cleared my throat of the phantom million stuck there, and answered her.

"I'm sorry. I'd have to get my three other detectives working around the clock, and the expense money wouldn't even pay their wages. If the cops and the other private detectives couldn't find the perpetrator in nineteen months, the chances of me doing it in thirty days are next to impossible. The million means nothing unless I catch the perpetrator. I don't think I'd do you any good, and I'd just be taking the last of your money. I'm still having a hard time believing your story."

I thought that would put the last crack in her dam but it had the opposite effect. She sucked it up and came back at me, a real fighter.

"You lost your whole career because of my husband."

"Not exactly. I lost my career because I was naive and I had an ego the size of this house. Your husband was just the object of a bad case of temporary insanity. Besides, you can't wave revenge in my face. Somebody already got it for me, better than I ever could."

"Then I only have one more thing to offer you," she said. She stood and approached me so we were eyeball to tear-filled, magnificent eyeball. My heart jumped and my breathing stopped. It seemed the erotic mysteries of the universe were about to be dumped into my lap. I wondered how I would say no if she offered. I wouldn't. She didn't. She did, however, read my mind, surprised and pleased at the effect she had. Then she set the smile aside and got back to business.

"I wasn't here when it happened, but I read the old newspaper articles and heard William talk about it constantly. You lost your job because you accused him of being involved in the murder of the mayor. You believed William wanted Mayor DiMarco dead because DiMarco was trying to stop all the high-rise building in the financial district and south of Market Street. William and his buddies had millions invested in the Market Street corridor. If DiMarco had been able to stop them, they would have lost everything."

"That's right," I said. "DiMarco would have put an end to all that horrendous building if Warren Dillon hadn't killed him in his own office. With DiMarco out of the way, the power downtown shifted from the save-the-city group to the developers. We got skyscrapers forty-eight stories above the San Andreas Fault, and your husband made millions."

I suffered an instantaneous fuck-up flashback, a mental replay of a young inspector ranting and raving to the press about corruption and cover-up after ex-cop Dillon received a measly four-year sentence for murdering the mayor. And I saw the same young inspector alone in his house on Telegraph Hill, crying like a lost child after he'd been fired and humiliated by the city for being "unstable," "irrational," "unprofessional," and "suspected of using illicit substances." My breathing went from zero to turbo, my chest heaving up and down as she talked.

"One night, a few months after Dillon was paroled, I overheard William talking in his den to a woman with whom you must be very familiar, Helen Smidge, Supervisor Helen Smidge. They were talking about Dillon getting out, they were afraid he'd talk and tell the whole story, how'd they'd pushed him into it, promised him they'd fix his trial and take care of him when he got out. They were talking about where to hide him and how much money it would cost.

"Several times I heard my husband having angry conversations with Dillon over the phone. William told him to keep his mouth shut and said he'd give him more money and have him moved to a different location. Then, about a year later, I heard on the radio that Dillon had committed suicide, and all day William walked around with a big grin on his face.

"In my husband's safe-deposit boxes, which I can't get to unless I'm acquitted, are diaries and records that he kept every day of his life. He told me once right after we were married that if anything ever happened to him I was to take all those records and diaries and burn them. He told me to make sure I got two particular diaries, the diary from the year that Dillon murdered the mayor and the one from the year Dillon was released and supposedly commited suicide."

She was telling the truth about the existence of the Farragut diaries. The last thing I'd come up with in my attempt to nail Farragut with DiMarco's murder was a former secretary who'd told me that Farragut kept meticulous diaries. My last official act as a cop was to request a search warrant and subpoena for Farragut's personal safe and safe-deposit boxes. When the judge refused I went crazy and made my second and fatal outburst to the media.

I asked my hands and knees to behave themselves, and fought the gagging feeling in my throat.

"I know where those diaries are, Frank, and I'll give you any one you want. You can have them all. You can have a record of every bribe, kickback, and dirty deal William and his friends ever pulled. But most of all, you can clear your name.

"A million dollars and the chance to vindicate yourself in front of everyone, Frank. All you have to do is find the people I'm looking for and prove what I'm telling you and everyone else— that I am not a murderer."

My first reaction was to run, to disbelieve everything, to let the whole ugly thing stay buried. That lasted five seconds, tops, and then the old fight started welling up inside of me.

I looked at her and saw the pain, the determination, the pleading. For the first time, the one question I'd been unable to shake since we met started to make sense.

Why was she doing this, if there really wasn't a burglar on the loose? Why would she go to these lengths, giving up what was obviously her last money to find someone if that someone didn't exist? She was desperate, but she didn't seem crazy.

She had offered me the ultimate reward, the one thing that could have gotten me to take her case: the chance to prove, once and for all, that I was right and the rest of them—the department, the city, everyone—had been wrong. I couldn't get revenge, but I could get something better: revenge's big brother, redemption.

I'd had some wild dreams of vengeance and vindication in my decade-long season in hell, but nothing, nothing like what was staring me in the face. All I had to do was find someone that no one else could find.

"I'll have a contract drawn up tomorrow," I said. "Where are the evidence files?"

She smiled a relieved but painful smile and led me down the hallway to a wood-paneled office. In the center of the floor were two pushcarts filled with identical boxes filled with files.

"Consuela and I spent days just copying them. The one on the right is yours."

I don't remember much of anything after that; loading the boxes in the Firenze Plumbing van, trading phone numbers, receiving five thousand in cash. I'm not sure what route I took home, if I passed any cars or saw any buildings or streets that may have looked familiar. I pulled into my garage, got out of the van, and loaded the boxes into the dumbwaiter I'd installed for my late grandmother, pressing the button that sent everything to the fourth-floor loft.

I climbed the stairs and exited onto the roof, taking in the San Francisco skyline, still numb, still afraid of what I was about to undertake. Along the Market Street corridor the hulking high rises blocked what had once been an uninterrupted view of the Bay. My endless reminder, my personal hammer from Farragut and friends that after DiMarco's murder, the city had been theirs for the taking.

Behind me I heard a heavy bellow, the sound a sea lion on steroids might make: the first foghorn in over a month. I turned and saw the first of the fog creeping above the hills of Sausalito, feeling as though a vise had been removed from my heart. The world had regained some equilibrium.

Until that night, I had tried to put the whole Farragut mess behind me. I thought I had finished suffering a decade earlier. I'd spent a month, postdismissal, as an inarticulate lump. My firing had made me so miserable I eventually bottomed out on misery. One day I forced myself to crawl out of the Fagen ooze and found that the sun still set behind the bridge and people still coughed in the movies. I counted my arms, my legs, my eyes, and my balls and still had two of everything. I paid my bar tabs and canceled my account at the liquor store and tore up several napkins on which I'd written the phone numbers of women who hadn't been able to quench the pain. I decided to go back to living.

But that night, looking at the desecrated San Francisco skyline, I realized that for ten years I hadn't been living.

I clenched my fists and shook them at the heavens, heart soaring, toes curling, and let the tears run down my face. I thanked God for my life and for the second chance to fight the fight that had almost killed me. Suddenly remembering I had neighbors all around, I looked to see if any of them had seen the lunatic flailing his fists on his rooftop, waved to the invisible gallery, smoothed my hair, and went inside. I remembered I had a job to do. The celebration would have to wait.

Downstairs, after I noticed in the mirror how horrible I looked in white coveralls, I changed to sweatpants and a sweatshirt and unloaded the dumbwaiter. Then I flopped in my leather chair and opened the first file, "Initial Incident Report," in the jacket marked PEOPLE VS. COLLEEN FARRAGUT.

I read until the sun came up.

4

*A*T SIX A.M. I climbed onto a mountain bike and speed-ped-
aled my way to Bugatti's Cafe on Filbert Street in Cow Hollow,
halfway between North Beach and the Presidio.

I ordered coffee and opened the morning *Clarion*. The trial was
front-page news, voluminous copy surrounding a large photograph of the magnificent Mrs. Farragut. Looking good in newsprint
is not easy. She looked good and then some.

An op-ed columnist wrote of the "seeming preponderance of
evidence" against Colleen, mentioned her "flimsy defense" and
how "skeptical" the police had been when they first heard her story
and decided to arrest her. He also spoke of her "sexual escapades"
with Tommy Rivera, ignoring the more bizarre activities of her
late husband.

He finished by mentioning that everyone in the world was
watching the trial and wondered whether the doctrine of "equal
justice for the rich" would indeed mean anything. The only thing
he didn't do was recommend a scarlet tattoo on her forehead.

I climbed back onto the bike and pedaled down Filbert Street
to Lyon, then turned into the Presidio.

The Presidio before seven in the morning is a sight and smell
to behold. The oldest military establishment on the West Coast,
it's filled with pine and eucalyptus trees that create intricate

patterns of morning light and shadow. Through the trees you can see the Bay and the bridge, the whole scene oozing a warmth and light that belie its function as a boardinghouse for war.

I'd ridden a bicycle so I could blend in with the scores of other riders and runners. I made a quick move off the road and into the trees along the wall behind the Presidio Heights mansions. The knobby tires bit deep into the black dirt as I glanced over my shoulder for anybody in uniform. Secure, I chugged my way to the highest house.

I ditched the bike and immediately confirmed what I'd gleaned from the other side the previous night: that scaling the Farragut wall was a mild commando feat.

I followed the wall downhill and after a dozen houses found what I was looking for: a section that almost anyone could climb. It was laid adobe style, meaning that the bricklayers never bothered to clean the excess grout from between the blocks. Several cracked blocks left toehold-size gaps, and the wall leaned inward. In a matter of eight quick steps, I had climbed it and was stationed on top.

I stood and walked casually along the wall past three or four mansions. I was wearing a pair of crepe-soled work boots and dark blue work pants and shirt. On the breast pocket of the shirt was a large white patch with red lettering that read CITY SERVICES, which meant absolutely nothing. I learned the trick watching *Mission Impossible* as a kid.

When I reached the back of the Farragut place I squatted down, staring at the French doors to the den. This is what a burglar would find. Was it feasible for someone, anyone, to pull such a stunt?

Had anyone climbed the wall at the point I had, looking for an easy mark, they'd probably have found the neighbor's doors closed hurricane tight, then found Farragut's wide open. Perhaps they'd even seen Farragut open the French doors, then disappear and reappear upstairs, fighting with his wife. A fifty-yard sprint to the wide-open doors and a house full of treasures. It didn't make sense, but it made junkie sense.

Desperate but doable.

As I rose, I noticed the curtains of Colleen's room being drawn. The windows were thrust open and Colleen stood staring out at the bridge and the Bay the way I've seen soldiers and marines stare when they thought they were seeing them for the last time. She was wearing a black lace bra and a tiny G-string, thin black lines running up over her hips.

She didn't move when she saw me. She wasn't self-conscious or embarrassed. I tried to read something in the steady gaze. I couldn't. I remembered the City Services suit and felt like Geek magazine's Man of the Month. She smiled, nodded good morning, and disappeared back inside.

It was then that I realized one more thing about my decision, one more reason to be glad she'd known of Farragut's diaries and put them on the carrot pole. I'd spend a month in her company, though never sure if she was the most calculating of killers or the most wronged of the innocent; it would mean a month in the soft, mesmerizing light of her beauty nonetheless.

I pedaled back to my house, mostly uphill, burning off a few pounds en route, and cursed turning forty as I stashed the bike. After a quick shower I called Zane Neidlinger at home to tell him I needed a seat in court for the day, and that it was very important to both of us to meet beforehand. He promised to have a seat ready and to meet me at Caffè Roma in an hour.

Within a half hour all three of my agency cohorts, Martha, Henry Borowski, and Arnie Nuckles, had gathered in the City Lights office downstairs to hear the boss's latest brainstorm. I don't know if they were more astonished by the fact that we were involved in the Farragut murder case, the million-dollar offer, or the Herculean nature of the task. I didn't plan to tell them about the diaries.

I'd always tried to stay out of the guessing game, rarely feeling an obligation to figure in advance if a potential client was guilty or not. Most of the time you didn't have to ask; it was the first thing out of their mouths. Usually you just tried not to yawn.

I told them what I'd heard and what doubts I had. Then I thought better of keeping the offer of the diaries to myself and told them about the remote chance that I'd be able to clear my name. They were Three Jaws Hanging.

I put the big question to them: why would Colleen Farragut invest half her remaining money, plus waste what precious time she had, unless there was something to her story?

Martha was the first to side with Colleen. She'd felt from the beginning that Colleen had been railroaded and the evidence against her was circumstantial.

Arnie was more skeptical but voted to proceed, promising his best effort. I knew he was doing it for my sake. Henry just nodded and smiled. He was in for the thrill of working on a case that amounted to a PI's wet dream.

I counted out three stacks of bills, fifteen hundred dollars each, keeping five hundred for myself for expenses. I told them that if we cracked the case, a quarter of the bonus money would go for new equipment and long-range operating expenses, I'd keep a quarter for myself, and they could split the other half million three ways. They'd have walked a barefoot mile on broken glass when I finished.

I gave each of them an assignment. I wanted Martha to check on Colleen's activities for the entire year preceding William's murder, to research her phone bills, credit card receipts, and her sexual escapades with Tommy Rivera. When she finished, I wanted her to look into Rivera himself. If we couldn't find the plates and the burglar, maybe we could uncover something to discredit Rivera. His testimony figured to be the most damning piece of evidence against her.

Arnie would work on William Farragut from the same angle: phone records, credit cards, all his activities during the year preceding his death, looking for anyone who might have threatened him. Henry's assignment was to check on any known burglars in the Bay Area, particularly those heavily into drugs and prone to spontaneous acts of violence. The police had already done extensive work on those subjects, so we'd be starting in their files and looking for mistakes and anything they had overlooked. That meant hours of reading documents.

There are a lot of stages in an investigation, and we were in the weirdest combination I'd ever seen, the preliminary round-up-the-usual-suspects phase and the eleventh-hour Hail Mary–Divine Intervention phase. When I mentioned the roughly thirty-day deadline and the fate that awaited our client, they headed to the loft to retrieve the files.

I grabbed my coat and sprinted down the hill to Caffè Roma on Columbus Avenue to meet Zane Neidlinger.

When I arrived he was ensconced at a corner table, a trace of cappuccino foam on his thin blond mustache, using the morning *Clarion* as a shield to ogle the behind of a blue-jeaned brunette tall enough to hunt geese with a rake. Zane was fifty-three years old, still blond, pink-skinned, and perennially wearing the contented grin of the aging satyr. He called it his fresh-fucked, just-got-paid look. He'd been a reporter for over thirty years and was that rarest of humans, one who never wanted to be anything but what he was. Irreverent, fearless, insightful, Zane was an encyclopedia of city history, a raconteur with few peers.

We met when he wrote a story about me, a fourth-generation San Francisco cop, a month after I graduated from the academy. He'd also written about me when I helped crack the Golden Dragon Massacre in Chinatown and was appointed head of the white-collar-crime division at the age of twenty-nine. When I was bounced from the department, Zane was there again, trumpeting my side of the story. Through his efforts, my career rose and fell under public scrutiny. In the end it was his defense of me that had almost single-handedly turned a lot of public opinion in my favor. I owed him a lot.

We climbed into his prehistoric Chevy and headed toward City Hall and the courthouse. En route he handed me a temporary press pass from a newspaper I'd never heard of and asked why I was so interested in the Farragut case, hinting that my previous battles with William were behind it.

First I swore him to secrecy. Then I asked him to be my eyes and ears for the remainder of the trial and to provide me with his notes and observations. I promised to make it worth his while. He'd known me long enough to realize I wasn't kidding.

I took a deep breath and told him. Jerking to a halt behind two shirtless Chinese boys unloading plucked chickens outside of a restaurant on Stockton Street, he made me repeat the part about the Farragut diaries.

It's hard to rattle a guy like Zane but his hands started to tremble on the wheel. He knew of the diaries and had coveted them for years.

Zane urged me to spare no effort in exonerating Colleen and securing the Farragut diaries and promised whatever help I'd need. In return, I promised to share the diaries with him alone. He reached over to shake my hand, visions of the Pulitzer Prize dancing in his head, as we headed to the courthouse.

We parked in the underground municipal lot near City Hall. As we climbed out of the car a black Cadillac with official plates entered, circled, stopped a few yards away. A bodyguard in a shiny blue suit exited and reached for the rear door.

We stared intently as Supervisor Helen Smidge emerged. Formerly Helen Smidgelewski, she was appointed to the board of supervisors to fill the vacancy when one of the supervisors succeeded DiMarco upon his death.

Three reporters materialized from nowhere to begin peppering her with questions about the Farragut case and her "close relationship" with Farragut. My heart jumped a little as another link between my wounded past and the events of the day fell into place.

Politics rivals television as our primary source of self-loathing and mediocrity. Out of a simpleminded narcissist with a sackful of inherited money and the insight of a fortune cookie, politics can make the future darling of city government, headed for the governor's office and beyond. Out of a friendless Ivy League nerd with a hundred-dollar smile and the sincerity of a laugh track, it makes a "dynamic leader" destined for the White House. It'll take a backwoods racist spouting jukebox idioms as a mask for the darkness and ignorance of his soul and make him a "voice for reason and moderation."

From a boring nonentity with an encyclopedia of clichés, the desperation of the unloved and the compassion of a baby peddler comes a woman such as supervisor Helen Smidge.

Nicknamed "Helen Smudge" by a San Francisco columnist for the oily stain she left on everything she touched, she had a physical presence that was impossible to forget, for all the wrong reasons.

The toes of her sensible shoes pointed so far apart it was hard to tell if she was making a left or a right. She had long, breadstick ankles with two lumps of calf pasted just below the woolen hem of her A-frame dresses. She was thick-waisted and neckless. Under a helmet of bleached and Varathaned hair was a set of eyes close enough to share the same socket. In spite of it, she had risen from a precinct political hack with a Rolodex full of bored housewives ready to mobilize for any cause or candidate she dictated to become a feared and omnipotent supervisor with a deathlike grip on the city's wealthiest elite.

She had also been William Farragut's number-one confidante, crony, and hatchetwoman on the board, as well as the principal recipient of his political patronage.

After Warren Dillon murdered the mayor, Smidge was appointed to the board of supervisors by DiMarco's conservative successor, Adam Reikling, the prime butt-boy of the sell-everything-to-anyone faction. The city instantly became a feeding trough for the high-rise developers and tourist hotel associations, with Farragut and Smidge leading the charge. Smidge had also been friend and mentor to former police officer turned assassin, Warren Dillon.

As Helen Smidge disappeared into the darkness under a canopy of "No comment," Zane and I made our way up the steps and into the flawless morning light. A few dozen homeless people had just awakened from their luxury accommodations on the park benches of their choice and sat watching all the commotion fifty yards away.

An impromptu press conference was being held on the front steps; there was a crush of people roughly the size of the crowd that attended Kennedy's funeral. As we hustled to the edge, Calvin Sherenian strode to the microphone tree to work the crowd. A French-Armenian orphan who was reared from the age of fifteen by relatives in the U.S., Calvin had put himself through Stanford Law School and was widely recognized as both judicial scholar and orator's orator. He was graceful, strong, witty, and eloquent enough to stir a crowd of Texans to weep for Saddam Hussein.

The sun balanced itself gracefully above the Hall of Justice, the sky a radiant blue backdrop. Everything grew quiet except for the cameras clicking and the sound of autowinders as Calvin fixed the crowd steadily with his gaze.

"I have asked to make this statement," he said, his voice instantly gripping the crowd, "to try to quell the frightening aura of hysteria that surrounds this case. It is my last public statement in this matter until after the inevitable verdict of not guilty.

"When I came to this country as a teenager, an orphan from a land of chaos and brutality, I was overwhelmed by the feelings of decency, hope, and fair play I found in my new home. Here, I said as I grew into a young man, is a land based on the rule of law and the sovereignty of justice.

"Occasionally that great vision is lost, as it has been in the case of Mrs. Colleen Farragut. She has been tried and convicted in absentia by the press and the office of the district attorney.

"On numerous occasions, I have been asked how I could defend the accused murderer of a lifelong friend and associate. It is because she is innocent, because I believe to the last fiber of my being that she is innocent, because I believe the circumstantial evidence against her is not sufficient enough to warrant an indictment let alone a trial and a conviction.

"William Farragut was my friend, but so is Colleen Farragut.

Over the past decade my friendship with Colleen has become as strong as it was with her late husband. I can think of no greater crime beyond the one already committed than to send an innocent woman to her death or to prison for the rest of her life. I have lost one friend to a horrible injustice; I do not intend to lose two.

"I ask now that we all let justice have its day. I will not speak again on this matter outside the courtroom, and I ask that you refrain from shoving microphones into my face and shouting out questions, as my inevitable refusal may, in its brusqueness, cause you ill will."

With a smile he turned from the rush of cameramen and reporters shoving microphones in his face and shouting out questions and ran inside the courthouse.

It was a marvelous performance, old Abe at the Springfield Courthouse getting in shape for Gettysburg, a Franco-Armenian Lincoln winning the hearts of a crowd in three hundred words or less. They wanted to acquit Colleen Farragut, perhaps torch the courthouse, and lynch the DA for good measure. It was a strange feeling for me, for many were the times I had hated Calvin for springing some swine the good cops of San Francisco had spent months throwing a net over. I was now his second-greatest cheerleader.

As the conga line of Betacams and notebooks followed Calvin, I told Zane I'd meet him inside and quickly made my way to the back of the courthouse.

I figured the "Police Only" entrance was out of the question, though a dozen reporters felt otherwise, doing the one-foot-to-the-other shuffle they do, smoking, stomping out cigarette butts, tossing coffee cups, waiting. One of them was collecting money and writing names in little squares on a piece of notebook paper. They had a pool going on what Colleen's sentence would be. The jackpot was her receiving the death penalty.

I went to the cafeteria delivery dock, found no one there. After fifteen minutes a string of a dozen small and large delivery trucks pulled into the driveway, followed by an unmarked gold van with the windows blackened out. I was unable to see who or what was inside. A few feet past me, the van stopped. The driver's side window opened and a long, graceful female hand with long, perfectly manicured fuchsia-colored nails chucked a piece of notebook paper in my direction. I snatched it quickly from the ground and opened it.

On it was written *How did you ever get the name Peekaboo Frankie Fagen?* followed by *Here's hoping.* It was signed with the same initial *C,* in the same lovely hand as the first note I'd received.

5

I MADE MY way past twenty-five reporters doing stand-ups at the entrance to Judge Marilyn Walters's courtroom, including one each in French, German, Spanish, Italian, and Japanese.

I flashed the press pass that Zane had given me to the deputy at the head of a line of five hundred people, many of whom had lined up outside the building before midnight. The deputy informed me there could be no photos taken of the jury, nor any at all after the proceedings started. I nodded my consent and entered.

Zane had staked out two seats in the front row behind the prosecution and eighteen feet from the defense table on our right. I squeezed past several other reporters and spectators and shimmied my butt onto the bench between Zane and a frumpy-looking female journalist yawning and wearing a badge that said FRESNO BADGER.

No sooner had I hit the pine than Calvin Sherenian swept in from stage left, followed by a pasty white boy in a pinstripe suit with his arms full of legal documents. The latter might have worn a sign that said BIG YAWN, NO BALLS but it would have been redundant. Zane whispered, "Bruce Bearden, USC Law Review. Arrogant little prick, completely anal-retentive. Calvin's research whiz and gopher."

No sooner had Zane finished putting the hatchet to Calvin's boy

Bearden than the two of them stopped in front of us. Zane and I put on our big howdy-how-ya-doin' smiles.

"Zane," said Calvin with a nod and the most sincere smile he could muster, "I figured you for a front row seat. You know my associate, Bruce Bearden?"

"Yes, we've met," said Zane, who faked a smile of his own and nodded at Bearden, who faked his best one back.

Then Calvin's gaze fell on me. "Mr. Fagen. Bruce, have you ever met the man they call Peekaboo Frankie Fagen?" Bruce shook his head almost indiscernibly, then shifted the stack of papers and stuck his hand out. It was soft, damp, like a fried-clam sandwich. "And what brings you here, Mr. Fagen?" asked Sherenian.

Before I had to fake an answer, the side door of the courtroom opened and an unarmed sheriff's deputy entered. The audience of professional and amateur peep freaks lunged to attention in anticipation of the prime exhibit, Colleen Farragut.

After a few moments she appeared, and the cameras started clicking. Colleen was obviously prepared for it; she walked with her head high, dignity overcoming fear, at least on the outside.

She looked right at me, then looked away without an inkling of recognition. Lawrence Ferlinghetti's poem came to me: *Women who needed despair to look beautiful/looked beautiful indeed/for there was despair/to spare.*

She took her seat as Calvin graciously slid her chair back for her. I wondered how she maintained her composure.

After everyone was seated, the bailiff called the jury. One by one they filed in. While they seated themselves, DA Jeffries shuffled papers, looking just a bit harried. In contrast Calvin, seated next to Colleen, looked relaxed, dignified, politely acknowledging the jury with a Mona Lisa smile of welcome. All but a few of the jurors acknowledged the presence of Calvin, the existence of the DA; when their eyes fell on the mesmerizing Mrs. Farragut they lingered for as many seconds as politeness and judicial decorum would allow. Only one of them actually stared, an old Mexican man who looked like a retired bank president. He'd have a hell of a story to tell when this one was over.

The bailiff called for everyone to stand as Judge Marilyn Walters entered. I knew Walters well, she'd been one of the fairest and smartest of all the judges I'd ever observed. Neither the defense nor the prosecution would find much favor, though if anything, she might temper some of Calvin's more dramatic efforts.

After the reading of the charges the prosecutor, Ian Jeffries, puffed himself up a touch and approached the jury. I could tell before he opened his mouth that he was going to try to out-Calvin Calvin.

"Your Honor, ladies and gentlemen of the jury. You are facing one of the most difficult tasks that a society can ask of twelve good citizens, to decide whether or not another human being should be deprived of her life or her freedom. In this case, with the charge murder in the first degree with special circumstances, a guilty verdict means death or life imprisonment without the possibility of parole. There is only one thing that can make this task a little easier, a little less troubling for you, and that is the overwhelming nature of the evidence that you will see and hear.

"The facts in this case will convince you that on a September evening over nineteen months ago, Colleen Farragut murdered her husband. She fired two shots from a .38 caliber pistol into his chest and left him lying in agony, bleeding to death in the den of his own home.

"And why did she commit this barbaric act? Because she was distraught over a pending divorce and a prenuptial agreement that would have taken away her mansion, her Mercedes, her platinum credit cards. She was distraught because a clause in that agreement stipulated that if she were caught having sexual intercourse with another man, she would receive nothing from her husband. And she was caught. She murdered William Farragut out of pure and simple greed.

"The defense, led by the vaunted and very crafty Mr. Calvin Sherenian, will cry circumstantial evidence. 'No eyewitness,' they'll say, 'no photographs, no tape recordings, no videotapes.' How surprising. A woman who holds both a bachelor's and master's degree from the University of California at Berkeley, who graduated in the top two percent of her class, an ambitious woman with a near genius IQ had the foresight not to murder her husband in front of a room full of people and to make certain no photographer was present. And for this, Mr. Sherenian will tell you, we should find her innocent. We should send her home with a sorry-we-bothered-you and hand her the millions of dollars she wishes to obtain over her husband's dead body.

"The high-priced Mr. Sherenian will tell you it's all a terrible coincidence: the maid's night off, the fact that the murder victim had informed her of his intention to divorce her a week prior to the shooting. He will put forth Mrs. Farragut's ridiculous claim that someone else shot her husband and ransacked the den while she was catching up on her beauty sleep.

"And who was this 'someone else' she claims was the actual murderer? A phantom burglar. Colleen Farragut will tell you a burglar did it, a burglar that nineteen months of intensive police work has yet to find a single trace of, a burglar who left no fingerprints, no clues, no physical evidence of any kind. A burglar that does not and never did exist.

"The prosecution will show you enough physical evidence to prove that Mrs. Farragut committed this crime. Then we'll put Mrs. Farragut's lover on the stand, and he will testify that months before she actually killed her husband, she offered him a large sum of money to do it for her. She was going to have her husband killed and pay for it with his own money. When her lover refused, she just did the job herself. We'll show you enough to make you quite ill.

"You'll hear some of the worst excuses, the weakest alibis ever concocted, all delivered with such convincing eloquence by the defense that you'll want to believe Mr. Sherenian when he tells you that day is night and bad is good. Don't do it. I implore, I beseech you, listen to the facts, listen to the truth, don't be fooled by any fast-talking charlatan in this courtroom." Ian bowed almost imperceptibly in the direction of the jury, hand on the buttons of his double-breasted suit, and returned to his chair.

It was a marvelous performance, Calvinesque in eloquence and inference. Jeffries had painted both Calvin and Colleen as rich, pompous asses ready to toy with the jury, used the standard ploy of shooting down the other guy's arguments before he got to present them.

Calvin was livid in his chair.

When Judge Walters called, he slid his chair back slowly and stood, staring sideways at Ian Jeffries with a steel-melting gaze. Then Calvin turned and looked down at the tabletop, regarded the knuckles of his left hand, raised his head to the heavens very briefly, sighed, looked at the judge and jury. After another brief glare at Ian Jeffries, he turned his attention back to the jury. He walked slowly toward them, every eye and thought belonging to him alone.

"I had an opening statement prepared; passionate, concise. But I'll acquiesce to my able opponent. I'll concede to him—and to you the jury—one point. I have the greatest faith that you will indeed judge this case strictly on the facts.

"But in his dramatic plea for a verdict based on fact, Mr. Jeffries argued for the exact opposite. He referred to me as the 'high-priced' defense attorney, a 'charlatan,' and warned you against any chicanery or deception. He in effect painted both the defendant and me as rich, arrogant, above the law. He will insinuate—no, he will state emphatically throughout this trial—that if a woman, even one as beautiful, intelligent, and compassionate as Colleen Farragut is, happens to marry a man from a higher social station than hers, or shows any 'ambition,' as he puts it, that she must be a whore and a murderer. If that's trying a case on evidence, I've been a dentist these past thirty years.

"My client is a party to a terrible crime, that *is* a fact. An unwilling party to a terrible crime, and that is this mockery of a trial.

"Since Mr. Jeffries has decided to make his attacks personal and superficial, to use character assassination and insults to try this case, let me break a long-standing rule, lower myself briefly to his level, and tell you folks what is really happening here in this courtroom.

"You see, ladies and gentlemen, a district attorney almost never tries a case himself. He's an administrator, he has deputies who try big cases for him. But Mr. Jeffries has a reputation for being excessively harsh on poor and minority defendants, for using the law to bash blacks, Hispanics, and poor whites."

Jeffries leapt to his feet screaming, "This is an outrage! I demand Mr. Sherenian withdraw and apologize. . . . " He could barely be heard over the tumult in the court.

Judge Walters banged the gavel. "Mr. Sherenian," she said, having to shout it several times over the din. I counted three blacks, two Hispanics, two Asians on the jury: seven out of twelve.

Calvin counterattacked before Walters or Jeffries could say another word.

"Your Honor, my client is on trial for her life, and Mr. Jeffries has made it very clear that not only her character but mine as well will become an issue in this trial. Justice demands that I be allowed to present an accurate picture to the jury. . . . "

"I'll give you some leeway, Mr. Sherenian, but you will withdraw your previous statement and you won't turn this trial into a circus."

"I'm only trying to prevent Mr. Jeffries from doing the same, Your Honor," he said, and then withdrew his statement.

Walters sat back uneasily.

Calvin started again. "Mr. Jeffries, as many of you know, is a candidate for state attorney general, and he is haunted by accusations of unfairness. So, he thinks if he shucks and jives through this case screaming 'Hang this tramp who married a rich man!' somehow, this equal injustice, this injustice for all will make him seem like the honorable, professional prosecutor he has never been.

"He has no case, he has no witnesses, he has no argument but to attack Colleen Farragut with the most vile and cowardly personal insults he can muster. I begged him time and again not to put an innocent woman through this ordeal. But the publicity was too great a temptation, so here we are, prisoners of a megalomaniac, a political hack, a political prostitute of the foulest odor."

With that, Calvin mocked the tiny bow of his predecessor, right hand over double-breasted, then returned to his seat.

The courtroom exploded as Walters banged the gavel and alternately shouted "Mr. Sherenian!" and "Order!" When it got quiet, all Walters could do was sit and glare at Calvin.

Walters had already lost a big point. The circus had come to town, to her courtroom, and Calvin owned the elephants.

The score was one to nothing, favor of Colleen.

6

*W*ALTERS TOOK BOTH attorneys into her chambers following Calvin's withering assault on Jeffries, where I'm sure she
chewed them out vigorously for the entire hour they were gone.
When they returned, she ordered the lunch break. Two jurors
actually looked over at Calvin and smiled.

Zane and I poisoned ourselves in the courthouse cafeteria, de-
claring Calvin's opening a landmark in the annals of jurisprudence,
then hurried back to our seats in advance of the stampede. As we
waited for the resumption of the festivities, a little clock inside my
head kept ticking *thirty days . . . thirty days. . . .*

Ian Jeffries called his first witness, Inspector John Naftulin. He
was in his late forties, with a chain mail canopy of graying hair, one
uninterrupted eyebrow resembling a furry windshield wiper, and
a nervous habit of constantly cracking his knuckles. I'd known John
from my days as the new kid in homicide. He was a tough, honest,
hardworking cop with a sackful of opinions and a quick tongue that
often got him in trouble.

"You were the first police officer called to the scene at fifty-six
fifty-six Park Drive, isn't that correct, Inspector Naftulin?"

"Yes. I was on Clement Street eating breakfast when the call
came over my walkie-talkie."

"And you wrote the crime scene report and became the chief
investigating officer in the case?"

"That's correct."

"And what did you find when you arrived?"

"I found the victim, William Farragut, lying on his back in the den of his home. He'd been dead for several hours; his body was stiff."

"In fact the coroner's report later indicated he'd been dead for over eight hours, isn't that correct?"

"Yes."

"And the cause of death, was it apparent to you at the time?"

"Yes. Mr. Farragut had been shot twice in the chest, once through the heart, once through the right lung."

"And you noticed this gun on the floor approximately twenty feet from the body?"

Ian Jeffries showed the gun to Inspector Naftulin, who identified it. Jeffries had it tagged and marked as People's Exibit One.

"What was the condition of Mrs. Farragut? Was she hysterical, crying?"

"She was agitated."

"Can you describe her for us?"

"She was breathing hard, her hands were trembling. She seemed . . . uncomfortable."

I figured it was time for Calvin to jump up and bark "Objection!" on the grounds that Jeffries was asking for conclusions and not facts. But Calvin sat stifling a yawn and a smile as Zane frantically scribbled notes next to me.

Several more times Jeffries did it, drawing out Inspector Naftulin's opinion that he was skeptical of Colleen's story right from the start. One by one the jury began to stare at Calvin. They'd all seen enough "Perry Mason" and "L.A. Law" to know that Jeffries was leading the witness, and still Calvin did nothing.

Then Jeffries got to the part I came to hear, the one opinion I was most interested in: Jeffries placed enlarged photographs of Farragut's den on a large bulletin board and asked Naftulin to use his "twenty-five years of police expertise" to tell the jury what he saw in the room.

"A fake burglary," was all he said. Jeffries asked him to elaborate.

"I've seen enough fake burglaries in my time," Naftulin said. When Jeffries asked how many burglary reports he had written in twenty-five years with the SFPD, Jeffries stated "close to a thousand, perhaps more."

I had seen hundreds of burglaries myself in nine years with the department. I'd seen a few dozen people try to fake burglaries to collect the insurance.

As Naftulin explained and every photograph showed, the contents of drawers were flung across the room, plants were dumped upside down, coffee tables flipped over. In reality, burglars go through drawers throwing out things they don't want. If you dump them, you then have to bend over, and burglars are inveterate nonbenders. Plants are rarely turned upside down, they're knocked over, usually landing on their sides and spilling dirt out like a cone. Tables are usually knocked at an angle, not overturned. Burglars, even the amateurs, are always afraid of making noise and are not prone to sending coffee tables crashing or scattering drawers about. The smart ones, the experienced ones, rarely knock over or break anything. Naftulin confirmed everything I'd thought when I saw the Farragut den and the exhibit photos in the evidence files.

It looked like someone had faked it.

And it didn't matter who had done it: whether it was some radical nut cases who shot Farragut and tried to make it look like a burglary or a vengeful killer trying to throw everyone off his tracks, the jury would think it was Colleen.

7

AFTER COURT RECESSED, ZANE drove me back to Telegraph Hill. We agreed it had been a rough day for Colleen Farragut.

Late in the afternoon session, Calvin had launched his counterattack on Inspector John Naftulin, attempting to hang him with his own rope. He honed in on Naftulin's opinion of the house, the Farragut wealth, the fact that Colleen had married into money. Calvin even got a flustered and belligerent Naftulin to admit that the charges he filed with the DA's office two days after the murder were based more on his dislike and mistrust of Colleen than on the evidence. I'd seen some ugly cases in my life, but this one was already bucking for the blue ribbon.

Unfortunately, what made the biggest impression on me, and I feared on the jury as well, were the photographs of a chump-change burglary. Despite Calvin's brilliant opening statement and cleverness in cross-examination, Colleen looked an inch closer to the noose when the day ended.

Arnie Nuckles was waiting at the office when Zane dropped me off. I've seen more encouraging faces at the morgue.

Arnie had spent the day checking William Farragut's banking activities, all two dozen accounts, starting the day of his murder and working his way backward. It was a job that would take a platoon of accountants weeks to do properly.

Arnie found nothing that appeared suspicious. No regular withdrawals of huge sums of cash, no series of deposits that snaked their way from an overseas account through a series of "front" accounts. Arnie learned that Farragut owned seventeen safe-deposit boxes at six different banks, plus three private safes. I was sure that several of them held his diaries, others the cash he used for bribes and kickbacks. Nothing, however, indicated that he'd been the victim of blackmail or extortion.

The Farragut clan, from William I on down, had built a formidible reputation for leaving no discernible trail throughout a hundred years of plundering the city. I envisioned old man Farragut III sitting at the dinner table, teaching young William IV how to run a proper slush fund the way most fathers instruct their sons in the art of hitting a curveball.

I asked Arnie about the girl who had been Farragut's S&M sweetie, but nothing that Arnie had found in Farragut's records immediately indicated who she was or where to find her. Naturally.

Nothing in the evidence files indicated that she had ever been found. That got my curiosity working overtime. Why hadn't the SFPD or Sherenian's army of PIs ever found her?

Finally, Arnie produced three phone numbers, the three Farragut had called most frequently, particularly in the days preceding his death. One was the number of his bosom buddy, Calvin Sherenian, one was the number of his political hack, Supervisor Helen Smidge.

The last was an unlisted number in Hillsborough that Farragut called every night between the hours of seven and eight. Through a friend of mine at the phone company, Arnie had learned that the nightly calls made by the murdered William IV were to Eileen Farragut, his mother.

This last piece of information was just one more in the string of surprising facts about the Farragut family, one I didn't remember from my previous pursuit of Willy IV. It made me wonder if Bluebeard wrote regularly to his mom.

I thanked Arnie, and after he left, I rose, yawned a jawbreaker, and went upstairs to exchange my courtroom apparel for a spare leather jacket and a Walther. Then I clunked back down the stairs, opened the garage, and fired up the Norton.

I slowed to watch the sun dropping behind the Golden Gate, fiery red, the shadow of the bridge moving over the Marina like a sundial on fast forward. It always amazes me to watch the colors of the city change as the sun sets, gold fading to pale metallic green, then deepening to a light iridescent purple as the last ray climbs Telegraph Hill and mingles with the first evening lights.

It had been twenty-four hours since I received Colleen's invitation to the opera and I was pushing forty hours without sleep. My head hurt, my eyes burned, and I had Eileen Farragut to deal with, if she'd see me.

I knew that keeping my arrangement with Colleen a secret was going to be tough; Eileen would be the first test.

Los Angeles may be famed for its traffic jams, but they do in eight or ten lanes what much of the San Francisco Peninsula is still doing in four. Bumper to bumper, the ulcer brigade returned to the suburbs, with me on the Norton burning a hole between the lanes, pissing off ten or twelve thousand people in the process.

My mind was all over the place. I thought of Colleen and the horror that awaited her. I thought of how the bastards had killed Kennedy and were still getting away with it, of how my grandfather had once tried to bust Farragut's grandfather and had gotten the same treatment I had. I thought that God was a bent quarter in a midnight phone booth.

I needed a night's sleep. I needed a job where no one went to jail or lost their life if I couldn't perform a miracle. I needed a long vacation with Colleen and two suitcases full of her favorite lingerie in a bungalow in the Caribbean, eating right and fucking like humans.

What I really needed was a break in the case. I wanted Eileen Farragut to tell me something she hadn't told anyone else, something that would lead me to her son's killer.

I exited the freeway, passing a sign that read WELCOME TO HILLSBOROUGH, which I doubted I was. One of the wealthiest suburbs in the country, it was also the home of the Hearst family of publishing and Patty fame. I pushed the Norton down streets so perfect, so clean, I suspected little gardeners hid in the bushes with pointed sticks, ready to attack any candy wrapper invading from some disrespectful ghetto to the north.

Arriving at the home of the late William Farragut III, I headed up the long drive. The house was another one of those Tudor-style monstrosities, and I was certain they'd be delighted to see an uninvited, leather-jacketed PI with long hair and a motorcycle.

I scuffed my way up the stone steps to the front door and pressed a button, which set off musical door chimes. A tiny peephole with a metal grate over it opened and a single female Oriental eye appeared.

"Francis Fagen, private investigator," I said, and held my ID up so the Cyclops could see it. I always saved "Francis" for the better neighborhoods, figuring the choirboy handle might offset the fashionably avant-garde Bowery appearance. I lowered the ID and told the eye I wanted to see Mrs. Farragut about the murder of her son. I held the ID up again. The eye didn't blink. I wished I'd had a spitball and a plastic straw. Finally the eye closed the peephole and left me hanging, reciting nonsense phrases, lyrics from bad songs like "Play That Funky Music White Boy" and wondering why private detectives never called first.

I'd waited long enough to earn a college degree when I heard latches being unbolted and the large wooden door swung open. The Oriental eye belonged to a short stout woman in her mid fifties. I thanked her in Cantonese as I entered. She was unimpressed. My Mandarin was equally unimpressive. I found out later she was Korean.

I followed the maid down a hallway like the ones in Colleen's house. Most were decorated in medieval decor: sawed-up bridge timbers, chairs and tables with flayed saddles for seats and backs. It proved again that taste and money rarely had intercourse.

The maid deposited me in a huge library where eightyish Eileen Farragut sat in a red chair wearing a green dress and black shoes, and didn't seem to mind. She was slight, silver-haired, and wrinkled as a catcher's mitt left out in the rain. She had fingers bony enough to pick a padlock, forearms that could slice cheese.

She looked me over from bottom to top without the slightest hint of approval. What struck me most were her eyes. Clear blue and years younger than their owner, they seemed to be crying out *Help me, I'm being held prisoner in the body of an old woman.*

"So you're the man who struck fear in the heart of my son," she said.

"That's twice I've heard that," I answered. "I must admit that it surprises me. I thought your son was only capable of one emotion." Open Mouth, Insert Foot Fagen.

But she smiled, looked me over top to bottom this time. "Greed is not an emotion, it's an institution with the males of the Farragut lineage." She said it with humor and life filling her eyes. "I remember you from your newspaper photographs, Mr. Fagen. You've gone to hell a bit, haven't you?" I didn't have much of an answer to that one. "I say, I've known a few private detectives in my life and you're the damnedest one I've seen yet. What is your business, Mr. Fagen?"

"I'm investigating the Colleen Farragut case. I think there's at least a chance she might be innocent. I was hoping you might help me. If she is innocent, that means the person who killed your son is still out there." It's deduction like that last bit that's going to get me in the PI Hall of Fame.

Eileen waved me to a chair. "I've answered a lot of questions already, but if you think it will help you I'll gladly answer more. Then you'll answer one or two of mine."

I nodded. I liked her already.

"Why did your son marry Colleen?" I began. She seemed a little surprised; I was sure no one had asked her that yet.

"Besides the obvious?" she asked. I nodded. Without blinking she said, "You know how most women are, here in the hedonist

65

half of the twentieth century; they show up for a first date in a garter belt and a pair of kneepads. Not Colleen. She made him wait, she refused to be impressed by his power or his money. He pursued her, not vice versa. After that, well, I hear she has incomparable oral dexterity."

I tried not to bust out laughing. "That's a noble trait, Mrs. Farragut, one I admire tremendously in a woman, but it's not a reason to marry."

"With William it was." She was serious. This was some family. Son finishes a hard day plundering the city, calls mom faithfully and lets her know what a good blow job the missus gives. Sigmund Freud should have had them on his greatest hits.

"Look, Mr. Fagen, I think you're trying to find hidden motives: did Colleen have anything on William, did she blackmail him or manipulate him into marrying her. The answer is no. My son was rich and handsome and very charming, although he had the Farragut curse, a soul blacker than a bottomless pit. He could have had a lot of women, damn near any woman he wanted, but he chose her. He was obsessed with her.

"I've oversimplified to make a point, Mr. Fagen, but Colleen was, in William's opinion, the most erotic and exciting woman he'd ever met. She didn't pursue him, he pursued her."

She was smart, smarter than I was. "So what happened?"

"To them? As I mentioned, my son had the family disease. His father, his grandfather—you know the Farragut history, I'm sure. They all had the attention span of an autistic child, especially when it came to human relations. He grew tired of her. Once he had her, he wanted what they all wanted: more. Something new and different. Something he couldn't have. Matter of fact, that particular curse is not limited to the Farraguts, at least where women are concerned. Most men are afflicted by it.

"In fact, Mr. Fagen, judging by your shoddy good looks, your lack of a wedding band, and your inflated sense of bohemian self-worth, you probably suffer from some of those very same afflictions."

Again I had to fight not to laugh out loud. She owned me.

"William called you every night, and I'm gathering that he kept very few secrets from you. Did he have any real enemies, people who were threatening revenge, who might have been capable of killing him?"

She looked at me, waiting for an explanation. I smiled and kept going.

"Right now, everyone is talking burglary, burglary. It could be someone came there to harm either William or Colleen, then tried to cover it up by dumping out drawers and stealing the two silver plates to make it look like a burglary."

"Yes, Ghiberti's plates. Among my son's most prized possessions." She hesitated, looked up, seemed to choose her words carefully. "My son had a lot of enemies, Mr. Fagen. He'd received a number of death threats over the years from radical groups in San Francisco and Berkeley. Crackpots like the people who kidnapped Patricia Hearst, Marxist groups. But the police don't seem to think any of them had anything to do with it, or they would have crowed about it in the media."

The police were right; any radical group or self-righteous wacko would have pumped it up for publicity value. I could safely move that theory to the bottom of the list.

"William's business opponents were a strange lot, Mr. Fagen, but most of them were his friends. People he'd bested in deals, people he'd defeated along the way. I despised my son's business tactics, the way I despised his father's and his grandfather's. But William never cheated a partner. The people he'd beaten always hoped he'd include them in his next venture. No threats, no blackmail, nothing. And believe me, he would have told me. His father died when he was only twenty, and I became his most trusted confidante. Myself and his lawyer, Calvin Sherenian, who became a surrogate father to him, were the two people closest to him."

I looked her in the eye, wanting to believe her. If what she said was true, one of my theories was probably wrong: that Farragut and not his possessions had been the target. That would bring me back to a bungled burglary. Or Colleen.

"Do you think Colleen killed him?" I asked.

She smiled. The great blue eyes floated over my face, softening. "No, I do not."

I was surprised and tried not to show it.

"I adore my daughter-in-law, Mr. Fagen," she said. "I thought she was the best thing that ever happened to Will. She used his money to try to help people. She wasn't one of those weekend liberals, she didn't help people to get her name in the society pages. She had heart, and she got her hands dirty. I can't imagine her doing something so stupid, even if she did want him dead."

She looked at me without speaking for a few moments, then added, "Look, Mr. Fagen. I hate being wrong almost as much as I hate being old. Colleen didn't have to kill anyone. Men swoon when she passes. She's smart enough and ambitious enough to get anything she wants without a man's help. I think the killer is elsewhere.

"Now answer one for me, Mr. Fagen. Why are you on this case? It can't possibly be for revenge in this ancient feud between the Fagens and the Farraguts. William is already dead. I know she has very little money left; she certainly can't be paying you very much. But every time I offer to help, she refuses."

I hadn't told her Colleen hired me, I merely said I was investigating the case. Lying about it now seemed futile.

"She gave me a retainer, and I'll get a very large bonus if I find the killer." I left out the part about the diaries. "She also asked that I keep my activities as quiet as possible, that I work strictly for her."

"If that is her wish, your secret is certainly safe with me. I wish you Godspeed, Mr. Fagen. Don't fail her."

I rose, thanked her, and headed for the door, wondering if I'd see her again, feeling grateful that my job sometimes brought me into the company of a woman like Eileen Farragut.

"Mr. Fagen," she called after me. I turned, glad to spend a few more seconds in her company. "If you need anything—if you need expense money, or reward money, or money for bribes—you'll call me. Without hesitation." It wasn't a question, but a kindly order. I nodded, thanked her again, caught the blue eyes smiling, and went out.

When I reached the motorcycle I looked back at the house. I was pleased and surprised by my reception, comforted by Eileen Farragut's conviction that Colleen was innocent, and troubled by the fact that I was a day closer to reckoning and still didn't know a damn thing more than when I'd started.

8

THE WORDS IN the evidence files started dancing and doing weird gyroscopic impersonations of the 49ers' cheerleaders when I decided I'd had enough. Dropping them on the table with the sinking feeling that nothing in them was going to help me anyway, I stood in front of the picture window and stretched, staring out at the dark waters of the Bay. I thought I saw the two bridge towers bowing toward each other like a pair of fencers. I was too tired to work and too wired to sleep.

I thought about Raymond Chandler and Dashiell Hammett, our two greatest writers of detective fiction, in that order, about how everything that happened in their stories, almost everyone the sleuth interviewed, virtually every place he went, produced a clue or a piece of the puzzle, and how unlike real life that was. For every piece of hard evidence you uncover you have to interview a few dozen bad liars and sift through a boxcar of useless information. I sensed I was going to break my own frustration record before I was through with the Farragut case.

The buzzer rang. It wasn't Arnie, Martha, or Henry Borowski, who all had keys. I cocked my Walther and put it in my back pocket, keeping my finger on the trigger, and went downstairs to answer the door.

As I approached I saw a tall, Grim Reaper–like figure, face

shrouded deep in the shadow of a hood. I didn't know the Reaper rang doorbells. I tensed a little, not having expected any hooded company, until I saw the long hand with the fuchsia-colored nails reach up and zip the hooded coat open. Colleen smiled at me through the etched-glass window. That woke me up instantly.

"Are you alone?" she asked as I opened the door. I nodded and let her in. She signaled to Consuela, parked across the street, that it was okay to go. Consuela nodded, then drove off.

"I'm sorry to barge in on you, but I just came from Calvin's office and I wanted to talk." She took the coat off, revealing the demure, businesswoman's attire she had worn to the trial that day. When she smiled the room seemed a little lighter.

"Have you eaten?" she asked.

"No, actually I'd forgotten all about it." It was just past ten. I went to a drawer and retrieved a menu from Fior d'Italia on Washington Square.

"My cousin Giuseppe is a maître d' at Fior, he'll have something sent over to us."

She selected the eggplant parmesan, I choose fettuccine vongole rosso. While I called and gave the order to Giuseppe, Colleen wandered about my office looking at my library of family photographs, many of which dated back to the Gold Rush. There were portraits of eleven of us in police uniforms, including my great-grandfather, Byron "Bunky" Fagen, my grandfather Arthur, my father, Francis Paul, and me, Francis James. Mine was taken on the day I graduated from the academy. Colleen grinned at the baby-faced rookie with the white-sidewall haircut and the smug determination, a twenty-one-year-old ready to right the world.

It was an impressive collection, and she looked at it with the intense, admiring eye of someone who loves both the city and good photography. Among the lot were some classics taken between 1850 and the Great Earthquake, showing the masts of schooners bobbing in the bay at Yerba Buena, the city little more than a booming but beautiful cow town.

The centerpiece of the collection were some prints of the 1906 earthquake and the resulting fires and destruction taken by the tragedy's greatest chronicler, Arnold Genthe, who had befriended my great-grandfather. She examined them intently as I opened a bottle of cabernet from the Cohn Winery in Sonoma. "Is that your house being built?" she asked.

"Yes. Those burly guys with the handlebar mustaches and denim aprons are my great-grandfather and his brothers. The child at the far right in the big picture is my grandfather. They were all cops, every one of them. That was 1887."

What was most impressive about the photos was the absence of landmarks in the backgrounds.

First, a shot from the top of Telegraph Hill, across the street. It showed North Beach and Cow Hollow without the Marina District, a grassy marsh that might have given birth to Swamp Thing. In the foreground was a muddy street with a wooden sidewalk and the Lombard Street cable car easing down, a line that no longer exists.

Most striking was Fort Point and the Golden Gate—without the bridge.

In several other shots, Coit Tower is conspicuously absent from the grassy knoll atop Telegraph Hill, and there is no Bay Bridge looming above and behind the Embarcadero.

"This house was built for the princely sum of seventeen hundred fifty dollars. I still have the receipts from the lumberyards and glass shops."

Colleen said, "Wow." I hadn't heard a bona fide *wow* in a long time, but I had to agree with her appraisal.

I jerked my head for her to follow me. Wine bottle and glasses in hand, I led her up the back stairs to my loft, where she remarked on my view of the bridge.

"I was surprised to see you in the courtroom," Colleen said. "I guess I was surprised to see you from my bedroom window this morning."

"I wanted to see how difficult it would be for a burglar to gain entrance from the wall. It isn't. I went to court because I knew they'd put John Naftulin on the stand to establish the crime and the crime scene. He's a good cop with a bad habit of talking too much. I was hoping he might say something he shouldn't have, give me a clue, an idea about where to start looking." My subsequent silence said he hadn't.

I set the table near the picture window, put out two dishes of antipasti I'd bought at Molinari's the day before, and filled our wineglasses. I told her I had a lot of questions and I wanted some answers. She nodded but said that once dinner arrived we'd stop, because it was difficult for her to eat when she was upset. I agreed.

I figured I had a good twenty-five minutes until the food arrived so I started with the two things most on my mind. First I asked about William's affair and how she found out.

"I got an anonymous phone call from a very nervous-sounding guy one day. He said his girlfriend was having an affair with my husband, he wanted it stopped, and he wanted money or he was going to the newspapers. After I caught my breath I told him I didn't care what he did. By this point in our relationship William and I were through anyway. I didn't give a damn if he was embarrassed in the newspapers. It was just a matter of time until he and I got divorced."

"You could have used it against him, tried to break your prenuptial, sweeten your settlement," I suggested.

"I'm not a blackmailer, Frank. I can't live my life like that."

"How long was this before William was killed?" I asked.

"He was killed in mid September, let me see . . . it was late July. About six weeks."

"Did you find out who the girl was, or if it was even true?"

"It was true all right. I have a friend who was an investigative journalist for *Mother Jones* magazine, Alice Stein. I called and told her about it, asked her if there was a way I could find out if it was true. I didn't want to go to a private detective. I've always thought they were kind of sleazy."

"Just the good ones," I told her. She smiled and went on.

"Alice followed William from his office one evening to the

Fairmont Hotel on Nob Hill. She actually rode up in the elevator with him and watched him enter a suite. Then she ran downstairs and rented the suite next door.

"She'd brought a listening device, the kind you attach to the wall, and she tape-recorded what went on." When Colleen hesitated I urged her to continue, sparing no details. I wanted to know who was the S and who was the M, if they took turns, if they had sex or just did the rawhide follies. I told Colleen different call girls had different rules, some were dominant, some submissive, some were switches. Most S&M professionals would not have sex with clients, although the Farragut cash might change that. Knowing the woman's peculiarities might make it easier to find her.

"They definitely had sex. William ordered her to dress up all in leather, thigh-high boots, black leather collar around her neck, black wrist and ankle restraints. Then he made her bend over a table, fastened her ankles to the table legs and her hands to the far end and whipped her with a riding crop, then spanked her with his bare hand. He made her count each stroke, made her beg him to fuck her. And then he did."

She was very cool about it, almost unemotional.

"Who left the room first?"

"He did. He told her to wait a half hour at least. She made a phone call, I figured it must have been the boyfriend, although we couldn't hear his voice over the tape. She called him Hawk.

"She lied to him, told him she was at a girlfriend's house. He obviously didn't believe her. He wanted to know if she was with William again and demanded that she give him the number so he could call back and verify where she was. They got in quite a row and she hung up on him."

"Sounds like this girl was an amateur."

"Yeah, that's what Alice said. I still have the tape if you want to listen to it."

"Yes, I do. Did Alice see the girl or get a license plate number or anything?"

"She rode down in the elevator with the girl, got a good look at her, but the girl left in a cab."

"How did he pay her?"

"Before they started he told her the money was in a drawer in an envelope. He told her to count it, to let him know if it was a 'fair price,' which is just like him, and she said yes."

"Description?"

"Five ten, blond, blue eyes, big boobs. A scar over the right corner of her mouth. I guess the boyfriend must have found out, because a week or so later anonymous messages started arriving at every newspaper in town. That's how all the rumors and gossip got started. The caller had enough details to make some of the newspapers print the story."

"I remember. Zane Neidlinger investigated and thought it was true. He said the girl had been seen at a number of hotels coinciding with the appearance of William, but no one knew who she was. Did the police or any of Sherenian's people ever find the girl or the boyfriend?"

"Calvin said it was better not to tell the police, that a private detective could find her just as easily and that we would be able to do things the cops couldn't in order to find out if she was involved. But the private detectives he hired never found her. They were all from the same agency, the Hayden Phillips Agency. Do you know it?"

I knew Hayden Phillips, a real swell guy. He was as low on the scale of evolution as you could get and still chew your lunch. He had the ego of an overpaid right fielder, the scruples of a washed-up movie producer, the heart of a five-dollar pimp.

He'd been a Treasury agent who left after twenty years to open his own agency. He got his start kidnapping children in custody cases, doping them up for the plane ride home. He also hired male models to seduce rich, lonely women, then kicked in the doors of their hotel rooms and photographed them doing the grunt-and-groan so their husbands could use the photos against them in divorce cases. He became so successful that his phone number was unlisted. He worked strictly for big law firms like Sherenian's.

The fact that they'd been unable to find the girl and her blackmailing boyfriend bothered me quite a bit. Phillips had some of the top PIs in the city working for him; the girl and her boyfriend were either long gone or dead.

"Has Calvin brought any of this out in strategy discussions? Has he thought of using this as a potential sidetrack, that a blackmail attempt was made and rebuffed?"

"Calvin said it was just another story that I couldn't prove."

Calvin might have been right about that one.

I asked her about her affair. She seemed a little more uneasy about that, but not ashamed. It was getting tougher to sit across from her when every move she made seemed erotic. Her long fingers wrapped around her wineglass, the glow of the lit-up city outside the window touching the angles of her face as she talked. Hearing the stories of her sexual escapades with another man was not going to be easy. Being professional was getting more difficult by the minute.

"I met Tommy Rivera when I got involved in a nonprofit organization called SOHO: Save Our Homes, Ourselves. They were buying up old and condemned buildings south of Market Street, teaching poor and homeless people to renovate them, then renting them to the people who did the work for very low prices.

"It seemed like Tommy had his life straightened out pretty well when I met him," Colleen continued. "I thought the program was a great one because it gave people skills and jobs and places to call their own. I started running into Tommy at parties and fundraisers, and he was all charm and warmth.

"I knew he liked me from the beginning, but he was cool, never made a move. I must admit that that intrigued me. He's very good-looking. Anyway, I ran into him about two weeks after I'd found out about William and the Bondage Queen. We went to lunch. I had two glasses of wine, I hadn't made love with my husband in a long time . . . " She hesitated, for the first time looking a little troubled.

"I'd never cheated on William before, but our marriage was really on the rocks, and I was still stunned by his affair. I was lonely and miserable. Tommy and I lasted a month, and at the time it seemed like one of the more enjoyable mistakes I'd ever made."

"When did it end?"

"A few weeks before William was killed. I found out that Tommy was living with another woman. Can you beat that? I guess I deserved it, a two-timer being two-timed. He'd also grown demanding and possessive."

"How did he react when you broke it off?"

"First he tried pleading, softening his attitude. When that didn't work, he just went nuts, calling at all hours, screaming that I just used him to do my husband's 'dirty work' for him. When I was arrested he called and offered his help if I needed it, but I didn't care. I was too hysterical to listen. A few months later he stopped by and tried to blackmail me, just like I told you."

"He concocted a story about you offering him money to have your husband killed?"

"Yes."

The door buzzer announced the arrival of dinner, a welcome relief. I went downstairs and brought the food back up, and we ate slowly, lingering as though neither of us wanted it to end. The moon laid a dazzling amber ribbon across the Bay, the lights danced in the city below as we talked and watched each other without any fears or reservations. I asked about her life growing up in the San Joaquin Valley.

"After my father ran away, my mother married the next man who asked her, a guy with a sixth-grade education who had a hard time holding a job. Outside of Modesto, a thirty-two-year-old woman with four daughters is not exactly A-list marrying material.

"Then they proceeded to have two more girls. Every year or so we had a family picture taken—his brother was always taking pictures—and you could see each sister wearing the same dress or blouse that the next bigger one had worn the year before.

"We were like slaves on this farm, baling hay, mucking out stalls, you name it. I remember when I was seven . . . " Her voice had gotten a little husky, and she took a sip of her wine. "I'd never had a toy of my own. I shamed my mother into making me one. You know what it was? A bicycle wheel. She nailed two sticks together into a T and all summer long I pushed that wheel with those sticks and thought it was the coolest thing.

"Then when I was fifteen, my stepfather made me stay home from a church picnic. He took me into the barn, said I was growing so fast he wanted to take some photos to remember me by. He was drinking, and I could just tell what he had in mind, but I was afraid of him.

"One thing led to another. . . . He told me to unbutton my blouse, then take it off, and every time I refused he got angrier. Then he grabbed me and started squeezing my breasts. I pushed him away and he slapped me and grabbed me again. I went crazy. That's when I bit the tip of his earlobe off and ran to a neighbor's house. I'd been keeping my baby-sitting money there so he wouldn't find it.

"A friend's older brother drove me to Salinas to catch the bus. I got to San Francisco that night, fifteen years old, with sixty-two dollars and the clothes on my back. Ten years later I married one of the ten richest men in the city. When I finally found out what sort of man my husband really was, he didn't seem a whole lot better than my stepfather. Just wealthier."

We looked at each other for a long minute.

Colleen wiped a tear from her eye. "I read in an old newspaper clipping that you speak nine languages," she said, changing the subject.

"That was a misprint. I speak five, six if you count two dialects of Chinese. It was pretty simple. My mother was from the Aosta Valley in Italy, where they speak French and Italian, so I had French, Italian, and English since birth. That made studying Spanish in high school very easy. I learned Mandarin and Cantonese from my friends growing up in the neighborhood. I picked up a few hundred words of German and Japanese, but not much more."

"William's mother told me that there has been a feud between your family and the Farraguts going back almost one hundred years. Is that true?"

"It's not much of a feud, really. It amounts to the Fagens trying to put the cuffs on the Farraguts for all the miserable shit they've done to people, with the Farraguts always winning. Do you want to hear how it started?"

"Yes, I do."

"The founder of the San Francisco Farragut clan," I began, "was the first William. He was a Welsh immigrant who got a real break during the Gold Rush. When all those boats starting arriving with thousands of would-be prospectors, even the crews jumped ship to strike it rich. Yerba Buena became a ghost port filled with abandoned wooden schooners.

"Farragut took over a number of the ships with the consent of the city and turned them into floating general stores, supplying tools, hardtack, maps, everything the miners needed. But he also had a soft heart, and he made a habit of extending credit to hard-luck cases and donating money to orphanages and charities. He died when William the Second was only sixteen, and within a few years, the son had started up where the father left off, minus a few unbusinesslike personality traits.

"William the Second, the first Farragut born in San Francisco, was the bad seed, the real architect of their little empire. He saw to it that compassion and charity became dirty words in the family vocabulary.

"He built his father's trading and supply business to its limit, then turned his attention to the city's other growth industry, construction. Even when the gold vanished, the population in San Francisco grew because of the town's wild reputation and because of the Bay, which drew shipping and commerce from all over the world.

"William the Second called in all the bad debts his father had on the books from failed miners who'd returned to the city looking for work. He made them pay off their tabs by working for Farragut Construction.

"He got land grants in exchange for bribes and kickbacks. He built stores, hotels, and cheap housing. He owned the tool supply company, a cement factory, and built a lumber mill. He bought up failed land claims in Santa Cruz County to the south and raped the land for its timber, leaving behind piles of slash and garbage.

"With hundreds of destitute men working for him twelve to sixteen hours a day, six days a week, for slave wages, his labor costs were reduced to almost nothing. Willy the Second was unstoppable.

"As if that weren't enough, he bought and bullied as many city officials as he could to keep building codes to a minimum, paid inspectors not to enforce the codes that did exist, and was one of the first to hire goon squads to beat and murder union organizers when the Industrial Workers of the World, better known as the Wobblies, tried to improve the conditions of the workers. For the above-named humanitarian efforts, he received numerous citizenship awards from a succession of well-paid-for mayors. Eugene Schmitz, mayor when the earthquake hit, was the worst. Every morning people willing to pay bribes for city contracts used to line up outside his office. The Farraguts owned him.

"When the quake hit, the houses Farragut had built south of Market Street collapsed. There are some great pictures of the old Victorians leaning against each other like drunks. The immigrant tenants found out the hard way that their houses didn't have poorly constructed foundations—they had no foundations at all.

"A small mob of hysterical Italian and Armenian immigrants, several of whom had lost family members in the destruction, marched over to Farragut's home. There were rumors, never confirmed, that they were carrying a long piece of rope with a noose custom-tailored for William the Second's neck.

"Somebody tipped Farragut off. He had several freelance Neanderthals and half a dozen corrupt cops surrounding him when they arrived. A screaming match started, and Farragut had the goon squad wade in and start busting heads with clubs and baseball bats.

"When Farragut left by the back entrance, he was confronted by a hysterical young Armenian whose infant son had been crushed to death when his rented flat collapsed. Farragut got a little incensed at the man's accusations, so he borrowed a pistol from one of his goons and shot the man between the eyes.

"A twenty-year-old rookie cop saw the whole thing through a back yard fence. When he tried to arrest Farragut, two older police officers stopped him.

"Then, when this rookie cop filed a report with his superiors, he got called into the mayor's office. The mayor, the chief of police, and a few others told him his vision had been impaired, his recollections inaccurate, and that a quick dose of amnesia would not only preserve his job but keep him from being prosecuted for filing false charges against a man of the stature of William the Second.

"The rookie cop was my grandfather, Byron Fagen.

"And so began the long and abiding love affair between the Fagens and the Farraguts," she said.

I nodded. We sat for a long while in silence, staring out at the city, glancing at each other. She was easily the most beautiful woman I'd ever known.

At midnight I called for a cab to pick Colleen up at the mouth of the alley a block below my house.

We stood in the alley's shadows, Colleen's face shadowed inside the hood of her coat. Turning to face me in the dim light, she said thank you and mumbled something about almost forgetting her problems for awhile.

She brushed the hood back. Her eyes played over my face for a few long seconds, making me a little uneasy. I fought it off and stared back into them, a brilliant jade even under the streetlights. I made no move toward her.

She put one long, warm hand along the side of my neck, and then she kissed me, the light smell of perfume stirring me, the warmest, wettest, softest kiss I'd been given in a very long time. I kissed her back, making no attempt to put my arms around her and hold her.

My heart pounded, I felt a little softening in the knees. She pulled back, smiled, then turned to see the cab turning the corner. She thanked me again for everything.

I opened the door for her and gave the driver the address as she got into the cab. Exchanging a last look, we said good night. I stood watching as the cab pulled away and disappeared down Greenwich Street.

I didn't know what was happening, and the scariest part was, I really didn't care.

9

I SPENT THE next few days running into more walls and roadblocks than the Volvo test dummy. One of the things I'd most admired about my former SFPD cohorts had been borne out in the Farragut case: they were relentless. They had run down every lead and "usual suspect" in all of California and half the western states.

They'd run hundreds of burglary suspects through the computer, eliminating most of them. In addition, they checked every one of scores of tips from people who thought they knew or had seen something relating to the case. Again, nothing.

The potential suspects among known burglars had been grilled, trailed, threatened with probation violations, offered immunity and preferential treatment for any information leading to the identification of the burglar. Nothing, not even the faintest clue.

Arnie had read the file of every suspect and picked out the ones who could conceivably have been the perpetrator. Henry and I repeated the efforts of the department, offering bribes, favors, anything we could to get a handle. We went everywhere from crack galleries to halfway houses to strip joints. I won a three-hundred-dollar bet, my only chance to defuse a very ugly situation, outside a biker bar in Oakland, when Henry easily whacked out two ex-cons who looked like bowling balls with hair. Henry enjoyed himself so much I had a hard time getting him to take the three hundred. It was just how bad things were going.

Next I concentrated on finding the phantom Bondage Queen and Hawk, the lovesick blackmailer. I had an artist visit Colleen's journalist friend, Alice Stein, who provided us with an astonishingly good description of the woman, down to bone structure, eye color, and the size and shape of the scar on the woman's mouth.

We visited the hotels where Farragut had used his credit card to charge rooms or buy dinners and drew more blanks. No one remembered or wanted to remember the blonde who had entertained William IV.

We tried bars, restaurants, nightclubs, anything that appeared on any of his credit card statements. We worked at a frantic clip, interviewing hundreds of people. Nothing.

We'd been on the case over a week, four of us working night and day, and nothing. When you added the years my family had been on the Farragut case, it seemed a hopeless eternity. I was just about at the end of my rope. My fears for Colleen were growing by the minute.

Then Arnie found a listing at the city assessor's office indicating that Farragut had been a partner in the Orso, a small, very exclusive hotel in Pacific Heights. A converted Mediterranean-style mansion only a half mile from the Farragut place, it was more like a posh boardinghouse where out-of-town businessmen could rent rooms by the month with services like secretaries and translators.

When I entered the place, I noticed an old friend of mine, Fred Worley, setting up the bar in the hotel's lavish dining room. Ignoring the stares of the desk clerk and indignant clientele, I walked into the bar and sat at a stool.

I'd known him since high school. I had boxed with him at Billy Newman's gym and studied Shorinji Ryu karate with him at Clarence Lee's studio in the Haight. He was the original stand-up guy, tough, a gifted actor who periodically went to Los Angeles for small film roles.

I showed him the composite of the mystery woman. He recognized her instantly. My heart jumped.

"I was working dinner here a few weeks before I went to L.A.

I've seen some beauts, but this one was something. Hard not to notice the scar on her mouth. She was nervous as hell, scared, guzzled down about three gin and tonics in fifteen minutes. She looked like a scared little girl in a woman's body. Long legs, phony boobs. When she went to the bathroom she left a copy of the personal ads from the San Francisco *Weekly Guardian*. I looked to see what she'd circled. It looked like she'd advertised for a sugar daddy, you know, "Tall, blond, wild imagination seeks very generous older man for discreet indiscretions.' She had the time and the address here written in."

"Did you see who she met?"

"After she went upstairs I saw a green Jaguar sedan pull up and in walked William Farragut, the guy who got murdered." He looked at me. "Shit, you think this girl killed him?"

"I don't know. Farragut's wife is the one they're trying to hang it on."

"Anyway, I saw Armando, the manager, come out from behind the desk, shake Farragut's hand, and give him a room key."

"Did you see him leave?"

"No, but I saw her leave. She came down, and there was a cab waiting for her. She didn't look so good. She was sort of dazed, wobbly, her hair was messed up. Actually, it was pretty sad. She looked like an amateur turning her first trick."

"Did you check her I.D.—get her name?"

"No. Sorry."

"You said it was just before you went to Los Angeles for a film. When was that?"

"Well, I left for L.A. on April first, April Fools' Day, kind of a good day to start your film career in Hollywood, right? Let's see . . . the newspaper comes out on Thursdays, and I remember this was Friday because it's always nuts in here Fridays at dinnertime. It was either three weeks before I left, or maybe two weeks, between March seventh and March fifteenth, as close as I can figure it."

I got down off the stool, dropped a healthy tip, and shook his hand. We promised to see each other again. Then I went out, climbed on the Norton, and broke all the speed limits en route to the *Weekly Guardian* office south of Market, where I barged in on Alan Jenkins, Zane Neidlinger's old protégé at the *Clarion*, now editor of the *Weekly Guardian*. I told him I needed to see back copies of the paper from two years ago and he took me to a large basement where the papers were stored in cardboard boxes by weeks and years. Within half an hour we'd found the ad I was looking for. Alan told me if the woman who placed it paid by credit card, they'd still have it in their computer.

Fifteen minutes more and I had the name of Lynne McBain, her American Express account number, and the address of her apartment in the Outer Mission. Fatigued as I was, I felt like a miracle had happened, like I'd found the Grail. On my way to Lynne McBain's apartment, I sobered up and realized I hadn't even begun to get close to it.

When I arrived I learned she had moved. I located a former friend of hers, a washed-out, strung-out-looking white girl living down the hall. At first, she didn't know what had become of Lynne, but a hundred dollars later she regained her memory. Lynne had bought a condo along the Embarcadero.

After canvassing every residential building on the waterfront, I found the one that had a mailbox in the name of L. McBain at the foot of Telegraph Hill, literally a stone's throw down the hill from my house. I pressed the buzzer, got no answer. I decided to wait.

I sat on the curb outside and stared at the open space above the Embarcadero Buildings, a space once occupied by an overhead freeway that had been destroyed by the "World Series Earthquake" in 'eighty-nine. It was the only improvement in the city's skyline in fifty years, giving everyone on the east side of town an uninterrupted view of the Bay.

I sat on the curb for an hour, watching the giant cargo ships passing en route to the East Bay. Once the West Coast's greatest port, the ships and the legions of longshoreman were now gone, working overtime in Oakland. The old docks and warehouses had become tourist restaurants, T-shirt shops, and cookie factories where pudgy tourists could get lost in thirty-seven languages. The stevedores had been replaced by dancing mermaids and cotton candy clowns. A city without a backbone, a beauty queen without substance, without heart, shallow and frivolous.

I thought about the Kiss. I hadn't seen Colleen in three days, though we spoke every evening on a secure line I'd arranged. She asked if she had offended me. She'd done a lot of things with one kiss, but offending me wasn't one of them.

As I sat waiting for Lynne McBain, Colleen was in court, a special Friday session. That meant the pace was accelerating and the end of the trial was a day closer than expected. I was going to see Colleen that night at my place, and I hoped I had something positive to tell her.

A green Morgan sports car with running boards and a leather strap across the hood made a ninety-degree turn at my feet, and sped toward the condominium complex behind me. It was driven by a blonde in big sunglasses with a distinctive scar across her right upper lip.

I caught up with Lynne as she bent into the trunk of the Morgan to remove packages from expensive Union Square department stores. She wore a short black skirt and spike heels. I approached quietly and offered her a helping hand.

She reacted with a start. I used my most charming voice and had my choirboy smile working overtime. It didn't help at all.

The eyes were pale blue, the scarred mouth a temptation to ask what happened. She had long, thin legs, a lean, almost hipless body, and two humongous, XXL better-living-through-surgery boobs with razor sharp cookie-cutter outlines just below the collarbone. The monster chest and skinny body looked like two bowler hats on a hat rack.

"Who are you?" she asked. "What do you want?" I pulled out my identification. She lowered her sunglasses, revealing cynical powder blue eyes.

"Francis Fagen. I'm a private investigator."

I could practically see her heart jump up into her throat. "And what do you want with me?"

"It's about William Farragut."

"I don't know anything about William Farragut."

"Really? I have a tape-recording of him tying you to a table at the Fairmont Hotel and whipping your fanny with a riding crop, so you must know something about him. I also have a copy of an ad you took out in the *Weekly Guardian* two years ago, along with your credit card number."

She got an instant case of the homicidal eye. "I got nothing to say to you, Mr. Fagen. You can call my attorney." She said "Mr. Fagen" the way someone says your name right before they shove you from a moving car.

"I'll call your attorney after I call the police, at which point you may be either a suspect in a homicide or a material witness. The cops will probably call the IRS, and I'm sure they'd just love to hear how a twenty-four-year-old unemployed woman pays for a seven-hundred-fifty-thousand-dollar condo, a forty-thousand-dollar car, and shops all day at Macy's and Magnin's." I waited for it to sink in. "Or, you can invite me inside, answer a few questions, and when it's all over, you can forget you ever saw me."

I was inside and sipping a cold beer before the minute hand on my watch moved. As I paced the living room, Lynne took the packages into her bedroom on the ground floor, leaving me to wonder what was in the loft on the second floor. When she returned, I asked.

"Well, why don't you come up and I'll show you." It was not the friendliest invitation I had ever had. As I followed her toward a heavy oak door, I had visions of a King Kong boyfriend looming behind. I unzipped my jacket, reached inside my coat, removed my Walther, and stuck it in my hip pocket, along with my hand. I thumbed the safety off.

At the top she unlocked the dead bolt and pushed the door open, revealing a pitch black, seemingly windowless room. She turned on the light and we stepped inside.

It was a sadomasochist's wet dream. The walls were completely covered in black leather held in place by silver studs. One wall was lined with whips, paddles, hand-carved wooden switches, leather handcuffs, dildoes for every occasion, and a hundred other devices not usually found at Rotary Club picnics.

Special features included a trapezelike device with leather restraints for fastening someone's hands overhead, tables for lying on and bending over, a stockade, two heavy metal cages and a large X-shaped frame with restraints at the four points. Prominent in the room was a large-screen TV and a video camera on a tripod, probably for recording the festivities for future family gatherings.

"You ever had your ass paddled, Francis?" She had her best leer going full tilt.

"Not since I got caught goosing Mary Louise Kennedy in the third grade. Didn't like it then, don't care for it now. Especially at your prices."

"Oh, no charge at all. I'll just slip into a corset, some fishnets, and thigh-high boots."

"Listen, lady, spare me the routine. I can see you're just thrilled about graduating from a nail to a hammer, but I really don't give a rat's ass how you make a living. All I want to know about is William Farragut."

Lynne wasn't finished yet. She smiled, walked over to a wall that wasn't really a wall, and pushed on a spot above her head. A door popped open. After examining the stack of video tapes inside, she picked one out, giving me one of those Jayne Mansfield third-rate come-on looks as she slid the tape into the VCR. I was tired and out of patience.

As the big screen kicked to life she doused the lights, and we sat in matching black leather chairs while on-screen a masked, naked man with half a hard-on was being tied to the bondage table by the leather-clad McBain. "Do you recognize him?"

I said that I didn't, not having much of a memory bank for those particular body parts. But when she started asking him if he was "ready" and he answered, "Yes, please," calling her Mistress, I recognized Farragut's voice.

After she whipped his little fanny carnation red, she went to the display wall, took down a leather belt, went to a drawer and pulled out a perfect plastic replica of a male member. Just before she drove it up the Farragut Highway, I realized it was a perfect reproduction of Farragut's own member. That's when I hit the stop button on the remote. The rich, they are different from you and me.

"Thanks for sharing that with me, Lynne. Nice trick, the dildo clone, probably make a nice addition to someone's Christmas catalogue. Let's talk about William Farragut, what do you say?"

She was exactly what Fred Worley had said, a little girl in a woman's body. She was just a scared, lonely kid, trying to play big, tough, and better. The whole facade was paper thin. She had shown me the tape to prove she had gotten the upper hand with Farragut.

I asked her about the blackmailing boyfriend, including enough detail that she was at a loss to deny anything. I told her I wanted to know Hawk's full name and where he was.

She nodded for me to follow her downstairs, where she opened a drawer and pulled out a newspaper clipping from an old issue of the *Clarion*, dated six weeks before Farragut's death. Then she handed me a copy of a death certificate, signed by the San Francisco County deputy coroner.

According to the article and the death certificate, Andrew Simcic, then aged twenty-four, had killed himself at a recording studio South of Market by firing a single shot from a .38-caliber pistol through his right temple.

"It would have been pretty hard for Hawk to kill William, since he supposedly killed himself six weeks earlier. And I was in Big Sur the night of William's murder, at Ventana, with a girlfriend. We danced at the River Inn until the bar closed, and eighty people saw us."

I asked her what she meant when she said Hawk "supposedly"

killed himself, and she burst into tears. She said Hawk had told her about the attempted blackmailing of Farragut several days before his death. He had been distraught when he found out she was turning tricks to support herself. He was a struggling musician, madly in love with her, and when he found out about Farragut he went crazy. Had Colleen paid the blackmail money, he planned to give it to Lynne so she would stop turning tricks.

"But he didn't kill himself. Look at the coroner's report. They said he was loaded on booze and pills and shot himself with a stolen gun. Hawk hated guns, he never drank hard liquor, and he never took pills. Somebody killed him. That's what I told the cops when they came. They didn't believe me."

"Did you tell them about him trying to blackmail Farragut or his wife?"

"No."

"How many times were you with Farragut?"

"Maybe thirty or so, I lost count. Every time it was different, but it always involved spankings or bondage. Once he had me fuck another girl while he watched. One time he just videotaped me masturbating. He paid me two thousand the first time, more after that. He was obsessed with me; he would have seen me every night, but I wouldn't do it. Once, twice a week was all I could handle."

"And what about the video I saw? When did you two decide to switch places?"

"It was my idea. I met this girl, she was in the life, S&M, she said it was a hell of a lot easier that way and men would go for it if you put it to them right. I talked Farragut into it. It was like, he'd already done everything else, he was bored. She knew this place, they made plastic replicas of gay porno stars' dicks. She came over one night and made a clay cast of William's. It was my chance for a little payback." She put her head down and wept softly to herself, no more facade, no more Bondage Queen, no more tough girl.

"Did he know you were videotaping him?"

She shook her head.

"Did you kill Farragut?"

"No."

"Do you know who killed him? Did you have someone do it for you to get even with him because you thought he had Hawk killed?"

"No." Tears were falling on her crossed arms and the front of her dress. There was nothing bitter or hostile in her voice, nothing that made me feel she was not telling the truth. She found a tissue, wiped her eyes, blew her nose. I gave her a minute to get her composure.

"How did Farragut reach you? Did he call you at home?"

"He never called me."

That one threw me. "How did he reach you?"

"A woman called me. She's the one who called when I placed the ad. She called and told me she had one of the richest men in California for me to see, that I had to see him and him only and submit to a blood test for AIDS, and that he was very kinky and would pay me a lot of money. A lot of money."

"Do you know who she was?"

"No. I only talked to her on the phone. She told me I had to go sit in this bar and have a drink so someone could look me over. I never knew who it was. She called me back the next day, said I was the one he wanted. She said her name was Evelyn."

"What bar did you go to?"

"Bajilla, on Market Street."

"What did the woman, Evelyn, sound like? Anything distinctive in her voice? A foreign accent, a Southern accent, maybe a stutter?"

"She had a raspy voice, she sounded older. She had one of those, she wheezed when she talked, you know, *hehhh*, like she was sucking in air real hard."

I knew who it was instantly, but I wanted confirmation. "Look, Lynne, if you'll give me a few more minutes of your time I won't bother you again. Provided you're telling me the truth. If Hawk was murdered, this woman might be involved. If you help me a little more, it might lead me to his killer."

She nodded. I asked if I could use her phone and was able to reach Zane at the *Clarion* offices just as he was returning from court. I asked him if he had any of the tape-recordings of the countless interviews he'd done with Farragut's stooge, Supervisor Helen Smidge. He said he did, that he had some of them in a collection he kept in his locker. I told him to go get one as quickly as his legs would carry him, put it in his portable cassette, and call me at the number I gave him.

We sat without talking, Lynne McBain and I, the only sound her sniffling as she tried to choke back tears. In the grand scheme of things, I really didn't have much sympathy for her. What sympathy I had I usually reserved for the poor black and Hispanic kids growing up in Hunter's Point, the homeless old people living in the Tenderloin.

Zane called back and told me he had a tape of a recent interview with Supervisor Helen Smidge all cued up. I handed the phone to Lynne. Her eyes lit up as she listened.

She nodded. "That's the woman who called me, who made all the arrangements. That's Evelyn," she said.

10

▼▼▼

I LEFT LYNNE McBAIN and returned to Telegraph Hill. Martha Walley was waiting with a report on Colleen Farragut, which she had written after reading the depositions and police reports in the evidence files. Arnie and Henry Borowski soon joined us.

Before I listened to any of them I called Lloyd Dinkman, an old SFPD friend in records. I asked him to make a copy of the police file and autopsy report on Andrew Simcic's death and bring it to my house when he finished his shift. He hemmed, hawed, then agreed.

I informed my team that I'd found Farragut's mistress, Lynne McBain, and confirmed a story that Colleen had told me, that McBain's boyfriend had tried to blackmail Colleen. I told them that the meetings between McBain and Farragut had been set up by Supervisor Helen Smidge.

That got their attention.

Then I told them about Simcic's alleged suicide, shortly after Colleen had rejected his demands for money, and what Lynne had said about the gun, the booze, and the pills not being part of Simcic's repertoire.

"They had him killed," said Martha.

"They being Farragut and Smidge," Arnie added.

"That's the way I figure it. After Colleen turned Simcic down, he called Farragut himself. Farragut probably freaked out, blamed it on Smidge. The onus would have been on her. Imagine how furious Farragut must have been."

"What does all this mean to Colleen's case?" Arnie asked. "If ol' Smudge had Simcic killed, it's not logical she would have killed Farragut even if Farragut was threatening her. He was her cash cow, her meal ticket; she'd be more inclined to try to woo him back. And Smudge was his ally, his pipeline to City Hall. She can't be a viable suspect."

"I think Arnie's right," Martha said, "but I think we should trace all the phone records of Smidge, this Lynne McBain, and Simcic. McBain has to be a prime suspect right now, regardless of her alibi for the night of the murder."

I agreed.

"One other possibility," Arnie said. "What if Smidge or Farragut did hire somebody to off Simcic? What if the guy turned on them, tried to blackmail Farragut, and Farragut didn't comply?" It seemed farfetched, but so was everything else in this case.

"I guess we have a decision to make," I said. "If Simcic was murdered, establishing a link between that and the Farragut murder might be a real long shot. I'm afraid to get sidetracked and waste what little time we have."

"I'll take it," said Martha. "I'm done with Colleen's files; I'll start on Simcic, McBain, and Smidge. If there's a link, I'll find it."

"A day or two, that's it," I said, the mere thought making me more nervous by the second. We were ready for Martha's report on Colleen.

Martha gave me one of those quick looks, like she knew of my attraction to Colleen and was about to tell me something painful. Martha can look at you and tell what color shorts you're wearing or the name of the girl you slept with a week ago.

"That crack they made about her giving his money away as fast as Farragut stole it was not far from the truth. You can't believe the organizations she supported: Children of the Night, Para Los

Niños, the women's shelter, St. Anthony's soup kitchen. Not only that, but she worked in all of them as well. This is some woman, Frank." I knew Martha was stalling, sugarcoating.

I asked her about the affair with Tommy Rivera. "I don't think she dumped Tommy Rivera, I think she wore him out. Thirteen expensive hotel rooms in one month in Marin and Napa Valley."

I suffered from the same apprehension as a lot of men. We all want the woman in our life to be a world-class lover but no one wants to know with whom she took her batting practice.

But there was nothing else of any value. Hours of reviewing documents had failed to give Martha any clues to Tommy's motivation for trying to blackmail Colleen, other than the obvious one.

After Martha, Henry, and Arnie left, Lloyd Dinkman arrived with a copy of the evidence file from the Simcic "suicide." I thanked him heartily, gave him an envelope with two hundreds in it, and promised him two of my season tickets to a 49ers game when the season started.

I had an hour or two before Colleen arrived for dinner, so I sat down and started digging through the file.

Several of Simcic's friends had told the investigating officers that he was depressed over the fact that the love of his life had become the mistress of some rich guy whose name they didn't know. None of them believed he was suicidal.

Two other things made me sit up and pay attention.

One was the report from the toxicology lab which arrived seventeen days after the alleged suicide and was marked confidential. It showed a very high level of the barbiturate Seconal in Andrew Simcic's blood. It also showed a blood alcohol level of .022 percent, almost three times the amount needed to convict someone of drunk driving. The combination of alcohol and Seconal should have made a blob out of Simcic, who was five feet nine inches tall and weighed only one forty at the time of death, provided he had no acquired tolerance.

I flipped through the file and found they'd done a work-up on liver and fatty tissue samples from Simcic's body, something the coroner often did when drugs and alcohol were a contributing factor in a violent death.

The reports confirmed what Lynne McBain had said about Hawk. There was no trace of liver scarring of any kind, and no trace of any drug residue in the fatty tissues of his body. The kid was not a drunk or a doper. With that level of booze and barbiturates in him, he was probably in a coma when he allegedly put a bullet in his head.

Nevertheless, the conclusion of the coroner's report was "death by self-inflicted gunshot wound."

But what really disturbed me were the two names attached to the report. The first was the assistant coroner, Dr. Michael Wentworth, a polyhidrotic pervert whose appointment to the ghoul crew had been arranged by Helen Smidge despite his shoddy med school record. He'd botched more postmortems than the rest of the coroner's office combined.

I had long believed that not all of his botched exams were accidents. Doc Wentworth had a drinking problem, a gambling problem, and on two occasions, vice officers had picked him up for jerking off in the bushes outside some poor woman's bedroom window. The story had been squashed and his job saved by someone at City Hall, probably someone named Helen Smidge. He was the perfect candidate for a postmortem hatchet job on crucial evidence.

The second name, however, was the real show stopper. The police report had been signed by Inspector John Naftulin, Investigating Officer. The same John Naftulin who handled the Farragut murder investigation and was the first witness for the prosecution at Colleen's trial. The same John Naftulin who had been second in command of the investigation of Mayor DiMarco's murder and had once gone on record blasting my allegations of a conspiracy to kill DiMarco and a fix in Warren Dillon's trial.

Little by little, the past was catching up with me, the characters trotting out of their graves to shake a bony finger in my face and say, *We're not through with you yet, Peekaboo.* It was getting more difficult to determine exactly whose case I was working on, Colleen Farragut's or my own.

11

I WAS JOLTED awake by the sound of my door buzzer. I'd nodded out in my reading chair, an evidence file over my eyes as though I might learn something by osmosis. It was six thirty, I assumed P.M., and that I'd been asleep for an hour and not unconscious for thirteen.

When Colleen entered, she looked strained, anxious, but still kept up a strong front. Once again, a tailored suit over a lacy white blouse did nothing to knock the edge off her beauty. In the afternoon light her eyes were still the most mesmerizing green I'd ever seen.

She took her coat off, sat in the chair I offered her, kicked off her high heels and accepted a glass of wine. A solid pull and she seemed ready to talk.

"How did it go today?" I almost hated having to ask.

"Not much different. More lab reports, fingerprint expert saying they were my prints on the gun, a crime lab guy reconstructing the scene, saying the shooter was to the inside of William, you know, William was closer to the French doors, like the shooter came from inside the house instead of outside."

Once again I wondered how she did it, how anyone guilty or not stood up to a murder trial. Being innocent and on trial for murder had to be the ultimate nightmare.

"What plans do you have for tonight, Frank?"

I hesitated for a minute, wondering why she asked.

"Evidence files. I still have a lot to cover." I left out the part about being down to the last three weeks and getting more nervous by the minute.

"Can we have dinner somewhere, somewhere I might not be recognized?"

Outside of Tonga, I wasn't sure where she had in mind.

"I have a friend in Santa Cruz," she said. "A retired schoolteacher, Virginia Riley. She has this great old Victorian house on Depot Hill in Capitola, a bed-and-breakfast place she runs in the summer. She lets me come down anytime I want."

She stood up, and my heart raced a little as I started sorting out all the reasons to say no; time, professionalism, my own fear that she'd be gone in three weeks if I couldn't find a way to save her.

"Look, Frank, I don't know how to put this," she said, sounding a little sad, and serious. "I'm not a fool; I know what I'm facing if you don't find the burglar. This may be my last three weeks of freedom. I've been thinking about this for more than a week." She hesitated, then said, "I haven't been with a man in almost two years."

The potential, I surmised, was enormous.

"I'm crazy about you, Frank. For years I've seen your newspaper photos, read the stories about you, heard William and his friends talk about you. I don't want you to think I'm a desperate woman reaching out for just any man. I could have done that anytime. And I'm not doing this to coerce you to try harder or do anything dangerous. I know you're doing everything possible. If I only have three weeks left, I don't have time to be coy or clever.

"I know it's a lot to ask of a man, to get involved with a woman he might never see again. But I don't want to go to prison without something to remember, wishing I had known you better."

She lowered her head and a few tears ran down her cheeks. Once again, she fought it off, wiping the tears away with her hands, looking at me, fresh tears magnifying the jade eyes.

My heart was pounding. It was tough to talk. "I had all these reasons worked out in case this came up," I said.

"Just say yes, Frank. Do what you want and not what you should."

"Yes."

Thirty minutes later, I parked the Corvette along the side of the road in the Presidio and made a mad dash through the woods, grateful that none of the photographers had staked out the stone wall behind the house.

When I reached the wall, I chucked a rock over.

Moments later a suitcase came over the wall, followed by Colleen, dressed in tight faded blue denim, tan cowboy boots, and sunglasses. She slithered down the wall, dropping to the ground.

We ran to the car, laughing, a little giddy.

I took the scenic route through the Sunset District, past the Cliff House and along the ocean on the Great Highway.

We were in Pacifica in a matter of minutes, despite the Friday night traffic. Once we had rounded Devil's Slide to the south, the traffic disappeared and the Pacific stretched endlessly ahead.

There are some great roads in the world, but Highway 1 from San Francisco to Santa Cruz and beyond to Carmel and Big Sur can match sights and stories with any of them.

This is God's back porch. An occasional farmhouse nestled among the hills, redwood forests, pumpkin farms, blackberry fields, spectacular beaches, green hills, jagged cliffs rolled by. We rode for a long time in silence, enjoying the sights, the smell of the ocean, the pine forests, the eucalyptus and redwood. It eased a lot of wounded spirit.

We passed the old whaling town of Davenport, now a haven for time-warped hippies, artists, and potters, past the beaches where I'd spent a lot of my summers as a child surfing and sunning: Hole-in-the-Wall, Red White and Blue, Four Mile. Many were hidden from the road, accessible only by winding, narrow paths filled with the fragrance of wildflowers.

To the left were the roads that snaked through the Santa Cruz

Mountains to Boulder Creek and Bonny Doon, thick with towering redwoods, pine and eucalyptus, roads with names like Pine Flat and Ice Cream Grade.

I told Colleen a story for each spot, each road, from my youth spent in paradise. I felt like a tour director for a dying woman, as though this was the only time she might see them, as if the gravity of her final visit had become an unseen weight, affecting the way I'd look at this road, these places for the rest of my life.

Capitola is another of the country's great towns, four miles south of Santa Cruz, a tiny village of four streets filled with shops, restaurants, a two-dollar movie theater, and enough charm to make you forget a lot of things you want to forget.

Virginia Riley's Victorian stood on Depot Hill overlooking the town, the oldest in a row of Victorians that had been built near the start of the century, all painstakingly restored and preserved.

Virginia had left Colleen a key and a note, telling her she'd had to go "over the hill" to visit her daughter in Los Gatos and would be spending the night. We had the run of the place, a creaking, antique-filled old house with a spectacular view of the ocean, the cliffs, the town. A burnt-orange sunset draped the western sky.

I called an old friend, a sculptor who worked nights waiting tables at the Shadowbrook, which overlooked the river and village. I asked for the private dining room downstairs, near the riverbank, offering a healthy bribe for the maître d'.

Colleen and I dressed in separate rooms, emerging tense, excited. She wore a skintight black dress of antique lace through which was visible a silky black camisole. The dress had a scooped, slightly revealing neckline and a row of buttons down the front. The hem was six inches above her graceful knees. She wore sheer black stockings and black patent leather pumps that made her only an inch shorter than I. She looked classy enough for a fashion layout, sexy enough to get a rise out of a dead man. I forget what I was wearing.

She slipped into a thin coat, presumably to prevent domestic upheavals as we passed through town. We took the back streets to avoid being seen, crossed the bridge over the Capitola River, hiked up a short hill, and got into the tiny tram car that is the Shadow-brook's trademark for the ride down from the parking lot.

As soon as I closed the tram door the car started its snail-like crawl down the hill. Colleen got a wild look in her eye, and asked how long it took the car to reach the bottom.

"At least a minute," I said.

She leaned into me, and I felt my hands on her hips, her leg between mine. We kissed, more intensely than the first time. The effect was dizzying. The world spun a little, the tram cable groaned beneath us, a tall pine creaked against another in the wind. I was hers, I was had. She kissed better than most women make love.

Opening one eye, I noticed we were approaching the restaurant and gently pushed Colleen away. She sighed and stared into my eyes, more alive and animated than I'd seen her.

The tram thudded softly to a stop, the door opened, and a family of seven, complete with bespectacled grandma wearing a blue corsage, nodded hello and told us to "have a nice dinner." We told them we would.

I tipped the hostess to lead us outside the restaurant, across a brick patio overlooking the slow-moving river, where several young couples paddled boats among the ducks and geese.

We entered through a door off the patio, Colleen causing a bit of neck strain, male and female, as we made our way to a large round table in a corner of the restaurant's lowest tier. We sat in our private corner, ate, held hands, smiled ourselves stupid. In the middle of dinner Colleen leaned over and kissed me, slid her left hand into my lap and started stroking, ever so gently.

The look on her face was subtle, restrained, her eyes searching to see how long the effect would take to reach my face, my voice. "How is it," she asked, not specifying the dinner or the warm feeling that had flooded the Fagen organ.

I croaked, "Great," and tried to eat, which is difficult with a hard-on.

She stopped for a second, unbuttoned a few of the lower buttons of her dress, folded it away from her leg, and put my right hand on the inside of her left thigh. I could feel the silk top of her black stocking, her garter belt, the smooth, hard expanse of thigh.

"I like to play a little," she said. "Do you mind?"

I called a cab to take us back to the house after dinner.

She led me into the living room, eased me down into a large, black leather armchair. "I saw you staring at my body the first time we met," she said, "when I was walking out of the box at the opera."

"Gee, and I thought I was so subtle."

She walked toward the fireplace, turned, faced me, smiled, looked down at the top button of her dress. She fingered it for a second, then popped it open. She looked at me, popped another one.

She worked it, enjoying it almost as much as I did. There was no hurry, no world outside. A few more buttons revealed the lace camisole, then a drum-tight stomach, an antique black satin garter belt, and the dream that springs eternal.

She walked over, slowly, the sound of spike heels on hardwood, sat in my lap and kissed me. Then she looked straight into my eyes. "I'm been thinking about this for a long time. Anything you want, Frank, all you have to do is tell me."

I was working on the list when my beeper went off. It startled Colleen a little, as it was in my jacket pocket and she was practically sitting on it. We were both excited, anxious, but I knew it couldn't be ignored, as only the City Lights crew had the number.

I looked at the beeper. The code number indicated it was Martha Walley calling me from the office. She always knew when I was having too much fun.

I told Colleen to hold the thought, went to the phone, and called the office.

"Martha, Frankie calling. What's up?"

"I think you better get up here right away, Frank. Arnie just called. He was listening to the police scanner in his car. An hour ago a bridge worker found a woman's purse in the middle of the Golden Gate."

I had a hunch what was coming. "Lynne McBain?"

"Yes. I just turned on your marine radio; the Coast Guard is going out any minute. They received a report of a body in the water, white female, blond hair. A cargo vessel saw her floating out by the entrance to the Bay. It's pretty foggy right now; it may take them some time to find her."

I went back into the living room and looked at Colleen standing there in basic black, looking a little self-conscious but no less seductive. I told her what had happened.

She put her dress back on, grabbed her coat and bag, and in less than a minute we were in the car and headed back up Highway 1 to San Francisco.

We'd just left the north end of Santa Cruz, where the road turns to a double lane each way, when Colleen looked at me and the night's excitement returned. Slowly, she unbuttoned her dress, stripping down to her camisole, G-string, garter belt, and stockings.

Then she leaned over, unzipped my pants, and proved that her late husband had not lied to his dear mom when he talked of her oral expertise.

We floated back to San Francisco in an hour flat.

12

▼▼▼▼

AFTER WE PASSED Pacifica and hit the south end of the city, I plugged my car phone into the Vette's cigarette lighter and called Martha Walley at the office. She told me the Coast Guard had gotten lucky: despite the fog they had located the body floating near the Marin County headlands. They had "dragged and bagged" her and were headed to Fort Point, where the cops and coroner were already waiting.

I asked Martha to assemble my photo gear—spare camera and high-speed film, tripod, telephoto lenses—and to be ready when I arrived.

Zane Neidlinger was in bed when I called to tell him the Coast Guard had found a floater relevant to the Farragut case, promising more when I saw him. He agreed to meet me at the observation point at the south end of the bridge.

We arrived back at Telegraph Hill, parked on the sidewalk, and sprinted into the office.

I wasn't surprised that Martha wasn't surprised to see Colleen. They both smiled as I made brief introductions. I told Colleen to wait, to go to my bedroom upstairs if she was tired. Henry Borowski entered from another room, and I told him to watch the house.

Martha and I got in the Vette and headed to Fort Point, little more than a mile from the house. Martha drove while I loaded film.

Zane pulled into the parking lot at the observation point seconds after we did. The three of us walked swiftly down the access road below the bridge and through the Presidio, stopping on the grassy hill overlooking the fortress at Fort Point, a hundred feet above the action. Most of the fog had dissipated at sea level, and a very bright moon illuminated six squad cars, three unmarked sedans, and a paramedic vehicle.

We took a minute to catch our breath, waiting for the show to start. Fort Point is the spot where the city and Bay were discovered, where Spanish explorers first landed. From there you can look up at the underside of the Golden Gate Bridge, feel its size and power, listen to the trucks passing, the wind whipping through its cables. I always remember it as the spot where Jimmy Stewart fishes Kim Novak out of the Bay in *Vertigo*.

Out past the bridge, three hundred yards away, we could distinguish the Coast Guard launch fighting the outgoing tide, pitching and yawing in a vicious chop.

I set the camera up on my shortest tripod as the three of us crouched in the bushes, anxious not to be seen. Through the telephoto lens, I scanned the small group gathered below us to see who the players were. I recognized only two of the half dozen uniformed officers. In the middle of the pack, however, stood the ubiquitous Inspector John Naftulin, and next to him Assistant Coroner Michael Wentworth. Let the charade begin.

The boat arrived and was tied up after a mighty struggle. Everyone crowded in as two baby-faced Coast Guard recruits passed the green body bag over the side. Several cops helped place the body on a gurney as the others shooed away a small group of gawkers.

Dr. Wentworth signaled everyone to stand back and zipped open the green bag. Someone held a strong, portable spotlight on the face, making it easy for me to photograph.

Wentworth removed a patch of tangled kelp from the long, stringy blond hair and turned the face toward the light. The eyes were wide open, bloodshot and glassy, and the skin was waxen, the scar on the right of her mouth chalky white and more pronounced. It was Lynne McBain.

Wentworth motioned for the purse that was found on the bridge, removed the wallet, and held the driver's license photograph up to her face. He turned and nodded to Inspector Naftulin as I clicked away on speedwinder.

Wentworth made a cursory examination of the body, turning the neck slightly, with effort, rigor mortis setting into the muscles. He checked for broken bones in the neck and face, which was bruised on the left side. It appeared her neck had been broken.

He then unbuttoned her gray blouse, revealing that both breast implants had burst, the skin ripped open by the 124-mile-per-hour impact with the water. One of the plastic breast sacs fell out onto Wentworth's gloved hand. He shook it off, unbuttoned her blouse further, revealing a mass of purple and blue discoloration on the right side of her ribs. Lynne just stared skyward as she was manhandled by yet another stranger.

Wentworth stepped back, apparently deciding he'd seen enough, and let the crime lab photographer take some shots of the body. I took pictures of Wentworth and Naftulin conferring off to the side. Zane scribbled notes and talked softly into a lavaliere microphone connected to the microcassette recorder in his coat pocket.

As they loaded Lynne's body into the meat wagon I fought off a momentary sadness, then urged Martha and Zane to crouch in the bushes until everyone left.

I rode with Zane back to the office and had Martha use my car to take the film to an insomniac photo whiz named Richard Beccari out in the Richmond District.

Once inside, Zane's face puckered in disbelief when Colleen descended the steps from my bedroom. I introduced them and he shook her hand politely. The pucker turned to one of those you-outdid-yourself-this-time grins.

"You want to tell me what's going on?" he asked.

I gave him the shorthand version, told him that Lynne McBain was the mystery gal who'd done the leather tango with William Farragut for several months before he died. I told him about Andrew Simcic's attempted blackmail, his supposed suicide, and the hatchet job that Inspector Naftulin and Assistant Coroner Wentworth had done on the Simcic evidence.

"You don't think this was a suicide either," he said.

"I just talked to her about eight hours ago. She was upset, but she sure wasn't suicidal."

Zane and I looked at each other for a long moment, then almost in sync we said "Flynn Pooley!"

"Who?" Colleen asked.

I thought for a minute before I answered. Once again, pieces of the past were falling into the current puzzle until past and present were virtually indistinguishable.

"Flynn Pooley was a crackpot geologist at UC Berkeley," I said. "Years before Mayor DiMarco was murdered, Pooley built a reputation by predicting a series of small earthquakes along the San Andreas Fault. He didn't use traditional methods—to put it mildly. He studied all this information: premature births in cows, household pets running away, the history of the fault slipping in patterns from south to north. He was the darling of the anti-high-rise movement in San Francisco.

"A lot of the land south of Market Street is just landfill; it's where the old Yerba Buena port was. Pooley said that if high rises were built along the Market Street corridor and an earthquake of 1906 magnitude, eight point one or greater, were to hit during the morning or afternoon rush hour, fifty thousand people could die. They'd be cut to ribbons by glass exploding from the windows of all those skyscrapers downtown. He said the glass and the bodies would be piled twelve feet deep."

I paused to let this sink in, and Zane took over.

"Flynn Pooley was a wild character. Smoked pot, hung around with Ken Kesey's Merry Pranksters, got arrested in a lot of peace demonstrations in the sixties. All the high-rise advocates—your late husband, the flunkies who took office after Mayor DiMarco was killed—they all despised him. Every time Pooley predicted an earthquake somewhere in the state, it happened. So his theories about the high rises gained credibility with each prediction. One day, about eight months before Warren Dillon snuck into City Hall and murdered DiMarco, they found Pooley floating in the Bay.

"His bomber jacket and wallet were in the middle of the bridge, near the suicide point, where all the jumpers climb over the railing."

"Just like Lynne McBain," said Colleen, visibly unnerved by it all.

"Just like Lynne McBain," I said.

"And you think Pooley was murdered?"

"Pooley was acrophobic," Zane told her. "Deathly afraid of heights. The medical report said he was high on pot and a mega-dose of LSD. They said he was so zonked he just decided to fly like Superman."

"I was on the police force then," I told her. "I'd been the head of white-collar crime for only six months. I knew your husband was bribing people, hiring private detectives, primarily Hayden Phillips, to get dirt on the opposition, the anti–high risers, trying to blackmail and discredit them."

"You think my husband had Flynn Pooley killed and made it look like suicide to discredit him and get him out of the way? And then William got Warren Dillon to kill the mayor so that his people could take over and build all those high rises?"

"That's exactly what I think."

"This sounds like we're living in some banana republic," Colleen said.

I watched as Zane disconnected his lavaliere microphone and rewound the tape he had made at Fort Point.

"Zane, where's the tape you played for Lynne McBain over the phone?"

"You mean the interview with Helen Smidge? I got it right here, I took it out at Fort Point to put in a fresh tape."

"Cue it up, will you? The same section you played for McBain."

The tape whirred as it rewound, then Zane hit the play button and we listened to Smidge droning on about her "role" in the city's future. But in the middle, Smidge's secretary buzzed and said, "Supervisor Smidge, your meeting with the mayor is postponed until four." I asked Zane if McBain would have heard that and he looked at the tape counter and said she must have.

"This is airtight," I said. "McBain realized the voice on the tape was the 'Evelyn' who had set her up with William Farragut, then heard the secretary call Smidge by name. She called Smidge's office, probably threatened to make noise about Smidge being Farragut's procurer unless Smidge did something about Simcic's murder. McBain must have thought it was Farragut who'd had Simcic killed. Maybe she realized Smidge might have been in on it and threatened her too.

"So Smidge arranges a meeting with McBain, ostensibly to meet her demands, maybe try to bribe her. Then whoever does Smidge's dirty work does a Flynn Pooley on Lynne McBain."

"It was the perfect night for it," Zane said. "Just like the night Pooley died. The fog was so thick, the video cameras that monitor everything from the towers of the Golden Gate couldn't have picked up anyone. Someone could have jumped out of a van in the middle of the span, dragged McBain five feet to the railing, thrown her over, then gotten back in the van, wham, bam, so long ma'am. Less than ten seconds."

"It also brings up another problem," Zane said. "Did McBain tell Smidge that you paid her a visit?"

"If she did," Colleen said, "they'll all know you're working on the case, and you could be their next target."

I had already realized that the next target could be me—or Colleen.

13
▼▼▼▼

"I<small>T ALL CHANGED</small> in the city after DiMarco's murder," Zane said, "just like it changed in the whole country when Kennedy was killed.

"Kennedy was no saint, but he made the Russians back down, he stopped the steel companies from ripping everybody off, he told black people the Constitution included them. And now he's a jerk for what, because he fucked Marilyn Monroe? This is a crime? Kennedy fucks Marilyn and the guys who came after him fucked everybody else. They robbed the country blind. That's just what happened here.

"DiMarco wasn't God, but he loved the city, he wanted to keep the high rises out, keep a place for families, for artists, a real city, not Disneyland North for a bunch of camera-packin' *turistas*. You know what's the saddest holiday of the year in this city?" he said, pouring a little more gin, testifying. "Halloween. There's no kids left. San Francisco has fewer kids per capita than any city in the world. The national average is two and a half times what it is here."

Zane muttered some more, abruptly realizing he'd had enough of both the gin and dissertation. He excused himself and left.

Martha returned with the blowups of the McBain photos. I looked them over closely and felt my hunch had been right: somebody had worked her over before they tossed her in the water. It increased my anxiety that she might have told her torturers my name. When Colleen arrived I set the photos aside so she wouldn't see them. She squeezed in under my arm, and I could feel the fear and tension in her body.

A new concern was added to my worries: Colleen's safety. They'd silenced Lynne McBain, quickly, brutally; if they even suspected Colleen were about to be acquitted, and that she might turn Farragut's diaries over to the wrong people, they'd do anything to prevent it.

I asked Colleen to spend the night and the following night, telling her I needed more information from her and that I could watch over her more easily this way. She agreed, trying to smile.

Pulling Martha into my office, I shut the door and told her what had happened with Lynne and the tape recording. I asked her to stay with Colleen until I got back. She took her revolver from her purse, slipped it into a clip-on holster and attached it to her belt at the small of her back, putting two speed-loaders in her pocket.

Henry was to do a serious recon of the neighborhood; I wanted to make sure that no one was staking out the house.

It was just past midnight when I left.

The body count was now four in the Flynn Pooley–Mayor DiMarco–Andrew Simcic—Lynne McBain string. Five if you counted Farragut, who I figured to be either directly or indirectly responsible for the first four.

I cranked up the Norton and headed straight for Bajilla, the bar where Smudge first asked Lynne McBain to wait while someone approved her for Farragut's consumption.

I arrived on Market Street barely four hours after Colleen and I had eaten dinner in Santa Cruz. Things were moving faster, taking shape, but the big picture was still not clear. I still had not found the burglar, or Ghiberti's silver plates. I prayed I was heading in that direction, that somewhere ahead there was a link between all this and Farragut's murder. I shuddered at what the consequences might be if I was wrong.

The most encouraging part, I reflected as I parked on the sidewalk and chained the Norton to a parking meter, was that I was starting to believe Colleen.

Bajilla, an upscale bar with a row of picture windows overlooking Market Street a few blocks east of the Castro District, was jumping when I walked in, Brazilian music pounding, the singer singing in Portuguese about his love for "dangerous lovers, dangerous lives." It always sounds better in song than it is in real life. I asked the bartender where to find the owner or manager. He examined me warily before directing me to the back of the club.

Shouldering my way through a polyglot crowd of gays, yuppies, converted rastas, and unemployed socialists, I found a door in the back with a sign that said EMPLOYEES ONLY. I knocked.

A male voice said, "Come in."

The owner, a tall, balding man in his early forties with a mustache and very white teeth, stood as I entered. He introduced himself as Sean Kaplan, extending a hand bigger and stronger than the body it belonged to. He was bespectacled, outgoing, and gay.

He asked how he could help me. I was too tired for subtlety. I showed him my ID, told him I was working on a murder case and that an innocent woman might spend the rest of her life in prison if I didn't find what I was looking for.

Kaplan studied my ID, looked at me twice. I said another prayer.

"You're the guy they called Peekaboo Fagen. I remember you. You were a hero to a lot of people, especially in the gay community, when you held that press conference and blasted the sentence Warren Dillon got for killing the mayor. I was a precinct organizer for DiMarco, I worked night and day for six months to help him get elected. It's a crime what they did to him, and to this city after his death. What can I do for you?"

"You keep all your back receipts, bar tabs, credit card slips?"

"Yes. We're required by the IRS to keep them for seven years."

"I need to see all the bar tabs from Thursday night, March 13, two years ago."

"They'd be downstairs. Have a seat and I'll get them for you. Would you like a drink, a glass of wine?"

"It's been a long day; I'd love a cup of coffee."

Sean opened the door and signaled for a waitress, a sinewy light-skinned black woman with close-cropped hair, and asked her to bring me coffee and anything else I wanted. I thanked them both.

The coffee arrived quickly. I stirred cream into it and tipped the waitress, thinking of Mayor DiMarco.

Alan DiMarco ranked among the city's greatest mayors. A former star high school and college athlete, he was an architect and historian. He was tall, ramrod straight, fair-skinned, and blessed with a resonant baritone voice. He was warm, unpretentious, and given to understatement, with little of the standard politician's facade.

As a lay minister who led the choir at the Reverend Cecil Williams Glide Memorial Church, a haven for San Francisco's most offbeat characters, DiMarco had periodically delivered sermons on a wide variety of Christian and human issues. He was also the nation's first openly homosexual mayor.

The son of a popular Union Street grocer, he was first elected supervisor from the city's Castro District. His appeal and popularity were great with people in all walks of life. He was a champion of the rights of the working class, women, and the disenfranchised, especially children. He was a staunch preservationist of the city's heritage and yet encouraged what he called "humanistic" redevelopment of the more decrepit areas. His friendship with the trade unions and city professionals had also been major factors in his political success.

It was a single event that galvanized his status in the city, occurring less than a year after his election as supervisor. Two gay men eating at an all-night diner on Market Street were taunted and harassed by a carful of punks from South San Francisco. When the gay men drove off, they were run off the road several blocks away, pulled from their car, beaten with lead pipes and baseball bats, and stabbed repeatedly. One of the men died, the other was maimed for life.

DiMarco asked to speak at an impromptu town meeting at a church in South San Francisco, near the homes of the four attackers. He asked people who hated or "didn't understand" gays to attend, a gutsy thing to do. Security was tighter than the President's. I was one of the cops assigned to protect him.

To a standing-room-only crowd he delivered an emotional speech, part plea, part sermon. "There is more to a human being than their sexual orientation," he said, a theme he reiterated often. "There is first and foremost the need to be accepted as a human being."

He read a message from the slain twenty-year-old's father, a construction foreman: "Whatever my son was, he was my son, and I loved him."

Then DiMarco quoted Christ's words: "What thou doest to the least of these, thou doest to me." He told the crowd, "I can only pray that you accept me. But I can demand that you don't beat me, or kill me, or burn down my house."

He ended with one of the most emotional statements in American history, the closing words from Lincoln's first inaugural address, praying that the spirit of hatred and violence be "touched, as they surely will be, by the better angels of our nature."

There weren't many dry eyes in the place. I stood next to him for three hours as he shook hands with everyone in the exit line. I realized then that he'd be the next mayor of San Francisco.

Sean Kaplan's return jarred me from my reverie. He had a stack of large green bar tabs in his hand.

"Here they are," he said, handing them to me.

I looked at them. "Your cash register stamps the time of each sale when the bartender rings it up?"

"Yes, it does."

"I want to find all the ones that have the first sale in before eight o'clock; let's say from seven fifteen, seven thirty on."

I separated the receipts that had credit card slips attached to them. Somewhere, somebody had to have made a mistake, I kept telling myself. That's all there is to detective work, the search for the fatal error.

In two minutes, I found a bar receipt for three Rémy Martins, the first at 7:33, a half hour before Lynne arrived, and the last at 8:40, shortly after she left. Attached to it was a Master Card receipt signed by Bruce Bearden. Bruce Bearden, Calvin Sherenian's smug junior-flip attorney. He'd worked for Helen Smidge that night, and probably on other occasions as well. And he had screwed up: either he had not brought enough cash or he never expected to be traced through his credit card.

I asked Sean if he knew Bruce.

"Sure, been coming here for years. He comes four, five nights a week, always trying to charm his way into some woman's drawers. He's usually not very successful."

"Do you have any idea where he lives?"

Sean went to one of two massive Rolodexes on his desk, found a business card.

"Yeah, this has his home number and address on it. He gave it to me months ago, told me if I ever needed any legal help to call him."

Sean copied the address and phone number down for me. I thanked him and asked him to keep my visit to himself. He said he would, and I believed him.

As I started out of the office, I saw Bruce Bearden walking in. He said hello to the bartender and waitress as he settled onto a stool. I ducked back into the office without being seen. Using the phone on Kaplan's desk, I reached Arnie on his cellular and asked him to pick up Henry in my Firenze Plumbing van and meet me outside Bearden's house in Diamond Heights.

Sean led me through a storage room, unbolted a delivery door, and showed me an alley leading back to Market Street. I figured Bearden would be ensconced at the bar for a while, exercising his nerd muscles. Sean agreed with me.

I unchained the Norton without Bearden seeing me, then

pushed it half a block from Bajilla's windows before starting it. Five minutes later I found Bearden's darkened house, and parked a block away. I did a careful recon on foot while waiting for Arnie and Henry to arrive.

14

ARNIE KEPT A GREAT set of burglar's tools in the Firenze Plumbing van. He was a wizard locksmith, and I figured he'd have us into Bearden's apartment easily, once I talked him into it.

You read a lot of crap in detective stories about guys just walking into people's offices, rifling through desks, breaking into people's houses like it's normal business. It's not. I had to fight off an unwanted case of the 'noids: the cops catch me, my PI license goes south, I spend six months in county sleeping with one eye open, trying to discourage the drooling proctologists from getting familiar with the Fagen posterior. As an ex-cop I wouldn't be a candidate for Inmate of the Year.

My hands were shaking, my insides churning as Henry hid himself in the bushes in front of Bearden's place to stand lookout.

It was an Edwardian-style house with large round windows. According to the mailbox, Bearden's apartment occupied the entire ground floor, with someone named Lipschultz living upstairs.

I deactivated the alarm system in seven minutes flat, then coerced Arnie into taking a look at the back door. We heard no evidence of a dog inside, nor any other form of life. I finally convinced Arnie to try his ring of keys on the dead bolt. Thirty keys and we had the mate, but the door lock was old and worn; it took Arnie five minutes to pick.

The apartment was large, filled with old, overstuffed furniture; neat and boring. I made my way to the front and tapped on the picture window to let Henry know we were in. We found Bearden's office and took a look around, careful to return everything we touched to its original place and position. Burglarizing a neatness freak requires a lot of extra work.

I took Bearden's high school yearbook down from a shelf and handed it to Arnie. One thing that struck me was the year he'd graduated: I knew Bearden was fresh out of USC, as Zane had told me, but the yearbook indicated that he was at least thirty-two years old. That meant there was an eight-year gap between his graduating from UC Davis and his entering law school.

There was a box of personal papers with a small lock. Arnie opened it in seconds. Inside was a passport stamped with over two dozen trips to Europe during the eight-year period between college and law school, each one with a stop in Zurich, Switzerland. As in bank account.

A look through his income tax statements revealed he'd worked for two major investment banks, the same firms that contributed heavily to Helen Smidge's campaign coffers and that had lobbied heavily for and financed the building of the Farragut skyscrapers in the Market Street corridor. Firms with millions to lose if everyone had listened to Alan DiMarco or a loose cannon like Flynn Pooley.

There was a record of Bearden's frequent-flyer miles on several airlines, dating back years, all of the payment columns on his personal records marked "cash." From Europe, he rarely returned straight home: he flew to the Bahamas, the Virgin Islands, a few times even to Panama. Places with bank secrecy rules rivaling Switzerland's.

The slush fund. Bribes and payoffs, smuggled place to place, in cash or cashier's check. No wire transfers, no records to trace. With all the business that Farragut did with the investment bankers, it's probable they put Bearden on their payroll at Farragut's or

Smidge's request, especially since he wasn't an investment banker himself. His degree from UC Davis was in anthropology.

We'd been on the premises almost an hour. We were both sweating, nervous. I was about ready to call it quits.

"Look at this," Arnie said. "And this."

In the yearbook was the inscription *To my best friend, the coolest guy in 8th period study hall (Ha! Ha!)* signed Adam Smidgelewski.

I knew that Adam was the nephew of Helen Smidgelewski.

A scrapbook photo showed Bruce Bearden, circa ten years old, on a Police Athletic League baseball team coached by Officer Warren Dillon and backed by Smidgelewski Printing, owned by Supervisor Smidge's father and uncle.

Bearden had been a friend of Helen Smidge's family since childhood. He'd known DiMarco's killer, Warren Dillon, as long as he'd known Smidge. Smidge and Dillon, I already knew, were lifelong friends. They'd groomed Bearden since he was a kid, almost the way that Smidge had found and groomed Warren Dillon to be her reactionary mouthpiece.

Arnie nervously checked his watch. "We gotta book it, Frank." We put everything back, double-checked that it was just the way we found it.

On a last-minute impulse, I decided to check the trash cans.

I found a note at the bottom of the one in the bathroom that read *10 g, meet J.N. Harris Street 9:00, reason w/ McB. first.*

Take ten thousand and meet John Naftulin somewhere on Harris Street at 9:00, try to reason with Lynne McBain first. And then what?

Where would he get ten grand? I began crawling around on the floor, patting the carpet, much to Arnie's consternation. I noticed one of the drawer sections of Bearden's desk was a rollout. I rolled it out, felt a round, hollow spot under the carpet, peeled it back to reveal a floor safe imbedded in cement.

Arnie got a stethoscope and went to work on the safe. I wiped sweat from both our brows as he twirled the tumblers and listened intently.

The phone rang on the desk by our heads, almost giving us both heart attacks. I turned the volume up on the answering machine.

"Bruce? This is Sean Kaplan over at Bajilla. Listen, we found a pair of glasses on the bar, thought they might be yours. Let's see, it's one forty-three, if you're headed home you should be there in about five minutes. You can call if you like, we'll be here."

It was Sean warning me. He knew what I was up to, he'd heard me on his office phone telling Henry and Arnie where to meet me.

We had to give up on opening the safe, but we'd found plenty. I turned the volume on the answering machine back down and we tidied up in about ninety seconds.

Before we left, I took a plastic sandwich bag out of the kitchen drawer and dropped into it the note Bearden had written about taking ten grand and meeting "J.N." on Harris Street at nine.

I passed Bearden on my Norton on upper Market Street. With the visor on my helmet down, he never even noticed me.

15

▼▼▼▼

*T*HE LATE AND very great writer Nelson Algren offered three pieces of advice I've always remembered: never eat at a place called Mom's, never play cards with a man named Doc, and never sleep with anyone who has more troubles than you do.

That first weekend together, I broke rule three vigorously with Colleen, who had more problems than anyone I'd ever broken rule three with before.

In between reading case files and studying new evidence and information, we made love like they were about to repo the equipment—which they just might. It was a loving, sweating, kissing, soul-shaking, heartrending, earth-moving, near record-breaking engagement. I had never known a woman who affected me in as many ways as Colleen did. It was as exciting as first love, as scary as sudden death.

We made love with our eyes open, taking in every moment, every sensation, no distance between us, neither holding back anything.

When I got back to work, I concentrated on Bruce Bearden.

Colleen had never heard of Bearden prior to the trial. Her chief impression of him was that he had an astonishing ability to remember hundreds of details from the case files, complete with cross-references and index numbers.

I got Zane to give up the remainder of his weekend and dig up Bearden's past. He uncovered plenty of surprises.

Bearden had been an orphan, adopted by a truck driver and his wife, raised with three stepbrothers. The father drank, the mother worked to help the family survive. It was unclear why they adopted him, although they did receive county welfare until he was eighteen.

He was a brilliant albeit disturbed adolescent. He had a black belt in tae kwon do, belying his wimp image. He graduated third in his high school class and in the top ten percent at UC Davis, but had been turned down at several law schools because he lacked financial resources. He might have been admitted to a lesser school and received financial aid, but the only places he originally applied were Berkeley, Stanford, Hastings, and USC.

After failing to be admitted to any of his first choices, he went to work as an investment banker for Harrison-Goldblume and Associates, a firm with close ties to William Farragut.

Calvin Sherenian eventually got him admitted to USC and paid his tuition. Bearden directed his anger at having been snubbed for eight years into his law studies, graduating second in his class. He had been with Calvin ever since.

Old neighbors said he'd been arrested twice as a teenager, once for sneaking into the San Francisco Zoo while drunk and throwing stones at some gorillas, and the second time for using his tae kwon do skills to beat up a much bigger kid. A check of public records revealed nothing, typical of junvenile offenses. According to a boyhood friend, now Bearden's bitter enemy, it was Officer Warren Dillon who'd had both arrests quashed.

I wondered if Bearden was actually dumb enough to do the job on Lynne McBain himself, or if the ten grand had been rejected by McBain and subsequently used to hire a killer.

The fact that Bearden had arranged to meet "J.N.," who I assumed was Inspector John Naftulin, was another very disturbing revelation.

I had always considered Naftulin a good cop in spite of his

presence on the crew that had lynched me. Now I figured him for involvement in at least two homicides, Simcic's and McBain's.

In addition to checking out Bearden, I sent Arnie to Big Sur to verify Lynne McBain's alibi for the night of the Farragut murder.

The same bartender who'd been on duty that night was there when Arnie stopped in. He claimed that a very drunk McBain had spent the night in his bed. Two of his housemates confirmed it. He never saw her again.

I had to believe that Lynne McBain had neither the guts nor the smarts to have William Farragut murdered. Finding whoever had taken Ghiberti's silver plates was my only real hope.

I had Henry Borowski begin surveillance on Bruce Bearden, staking out Bearden's place from half a block away in the Firenze Plumbing van. When Henry tired, Martha would take over. I thought of having Martha sidle up to Bearden, use her charms to draw whatever information she could from him, but rejected the idea as far too dangerous.

Somehow, Colleen's affection and the intensity of our feelings created a grand buffer that helped to block the fear. As soon as we took our hands off each other, as soon as I opened up another evidence file or received another report from Henry or Zane, my stomach started churning and the anxiety grew.

I had to find the link between all of this and Farragut's murder, the last piece in the puzzle. I had decided to concentrate on two things.

The first emerged when Arnie made a startling find in the evidence files under "Miscellaneous Reports." There had been three similar burglaries in Pacific Heights and Presidio Heights during the eighteen months preceding the Farragut shooting, and all were still unsolved. The burglars had similar MOs: nighttime entry through a rear or side entrance concealed by a large wall or hedge. None was a professional job. Things had been knocked over and spilled, lights left on, tools taken from storage rooms and used to pry open drawers.

Things of no value had been taken: a woman's favorite hat, a telephone answering machine, two bottles of wine with the owner's name stamped on the label. And the burglars had only hit a few rooms in the enormous houses; they seemed to know right where the good jewelry was kept, which drawers to look in, which closets to rifle.

They were amateurs, but they had cased the places prior to the break-ins. They might actually have been inside the houses before the burglaries.

Follow-up police reports stated that no common denominators had been found amomg the victims: none of them had the same cable installers, laundry service, gardeners, anything.

There was not a single follow-up report filed by Hayden Phillips or any of his private detectives. Reinvestigating the three burglaries should have been their highest priority. A major issue was relegated to the junk pile.

The second thing I focused on was Colleen's previous lover, Tommy Rivera. I knew he'd be testifying soon and his involvement in Colleen's prosecution had bothered me since she'd first told me. Why would Rivera go through such an ordeal, committing perjury to convict what he must have been sure was an innocent woman? Why would he lie on the witness stand with half the world watching? There had to be more to it than jealousy or revenge—if he was lying.

I called Colleen into my office. She came in smiling, dressed only in a black satin teddy that came to just above her hips, a thin black string between her cheeks, exposing legs and butt and Frankie's carnal weakness. I smiled back. I went over, put my arms around her, backed her to the closet, pulled out a black robe, wrapped it around her and tied it at the waist.

I was getting ready to ask her about the burglaries in her neighborhood when the phone rang.

It was Henry Borowski. "Bearden is leave house now, he carries big briefcase, haves nervous face, lookink everywhere around before he gets in car."

"Follow him and keep me posted on the cellular."

I told Colleen to stay inside and do exactly what Martha told her, grabbed my own cellular, and ran to the bike.

Plugging in the adapter, I started the bike and tore off down Lombard. I sped through North Beach, past the cappuccino liberals, hit Broadway, and headed through the tunnel. When I popped out on the other side near Van Ness, I hit the speed-dialer and got Henry in the van.

"He iz go toward Great Highway, past zoo."

"Stay with him until I catch up," I told him. I figured the fastest route was out Fell Street, through Golden Gate Park to the Pacific Ocean and the Great Highway.

If Bearden turned north on the Great Highway, he'd be coming straight at me. If he was going south, I could probably hit ninety or a hundred on the beach-hugging four-lane highway heading to Pacifica.

As I sped through the park, Henry called, saying Bearden had turned south. The entire coast along the Great Highway was heavy with fog. It made it harder to speed and greatly improved the chances of dying.

I caught up to Henry, struggling to stay close to Bearden in the fog. The visibility was about a hundred feet as we headed down the Pacific Coast Highway through Pacifica, to Sky Line Boulevard, turning south toward Woodside. We'd put Bearden "in the cradle," me in front in case Henry lost him, Henry on his tail.

Bearden turned off the road in Woodside and headed for a large farmhouse on top of a hill. With the fog clearing, there was an expansive view of the surrounding Santa Clara Valley and the San Francisco Peninsula. I circled back to see Bearden speaking into an intercom box at the gate. It opened and Bearden drove in.

Henry and I stopped at a deep turnout a hundred yards from the drive, a spot with a good view of everything. I grabbed the infrared binoculars from the van and we ran up a hill in time to see Bearden get out of his car.

Through the green haze of the glasses I saw a figure step outside the farmhouse. Rigid bearing, aquiline nose, disappearing hair:

Calvin Sherenian coming to greet his protégé. Bearden handed Sherenian the large briefcase.

It got even more interesting fifteen minutes later when Tommy Rivera arrived and drove through the gate.

Bearden and Sherenian both came to the door to greet Tommy Rivera. They shook his hand, looking nervously about to make sure Tommy was alone. Henry had a camera and telephoto lens prepared. Using his shoulder for a tripod, I snapped a couple of quick photos.

The three men entered the house. I couldn't figure it.

Rivera was the prosecution's witness, the guy trying to bury Colleen. So why were Calvin and Bearden, the defense, meeting him down in Smokey Bear country?

I got a little excited, hopeful. Maybe they were paying Rivera extortion money. Perhaps they'd called Rivera, asked for a meeting and were acquiescing to his demands. If he recanted his affidavit, refused to testify, the remaining evidence against Colleen slid back to circumstantial. Her chances for acquittal would grow tremendously, back to a merely scary fifty-fifty.

Soon after, paranoia began to serve me well.

I called the office and asked Colleen who would be the administrator of William's estate if she were unable.

"Calvin Sherenian, why?" I told her I was just curious and suggested she try to get some sleep.

I was afraid to say it aloud, to tell Henry what I really suspected.

Calvin and Bearden could easily have been bribing Tommy Rivera to recant his testimony. But the longer I thought about it, the more I doubted it. Too many people had too much to lose if Colleen were acquitted and Farragut's diaries fell into her hands. They all feared that she'd turn them over to the newspapers.

I feared the worst.

Calvin Sherenian was trying to get Colleen convicted. He was paying Tommy Rivera to testify against his own client.

16

▼▼▼▼

WE TRIED TO eavesdrop on the conversation inside the farm-house, sneaking up to the building, listening with stethoscopes, creeping near windows. Nothing. They were inside somewhere, out of enhanced-listening range. All we got for hours worth of effort was sewer breath, splinters, a few minor ankle sprains.

I called Arnie and had him get his cousin Phillip out of bed. Phil McPherson is an Alameda County sheriff's deputy, an ex–Army Ranger and former boxer, weight lifter, martial artist, and SWAT team member. I could sleep in Beirut with Phil guarding me.

I had a working defense plan for my own house, as I'd sheltered a number of witnesses before. Triggered by my suspicions of Calvin's treachery toward his own client, I decided to go to my version of ready alert.

Martha would sleep in the room at the top of the steps, protect-ing the access to my bedroom, where Colleen would sleep.

There was a seldom-used security system with exterior cameras covering all the doors and first-floor windows in the house, a gift from a security company I'd sent dozens of customers to. From the monitor inside the garage workshop, Phil could watch every en-trance. When Phil arrived, I instructed Arnie to recon the neigh-borhood once again. He would also be Phil and Martha's backup.

At four thirty in the morning we returned to the farmhouse in

Woodside, listening, finding nothing. We contented ourselves with waiting across the road for everyone's departure.

At 5:35 A.M. Tommy Rivera walked out, carrying Bearden's black briefcase, beating the sunrise by less than fifteen minutes. I got a few more quick photos, this time from a tripod set on a tree stump a hundred yards from the house.

I left Henry to follow Bearden while I tailed Rivera back to the city, riding the Norton without lights. About twenty minutes later we'd reached Pacifica, when Henry called over the cellular to tell me Bearden and Sherenian had left and were headed in the same direction.

Tommy arrived at his house in the Mission District at a little past six. I found a spot to park the Norton where I could watch the house without being seen. Tommy reappeared at exactly 7:50, showered, groomed, and dressed in a blue pinstripe suit. Court clothes.

He looked around nervously as he got into his car, then drove straight to the courthouse.

Henry called and told me Sherenian was leaving his building. All of a sudden, I realized I'd made a potentially dangerous mistake. What if Calvin called Colleen, found out she had stayed away from home, grew suspicious and decided to have her followed?

I called home frantically and got Martha. She'd called Consuela the night before and had Consuela activate the call-forwarding so Colleen's number would ring on my private line without detection.

Calvin hadn't called. Martha had already phoned for a cabdriver we trusted to take Colleen home. Phil would escort them through a basement maze below my house and out through a neighbor's garage a block away. Martha and Phil would follow the cab in Martha's car to within a block of Colleen's house.

Calvin sent a car and a driver to transport Colleen to court every morning. I worried for Colleen's safety but didn't figure they would make a move against her en route to the courthouse, in broad daylight. I thought of having Phil or Martha tail Colleen, but I was afraid they might be spotted.

I went home, showered, shaved, dressed, and guzzled strong coffee to fight the effects of another night without sleep. Then I headed back to the courthouse to see if Tommy would testify, and if his testimony would confirm my suspicions.

17

*A*T 10:20 A.M., Tommy Rivera walked into Judge Marilyn Walters's courtroom and prepared to take the stand. The media squirmed and frothed like sharks in shallow water.

This was what they came for, the main event, the Lions and Christians part of the show, the "Ladies and Gentlemen . . . the Rolling Stones" portion. It's what got their lace panties wet, their little peters twitching. The good stuff, the above-the-fold-stuff, the lead-in to the first hemorrhoid commercial. Big. Bigger than massacres in Eastern Europe, famine in Africa.

The rich widow, the wicked tramp of Presidio Heights. Farm girl. Teenage waitress in a tits-and-ass joint. Society do-gooder with pinup beauty. The woman who married it all and then shot him, the suspended millions, the gas chamber, the cold cell at Frontera with the bad light and terrible wardrobe.

Now the Latin stud with the golden hammer, the record, the charm, the degree from Berkeley. Info on the heartless bitch and dead hubby, good shit, inside dirt, dick-in-the-middle-of-it stuff.

The media pushed and shoved and cursed each other in the hallway until Walters sent two bailiffs to restore order. They peered through the doors as they swung open and shut for the deputies. Pleading, baggy eyes. Watery eyes, high-test-coffee-and-menthol-cigarette eyes. *Give us anything,* they pleaded. Bestiality, bondage, maybe a little Lesbian Home Porno!! Dare they dream of . . . satanic ritual? Did she nibble on the body? *Help us, please.* . . .

After the bailiffs made a few terse but highly believable threats, they became quieter, more rigid. Mummylike.

Tommy Rivera was sworn in, Ian Jeffries approached.

"Please state your name and occupation."

"Thomas Angel Rivera." He sniffed a little, pulled himself up in his seat. He gave Angel the Spanish pronunciation. "Ahn-hel."

He was an impressive sight. Lean, slick black hair, obsidian eyes, conservative suit, white shirt, colorful tie, handmade shoes. The street kid who'd made it, the glib outlaw with the master's degree from Berkeley. Connections downtown, good seats everywhere, the really big parties. Headed for the supervisor's office? Too small. Rivera was ready for his own Series, a big stage for a new matinee idol.

He was so taken with himself he neglected to answer the second part of the question.

"And could you state your occupation."

"I'm a special consultant to the Office of Redevelopment."

"And what do you do in this capacity?"

"I examine renovation plans and projects, make recommendations to the director and to the mayor's office. I meet with private parties, developers: I try to cut red tape, follow the guidelines set by the city."

He looked at Colleen for the first time, who looked back, quietly staring him down. Rivera turned back to Ian Jeffries.

"Mr. Rivera, after you give us your testimony the defense is going to try to discredit you as a witness, say that you lived a life of crime as a teenager, that you are not an honorable man, that you are not to be trusted. I'd like to clear the air about who you are, where you came from, and what you've done."

"I have nothing to hide, as long as I get a chance to tell the whole story."

"You were born and raised in San Francisco, in the Mission District, is that correct?"

"Yes."

"What was your mother's occupation?"

"She was a prostitute."

"And your father's occupation?"

"I never saw my father. My mother told me several different stories about who he was, depending on how drunk and loaded she was at the time. All I know was that he was one of her tricks."

"You are the oldest of five brothers and sisters."

"Yes."

"And what was your relationship to the other children?"

"I was their surrogate father. I cooked their meals, made them breakfast before school, washed their clothes."

"How old were you when you began caring for your siblings, Mr. Rivera?"

"I was eight. Maybe younger."

"What else did you do for them?"

"I supported them financially. I think I was nine when I assumed that responsibility as well."

"How does a nine-year-old support four other children?"

"By stealing. First it was things that were left in neighbors' yards and in unlocked garages. Then I graduated to car stereos, fencing stolen merchandise, things like that."

"How old were you when you paid the family's rent for the first time?"

"I was nine. The landlord came and threatened to evict us—my mother was so loaded she didn't care. So I broke into someone's house and stole their stereo and a few watches. I would have stolen the TV but I wasn't big enough to carry it."

"The records show your mother received welfare payments, and you say she worked as a prostitute. What did she do with the money she got from those two sources?"

"She spent it on dope and booze."

"Have you ever done drugs, Mr. Rivera?"

"Not even once in my life."

"When were you first arrested?"

"When I was sixteen I was arrested for grand theft auto and fencing stolen auto parts. I was sentenced to eighteen months in juvenile hall. While I was there I stabbed an older boy who tried to rape me, and I wound up doing a full two years."

Never mind that the other boy was half Tommy's size and claimed Tommy tried to extort money from him.

"What happened to your family while you were in jail?"

"One of my mother's tricks cut her to ribbons with a beer bottle and she bled to death. The county put my brothers and sisters in foster homes."

"Were you ever arrested again?"

"At eighteen I was arrested for stealing typewriters from an office building. While I was in jail I met a counselor, a Roman Catholic priest who befriended me, who tried to help me. Father Mario Vargas. He taught me how to read and write, and I fell in love with books and with learning. I earned my high school diploma while I was in San Luis Obispo Men's Colony."

"What did you do after your release from jail?"

"I enrolled at the City College of San Francisco, got my associate degree in social welfare. Then I transferred to the University of California at Berkeley, where I earned a bachelor's and a master's degree, the first in urban planning, the second in architectural design."

"Have you been arrested for any crimes since you first enrolled at City College?"

"No."

Proof positive that either the cops had been sleeping during that time or Tommy had refined his techniques.

"How did you meet the defendant, Mrs. Farragut?" Ian always called her Mrs. with an oily marinade of condescension. Never by her name, to remind everyone that she was the lesser half of Farragut & Farragut, the murderess shadow of William, whose name he used with great delicacy. Calvin might have objected to the Mrs.-and-William dichotomy and won. At least he'd have gotten it in the record, in the jury's mind. My uneasiness was growing.

"I met her at a number of social functions. Fund-raisers, primarily, for the urban renewal project I ran called SOHO: Save Our Homes, Ourselves."

"How did you come to run SOHO, Mr. Rivera?" Addressing him with just the subtlest note of respect, reverence.

"I founded it ten years ago, when I was twenty-eight. I got the city to give people back their condemned housing provided the occupants renovated it, turned it into real homes. We got city funds, state funds at first, plus private donations. Mrs. Farragut was one of our biggest supporters."

"You knew her well, then."

"Very well," he said, and allowed himself a smug little grin. *Yes*, the hot media breath begged silently behind me, *how well? How good was she, Tom? Did she sing soprano in the midnight choir? Help us. . . .*

"How long ago did you meet?"

"About four years ago."

"And how friendly did you become?"

"Real friendly."

Rivera's face underwent a strange metamorphosis, slow, subtle, reflecting a much more animated interior, from coy to worried. A nervous smile appeared on his lips.

"Friendly to the point of sex, Mr. Rivera?"

"Yes."

"How many times?"

Tommy leaned forward, almost resting his chin on the oak rail in front of him, an intense look transforming his features yet again. Everyone seemed to lean a little forward with him.

"Are you talking about . . . multiples? Say we're in a hotel room, four, five hours, we do it, three, four times, does that count as one encounter, or three or four?"

Then he leaned back. He owned the place; even the judge

fought to keep from showing any reaction. I could hear little hands scribbling away all around me.

"That's one encounter, Mr. Rivera." Heh, heh—Ian sorry he never got to do her himself.

"Perhaps ten times . . . yes, that would be about right." Tommy fighting the nerves again.

"Over what period of time?"

"A month."

"Ten times in one month?"

"Yes."

Colleen looked ready to die, ready to scream, anything to put an end to the horror. She struggled visibly to keep her composure.

"Where did these encounters occur?"

"Hotels outside the city limits, where she would be less likely to encounter people who knew her. Marin County or Napa Valley."

"Never at your place or at hers?"

"No."

"Why didn't you go to Mrs. Farragut's place?"

"It might have gotten a little embarrassing if her husband walked in. I know it would be for me."

They were eating it up, even if he was sweating, swallowing nervously. Something was bothering him. He held his head up, took a long slow breath, sucking it up as Ian Jeffries waited.

"Big hotels, nice hotels, Mr. Rivera?"

"The biggest, the nicest."

"Expensive?"

"Yes."

"Who paid for them, Mr. Rivera? Who footed the bill?"

"She did."

That's right, Ian, the scarlet letter on her chest. Fucked this slick dude with the old man's money.

"Identify her, please."

"Colleen Farragut. Mrs. Farragut, right there." He pointed.

"How do you know she paid for all those rooms, Mr. Rivera?

Did you ever see her pay for them at the desk?" Smelling blood, Ian drove the knife home.

"No, but I've seen several of the receipts on the dresser, on the nightstand." He put a wisp of Valentino in the nightstand crack. Subtle, but it registered. Minor, minor crowd ripple.

"You had room service, good wine."

Calvin objected and was upheld. He looked clumsy, desperate to slow the juggernaut. Exactly what he wanted.

"How much did the rooms cost?"

Calvin objected again, got himself overruled. Even Colleen grimaced this time.

"Three hundred, four hundred dollars a crack. More, sometimes, come to think of it; even six, seven hundred." Tommy was about halfway to a blown gasket, working at his tie, his collar.

"Why did it end?"

"She asked me to do something crazy."

Foot shuffling, notebook pages turning in unison.

"How crazy?"

Tommy's face was straining like an overfilled balloon. He tried to answer, swallowed, tried again. To me it was an act, but the jury seemed to see it differently. They looked mesmerized.

They didn't see Tommy lying. They hadn't seen him come out of the farmhouse in Woodside. They saw a guy distraught about having to rat out his ex-lover. A tortured hero. I could have died watching.

"Take your time, Mr. Rivera, we know this is not easy."

I looked around the courtroom, saw that Sherenian and Bearden hadn't cracked a wrinkle. The two of them, Zane, and I, we were the only ones who knew what Tommy was really up to.

"She wanted me to find some guys to kill her husband," Tommy finally said, blurting it out after a struggle. He swallowed, asked for a glass of water, drank, nodded his thanks to the bailiff. "She offered me a lot of money."

"How much money?"

"She never mentioned a price. She just . . . she just said, 'You know a lot of bad people. Find two guys you trust, I'll give you money to pay them, then send them away.' She said she'd pay them well."

"And you?"

"She said I'd be a very wealthy young man."

"How did you react?"

"At first I didn't believe her, but then she just looked at me and said it wasn't a joke." He rubbed his eyes and the bridge of his nose slowly.

"I was so astonished, I couldn't say anything. Here I was, I tried to fix my life, I tried to crawl out of this hole I came from, and she comes along, she makes me feel like I'm the love of her life, and then she asks me to get somebody to kill her husband."

"Did she tell you why she wanted to murder her husband?"

"Not that night, she didn't. It was another time."

"When did she tell you why she wanted her husband killed?"

Tommy hesitated, looked confused, blurted out, "Ahh, at a hotel in Sausalito. It was my birthday, July seventh. We were in a hotel room in Sausalito."

"Which hotel?"

"The Bay View. It was my birthday," he said again.

I looked to see how Colleen was holding up, but I caught something more interesting: Calvin reacted with a start to Rivera's statement about when and where the offer took place. So did Bearden. Calvin leaned over and whispered to Bearden. If the jury caught it, it looked natural enough—his client had just taken a fatal shot. I smelled a screwup.

"So you saw her again, you were with her after she made you the offer, correct?"

"One time. I was in love with her. She called me, she knew it was my birthday, she said she was sorry. I tried to pretend it never happened, but I had to ask her why."

"And what was her answer when you asked why she wanted her husband killed?"

"She said she hated him, that he cheated people, didn't care about anyone, just money. She said he was an animal. She also said he had a girlfriend."

"So she appeared jealous."

Calvin ignored a chance to object.

"I don't know if she was jealous," Tommy answered, then spat out, "she just hated the guy. She thought she'd married a monster."

"Did she tell you about her marriage contract?"

"Yes, she said she had a prenuptial agreement. She told me that William was going to divorce her and she would lose everything."

"How many times did you talk about the murder?"

"Just those two times."

"And what did you tell her?"

"I told her she had to be crazy. I told her she would get caught."

"You had no other contact after that night?"

"No."

"And after her husband was killed, did you try to contact her?"

"Yes. I was freaked out, I wanted to know if she really did it. But she refused to talk to me."

"Why didn't you come forward with this information right after the murder?"

"They arrested her a few days after. I thought they had her, I thought she'd just plea-bargain and get one of those rich-people's sentences, you know, eighteen months playing tennis in some country club somewhere."

Calvin objected. Walters upheld, struck it from the record.

"When it seemed certain there was going to be a trial, that she was going to deny everything, I called the district attorney's office. They asked me to testify." Tommy was cool again, seemingly in control, the volcano subsiding.

"One last question, Mr. Rivera." Ian gave it the good pregnant pause. "That first night she brought it up, did Mrs. Farragut say how she wanted to have her husband killed?"

"Yes."

"How?"

"She said . . . her idea was to fake a robbery, get two guys to shoot him and make it look like a robbery attempt." Tommy got it out, growing more emotional. "It was ridiculous, but she was desperate."

"What was your reply?"

"I told her she'd get caught."

"Thank you, Mr. Rivera. I have no further questions at this time, but I'd like the option to recall this key witness later."

Walters granted his request, thanked Rivera.

Instead of moving to cross-examination, Calvin asked for time to confer with his client. Judge Walters banged the gavel, granted a short recess, and the jury was excused. After they left, the bailiffs escorted Colleen, Calvin, and Bearden through the side exit. I waited until they closed the door to follow the shuffling crowd into the hallway.

Rivera's testimony had been very, very deadly. And not a word of it was true. That was the one part of Colleen's story I believed without question: Colleen could never have been so stupid as to ask someone she'd been sleeping with for a month to have her husband killed.

I was believing her story more and more by the minute.

And I now had a new target, a new weak spot in the fabric of lies.

Tommy Rivera.

18
▼▼▼▼

CALVIN'S CROSS-EXAMINATION OF Tommy Rivera was spirited—and meaningless. He passed briefly over Tommy's criminal past, ostensibly trying to discredit him, but not trying very hard. He challenged him on his recollections, on his delay in going to the police, never once asking if he had tried to blackmail Colleen.

I cast sideways glances at Calvin and Bearden throughout, to see if they were doing the same with me, to try to find any hint that Lynne McBain had told them of my visit, or that Bearden had detected that anyone had been in his apartment. If they knew, they were too good to let on.

Tommy Rivera got stronger as the cross-examination went on. Calvin looked defeated, Colleen despondent.

When Judge Walters banged the gavel at the end of the day, you could hear the bell tolling.

I had a very simple system worked out with Colleen. At a prearranged time every evening, she would climb the wall behind her house, where Henry and Martha waited outside to bring her to Telegraph Hill. As I waited for her to arrive the night of Tommy's testimony, I knew I had a major league problem, one not uncommon in my line of work.

I was duty bound to tell her what I'd found about Calvin's

treachery, but I was afraid. I was afraid she'd crack, that even if I told her to say nothing to Calvin and Bearden, they'd sense it in her attitude toward them, that something she might say or do would tip them off that I was on to them.

I was also legally and ethically bound to tell the court if I discovered a crime in commission, especially one as grave as tampering with the judicial system. Right then, that was the least of my worries.

I knew I couldn't tell Colleen just yet. For the first time since she'd hired me, I held a small coign of vantage.

If I couldn't find the burglar by the end of the trial, I could always step forward with the photographs of Calvin and Bearden meeting with Rivera in Woodside and derail the process through a mistrial. That would buy Colleen another six months and probably get Calvin and Bearden disbarred, at least temporarily.

But that still wouldn't save Colleen. Ian Jeffries would refile and Colleen would have to do it all again. No assets released. No money, no diaries. Finding the burglar was the only real end to the nightmare.

When Colleen arrived I asked for her help. I mentioned nothing about Sherenian or Bearden, their treachery, or Bearden's involvement in McBain's murder.

"Tommy Rivera testified you made the murder proposition at the Bay View in Sausalito the night of his birthday."

"I never offered him anything, that smug, lying little *bastard*." She was so angry she was shaking. I gave her a minute.

"We were in a hotel room in Sausalito on his birthday, that part is true," she said when she'd calmed down enough. "I remember it well because it was the next day that William confronted me about my affair with Tommy."

"Tell me what William said. How did he find out?"

"He said he had 'evidence, hard evidence.' "

"Did he say what kind?"

"Not really. He said 'irrefutable evidence, the kind that stands up in court.' Those were his exact words."

I thought for a minute, had the answer. She pulled it out of me.

"If he had stand-up-in-court evidence, he didn't mean a sighting by a friend or aquaintance. Did you ever enter a hotel lobby together, leave together, were you ever seen holding hands or kissing in public?"

"Never. We were fanatically discreet. We always entered and left separately, never went near each other in public."

I drifted off again, reluctant to tell her what I thought.

"You said we'd work together, Frank. Tell me."

"I think your husband or Sherenian had their private detective, Hayden Phillips, bug your room, or worse, make a video."

"Oh, God" slipped from her lips, and I knew that if there was a video it would be a beauty. Even the audio would be a blockbuster.

"Your husband would never have pulled a stunt like that without involving Sherenian, and Sherenian always uses Phillips. This is right up Hayden's alley; he built half his agency by trapping women with their lovers so the husbands could use the evidence in divorce proceedings. You're sure it was the very next day, the day after you and Tommy celebrated his birthday in Sausalito that William confronted you?"

"Absolutely."

"Then Tommy may have made a fatal mistake on the witness stand. If a tape was made of you two that night, William would have confronted you the next day. In my experience, no man waits a week before confronting his wife with evidence like that. And the tape would prove you never offered Tommy money to have William killed."

"You're right. William started the whole argument by asking where I'd been the night before, what had I been doing? And if I tried to pull a stunt like that, offering money to have my husband murdered, and William found out, don't you think he would have done something about it? Gone to the police, had me arrested, something—anything? My God, that tape could prove that I never offered Tommy a thing."

She put her face in her hands as if she was trying to rub the pain, the fatigue away. "This is just great. Instead of dying in the gas chamber I can die of embarrassment while the whole world watches the tape. I can just see it, those nice newspaper photos with black strips across your tits and your butt."

"That won't happen. All that's important is the audio part. We could kick Tommy's testimony, prove he's lying."

"That still might not get me an acquittal. This is a nightmare, Francis."

"Let me worry about it. Let me find out where the tape is."

I figured Calvin had the tape. Farragut always hid behind his lawyers.

If I could get it, it would give me one more monkey wrench to throw into the works if I couldn't find the burglar. It would also strengthen my chances of nailing Sherenian, Bearden, and Rivera for perjury and conspiracy to obstruct justice.

All I had to do was burglarize Calvin's home and office and find the right tape.

I showed Colleen the reports Arnie had found of the three similar burglaries committed in her neighborhood in the months preceding William's death. I asked what she knew about them.

"Only what I read in the files," she said. "Calvin told me the police had investigated and found no connection between them and the burglary at our house."

"And Hayden Phillips found nothing either?" I asked.

"I don't know. I guess not, or they would have made an issue out of it. There's a lot of burglaries in those neighborhoods. Calvin just said there was no link."

I handed her the burglary reports for the homes of the Schmid-baums, Castellanos, and Rosenzweigs.

"Do you know these people, Colleen?"

"Yes. I know them well. They're involved in a lot of the same things I am—charities, fund-raisers, gallery openings."

"Do they throw a lot of parties?"

"Yes, as a matter of fact. You know, lawn parties, fund-raisers for political causes, for homeless missions. They're very active."

"Did any of them have parties around the time of the burglaries?"

Colleen looked at each name and date carefully.

"The Schmidbaums and Castellanos did for sure; I went to both. I remember when they were burglarized. The Rosenzweigs, I'm not sure. . . . I think they did, but I missed it. I think they gave a big party before William was murdered, a few months before, but I had tickets to see *Cats* at the A.C.T. that night and I missed it."

"Did Tommy Rivera go to those parties?"

"I don't remember, exactly, but—wait. Yes, he was definitely at the Schmidbaums', that was the first time I'd seen him in a long time. The Castellanos' party . . . yes, I remember seeing him at the Castellanos' because he spoke Castilian with Castellano."

I asked her to call Mrs. Rosenzweig to see if Tommy had been to their party the night Colleen had gone to see *Cats*. Before she did, I activated the "bug catcher" to see if my line was tapped. It wasn't.

Mrs. Rosenzweig confirmed that Tommy Rivera had been to the party at their house six weeks before they were burglarized.

19
▼▼▼▼

CALVIN'S TREACHERY AND Rivera's testimony went a long
way toward convincing me of Colleen's innocence. It also helped
me to stop mistrusting her. It broke down a wall that I kept my
strongest feelings behind.

What I imagined was a serious case of oh-Lord-I-think-I-love-
her had really been a devastating wave of want and passion, plus
that rarest of all things, recognition of a kindred spirit, a soul mate.

To trust is to go beyond the last barrier, to let go of the fear one
clings to like a life jacket. In my case, I had more than ordinary
cause for apprehension.

That night when we made love, it was deeper, stronger, slower,
looking and kissing, body watching, staring unwaveringly into
each other's eyes. There was no distance between us, the barriers
were gone.

I hadn't felt that in a long, long time. I'd never felt it stronger.
We'd turned the corner from fucking, sweet and urgent as it was,
and we were fucking better than ever, everything fearless, everything open.

Four hours of sleep and I was back in the hunt.

I prayed Tommy Rivera was the last piece in the puzzle, that
I was creeping up on a merciful end to Colleen's nightmare, to the
long Fagen nightmare, to my own protracted horror.

I made breakfast, and while we ate I alternated between looking at Colleen and worrying somewhere out in space. She noticed it, the worry, the wondering. The gravity of what awaited her was now weighing on my heart as well as my mind.

Just before she left I nonchalantly asked her to keep tabs on Calvin and Bearden, their schedules, the places they went after court. When she asked why, I told her I was afraid to run into one of them while running down information and leads. She seemed to buy it. We kissed good-bye, and then Martha and Phil took her through the basement to Martha's waiting car. The simple act of sneaking her in and out, of protecting her, of being with her, was becoming more dangerous, more difficult.

Two minor league screwups, I thought when they'd left, two small but crucial mistakes that had turned the whole thing around, given me hope, direction.

The first was the fact that Fred Worley, my old acquaintance who tended bar at Farragut's hotel, remembered Lynne McBain, and remembered reading the personal ad she left unattended.

The second was that when Bearden had checked out Lynne McBain, he'd paid for his drinks with his credit card, leading us to the discoveries we'd made in his home, the note about meeting J.N. with ten grand. That in turn had led me to tail Bearden to the meeting with Sherenian and Rivera in Woodside.

Too close. Just thinking about it made me nervous.

All I had to do was break into Sherenian's home and/or office and find a tape of Colleen's rendezvous with Tommy at the hotel in Sausalito—and risk losing my license and being thrown in jail. Before the Bearden break-in I hadn't committed burglary on a case in seven years; now I was working on my second one in a week.

A half hour later, Martha, Arnie, Henry, and I met in the City Lights office and went over recent developments.

"I'm convinced that Helen Smidge had both Simcic and McBain killed, and that Bearden or John Naftulin either did the killing or hired the killer. Whoever did it probably did Flynn Pooley as well." I pointed out that if Calvin could get Colleen convicted, he would be named executor of Farragut's estate, and would be free to destroy Farragut's diaries, sending the whole dirty history up in flames.

I waited a second for it to sink in.

"There's something that has bothered me about Tommy Rivera testifying since I first heard the story," I went on. "Colleen says she refused Tommy's ludicrous blackmail scheme. So what does a guy with half a brain do in a situation like this?"

"He gives it up," Arnie cut in. "Next case. Nobody but a moron would get up there and lie on the witness stand just to get revenge on somebody."

"That's right," I said, "nobody but a complete moron would actually go through with a stunt like that. And Tommy Rivera is anything but a moron."

"But they bribe him," Henry said, "ve see guys have meeting, make deal, he comes out vith briefcase probhubly stuff vith money."

"I still say there's more to it than that, Henry."

I gave each of them a copy of the police reports Arnie had found. "Three burglaries, all with similar MOs to the Farragut burglary, all in Presidio and Pacific Heights mansions, within eighteen months of the Farragut killing."

"Similar, but not identical," Martha said.

"That's what Inspector Naftulin and his crew decided. Not that I believe a word he says."

"That doesn't mean they're necessarily wrong," she came back.

"There were parties at all three of the burglarized houses within six to eight weeks of the break-ins," I stated. "Fund-raisers. All three of them were attended by Tommy Rivera. You'll notice that Hayden Phillips retraced the cops' steps, except there's no mention of these burglary reports."

"Vich means Phillips probhubly did verk, but not report all he find."

"Exactly. He was more diligent than Naftulin, because he had more time, more manpower, and because he desperately needed to find the real burglar. He wanted to find them so he and Calvin could make sure no one accidentally turned up to ruin the lynch party they had scheduled for Colleen."

"Which means," said Martha, "that maybe he did find the burglar in these cases."

"That's exactly what I believe," I said, "which brings us to the missing link. Now, I think that Tommy Rivera would have been too afraid to go to Calvin with that ludicrous blackmail story and ask for hush money. He knew Colleen must have told Calvin, he knows Calvin is a shark and must have been waiting for Rivera to try it again so he could nail him. One of two things could have happened.

"Calvin could have sent his butt-boy, Bearden, to get Rivera to testify against his own client."

"That's dangerous," said Arnie, playing devil's advocate. "Tommy's offer to Colleen was that he *wouldn't* testify. Actually getting up there and testifying is another story completely. Tommy could turn on Bearden and Calvin, blackmail them for even more money after the trial. He could also dump it in their laps if something went wrong. Calvin would not take a risk like that with a guy like Rivera."

"Unless they had something on Tommy," Martha said.

"That's exactly right," I concluded. "Tommy's testimony yesterday is what made it click in. What was Tommy's regular line of employment before he got religion? He was a burglar. He was a great burglar. I went after him once; we knew he'd broken into dozens of places but we could never catch him. An old girlfriend ratted him out, told us where he hid the merchandise. We nailed him when he went to retrieve the stuff. If it wasn't for that, we might never have gotten him.

"Which brings us to the second and most likely possibility: Hayden Phillips found the real burglar in those other three jobs and discovered Tommy was involved. I doubt Tommy did the burglaries himself, he's too smart for that. But he set them up. He cased the places during the parties, then sent his stooges to do the dirty work.

"Now, Calvin knew the case against Colleen might not be strong enough to convict her. If she goes free, she gets William's diaries and turns them over to the newspapers. A lot of rich guys, himself included, get a lot of time wearing dresses up at Folsom.

"Calvin knew that in order to get Colleen out of the way and get the diaries, he had to do two things: he had to turn in the worst performance of his career, and he needed to get one more piece of evidence against her. Which Rivera could provide, if Calvin could manipulate Tommy without fear that Tommy would turn on him later."

"So Sherenian sends Bruce Bearden to see Tommy. They have Rivera in a vise. They know he tried to blackmail Colleen, and they know he engineered the other burglaries. Tommy's facing ten, twenty years, maybe more if they can make it look like Tommy did the Farragut job too. But they give him a way out."

"All he has to do is go through with his threat and testify against Colleen—with Sherenian's expert coaching. Instead of going to jail, Tommy winds up a rich man and gets revenge on Colleen for dumping him. And the chances of his coming back on Sherenian are slim and none. If he messes with them, or messes up somewhere, they can send him away for a long, long time."

"Pretty simple choice for a guy like Tommy," Martha said.

"And that brings us to the big question," I said. "If Tommy was involved in the previous burglaries, was he also involved in the Farragut burglary?"

"He'd been in the Farragut house before," Martha said. "I remember seeing a newspaper photo of a SOHO fund-raiser at the Farragut mansion, and Tommy was standing next to Colleen."

It was the first I'd heard that Tommy had ever been in the Farragut house, but it fit perfectly.

"That means if Tommy did engineer the Farragut burglary as well, he's a shoo-in for murder one for masterminding a robbery that resulted in murder."

"Technologically he would be Farragut's murderer," Henry concluded.

"Now all we have to do is find the burglar," Martha said, "which is where we came in. And hope that somebody hasn't sent them to Uruguay or the bottom of the Bay, which seems to be a favorite dumping spot. Then we have to connect them to Rivera."

"And we also have to hope that either Calvin or Hayden Phillips didn't get Ghiberti's plates and destroy them," Arnie added. "They might be our only physical evidence."

We also had to hope that I was right. We were doing a lot of hoping.

Martha asked for the game plan. The clock was running, and everyone was on edge.

"An all-out assault on Tommy's involvement in the burglaries. I want each of you to take a file and go out and visit the Schmidbaums, Castellanos, and Rosenzweigs. Ask them if there's anything that they can add, any piece of information that's come to them weeks or months after the burglary. Were any items taken that weren't discovered missing until later, no matter how insignificant. A scarf, a handkerchief, anything.

"Tommy's old rap sheet is easy to get, I can have Lloyd Dinkman run a copy in no time. What I'm interested in is what he's done since he supposedly went straight. I want to know every move he's made. I want phone records, credit card receipts, names of old girlfriends, old running buddies. We're going to start twenty-four-hour surveillance on Bearden and Rivera. Bearden's the one doing the dirty work; Calvin's smart enough to let his flunky handle all that. Colleen will tell me about all of Sherenian and Bearden's activities, but she doesn't know about any of this yet. I haven't told her that Sherenian wants her convicted."

"That's dangerous," Martha said. "Not to mention unethical."

"I know. But right now I think we have a slight edge on them. I don't think Lynne McBain told them about me, or they would have made some move already. My guess is she just told Smidge she heard her voice on a newscast or an interview and recognized it. If I tell Colleen, she might accidentally tip them off that we're on to them."

"There's one other thing I want to do. Rivera and Colleen really were in a hotel room in Sausalito on his birthday two years ago, which he claims is when she offered him money to murder her husband. It was the next day that Colleen's husband confronted her about her affair with Tommy. Farragut said he had solid proof, proof that would stand up in court."

"Probably an audio or video recording," said Martha.

"Right, and I think Hayden Phillips made it and gave the tape to Sherenian so William could use it against Colleen in the divorce proceedings. If we can get that tape from Sherenian, we can use it to prove Colleen never asked to have her husband killed, and that Rivera lied on the witness stand. That and the photos of Calvin and Bearden group-groping the prosecution's star witness would trigger a mistrial and maybe even get Sherenian and Bearden disbarred and sent to jail."

"That might not save her from a retrial," Arnie said, "and that also won't get you Farragut's diaries. The longer those diaries are out of our hands, the greater the chance of someone else's getting to them and destroying them."

"That's why we have to nail Rivera and find the burglar," I said. "After we break in to Calvin's place and find a tape of Tommy and Colleen in the hotel."

"That's the riskiest stunt of all," Martha said. "If we get popped for breaking and entering we'll be in jail waiting for her when she arrives. There won't be anybody to help her."

I just waited, looking at their three gloomy faces. Martha agreed first, then Henry and Arnie.

"One last thing just occurred to me," I said. "What if Tommy Rivera does screw up somewhere? How's he going to explain his sudden, newfound wealth? As much as they have on him, he's still a loose cannon, and this group obviously hates loose cannons."

"They're probably phoning his measurements in to the undertaker right now," said Arnie.

"And we need him alive, at least until the trial's over," I added. "That means that while we're running surveillance on Tommy, we might have to stop somebody from killing him."

20

▼▼▼▼

*T*HE SIMPLEST APPROACH to detective work is to look for
flaws. A weakness in the story, a mistake, a tiny lie, an alibi that
doesn't coincide perfectly, a parking ticket near a crime scene, a
telltale credit card receipt.

I have another rule that has always served me well: when you
want something on somebody, forget about his friends. Known
accomplices, past partners in crime—all they will do is lie to you
and tip off the suspect that you're on his tail. Give me an enemy
every time.

Someone who's been double-crossed, cheated, unpaid. A betrayed partner, a jilted lover, a spiteful neighbor, a vindictive wife.
When I have to get something on a suspect, I search the court
records for delinquent alimony and child support payments, un-
collected debts, assault charges, lawsuits.

I spent the morning studying old files at the *Clarion* building,
compliments of Zane Neidlinger, going over newspaper clippings
and microfilm files of everything they had ever written on Tommy
Rivera.

That's when I found her, kind of cursing myself for not thinking
of it before.

Angela Estrella.

Angela was born in the Mission District, daughter of Guatemalan immigrants, a high school cheerleader and debate champion, now a community activist. She graduated from S.F. State six years after I did and quickly became the head of Social Services in the city.

She had been a director of Para Los Niños, an organization that helps poor and homeless children, plus a dozen other groups. She was appointed to the board of directors of Tommy's SOHO project when they started getting massive grants from the city and state. According to one of the articles, she resigned from the SOHO Board over "unspecified differences" with Rivera.

Angela had been a supervisor at Social Services during Tommy's three-year tenure as a caseworker.

From various other articles I learned that eleven years earlier Angela had married a prominent expatriate Chilean architect, a former Allende supporter and Pinochet hater named Francisco Mena. From the circulation department of the *Clarion* I got their address in the Mission District.

Five minutes on the Norton and I was ringing Angela's doorbell. Her house was a beautiful restored Queen Anne Victorian overlooking Dolores Park.

Angela answered the door wearing an apron and wiping flour from her hands.

"I'm Francis Fagen," I said, holding up my ID. "I'm a private investigator. I'm working on the Farragut murder case. Can I ask you a few questions?"

"Is this about Tommy Rivera?"

I nodded. She opened the door and invited me in.

We trudged up the endless steps that sadistic architects designed into half the houses in San Francisco, arriving at a rambling, sun-filled upper floor filled with paintings and sculpture by Mexican and South American artists.

Angela led me into an enormous parlor with a view of the park, where she called for someone named Anna to come and remove the two children who had now clung to her, staring at the leather-jacketed stranger. Anna appeared, heavyset and Nordic, and took the children, promising to return with tea.

"Are you the same Fagen that got kicked off the police force over the DiMarco murder?" she asked. "You had some kind of nickname . . ."

"Peekaboo," I said.

"What can I do for you, Francis?"

"How'd you know I came about Tommy Rivera?"

She went and pulled shut the heavy sliding door that closed off the parlor.

"I've been waiting a long time for somebody to nail that sleazeball piece of human garbage. I read in the paper this morning about his testimony against Colleen Farragut."

I waited patiently while she looked down for a moment, gathered her thoughts.

"You don't know the kind of stuff Tommy has done to people, Francis. You don't know." she said.

"Tell me."

"He's lying. Colleen Farragut never asked him to have her husband killed, I don't believe it. I knew her when she sponsored SOHO, when I was on the board of directors. She was kind, she cared about people. She had a real heart."

"How do you know he's lying? How can you tell for sure?"

She shook her head slowly, almost embarrassed.

"You worked with Tommy at the Department of Social Services. Were you his supervisor?" I asked.

"Yes. I hired Tommy Rivera. I brought him into the department. I was his supervisor for three years, until he got SOHO off the ground and started working there full time."

"What did he do, Angela? What can you tell me about him?" I was starting to sound a little desperate, and I didn't like it.

"He used people. He left the Welfare Department because he was forced out, they were going to fire him. He is an evil man, he speaks for no one, not poor people, not Hispanics, no one but himself."

"Why was he going to be fired?"

"He used to make deals with the welfare recipients. Women he'd caught committing fraud, women who didn't quite qualify or who wanted more money than they were entitled to."

Anna knocked, and we waited patiently as she brought the tea and then departed.

"Be specific, Angela. I need to know."

"He used these women. He found the best-looking ones, gave them extra money, gave them payments for five kids when they had only one or two."

"And for this, they gave him sexual favors?"

"Yes. And kickbacks. Sometimes even more than that."

"What do you mean, more? What else did they give him?"

"They did things for him . . ." She was clearly having a rough time just talking about it. "They sold dope in their neighborhoods. I know because I heard from a very reliable person."

I looked at her and waited.

"Three different women on welfare had jobs working as maids in big houses. Tommy knew about it and let them keep their jobs, provided . . ." She had to struggle for a few seconds to keep her composure.

"Tommy made them scout out burglary victims for him. They wrote down things about the places they worked, made a list of all the valuables. Then he'd send people there when he knew the owners were not home.

"I got an anonymous call one day, a woman told me Tommy was doing this to her sister. She said her sister knew of two other women to whom Tommy had done the same thing."

"Rivera was the sister's caseworker?"

"Yes."

"Do you know the names of any of the women?"

She shook her head.

I asked a few more questions without learning much, and when she showed me out I promised to tell no one of our conversation if she would do the same. She agreed.

Back on the street, I unchained the Norton from a no-parking sign and kicked it to life. I hadn't asked why she never reported Tommy when she was his supervisor, or why she accepted a seat on the SOHO board knowing what she did about Rivera. From the newspaper articles I'd studied, I knew that Angela had married Francisco Mena exactly two months after Tommy Rivera left the Welfare Department. That was eleven years ago.

On the mantel in Angela's living room were photographs of Francisco and their four children. The oldest, a girl of about ten, bore a striking resemblance to Tommy Rivera.

Maybe Francisco Mena had never noticed.

21
▼▼▼▼

*I*T WAS MIDAFTERNOON when I finished lunch at Franchino's on Columbus. I had lingered over the osso buco, thinking it all over.

One of the burglars at the Schmidbaum house had definitely been a woman, not a very bright one, who left lipstick and teeth marks on a piece of cheese. She'd probably been the one who'd stolen Mrs. Schmidbaum's favorite hat.

Angela said Rivera had used women from his caseload to commit burglaries for him. A real stand-up guy, the more you knew about him. Was it possible he still used his connections from his days as a caseworker?

A wave of anxiety went through me. I just wanted to fold, to find a hole to crawl into and pretend none of this had ever happened. If I had guessed wrong, if any of the story I had pieced together proved untrue, it was Colleen who would pay the most terrible price.

I fought off the panic. I made myself believe I was right. Tommy had once been an ace burglar himself. He had switched to using poor, desperate women to do his bidding. My longest hunch to date was that he was still using women he'd met during his days as a caseworker.

Originally, the trial was expected to last a month. But with a

Friday session, and short appearances by Tommy and several of the witnesses, the pace was accelerating.

I had two weeks or less.

I paid the check and, for privacy, asked to use Franco's office phone. I had memorized Angela Estrella's number off the phone in her living room. I called and asked if she still had any friends at Social Services. She said her brother worked there as a supervisor. I told her I needed her help to nail Tommy and keep Colleen from going to prison.

"Anything," she said. "Just tell me."

But when I told her she balked. I wanted a copy of every case Tommy Rivera had handled in his three years at Social Services, the name of every female who ever received even a single payment through Tommy's docket.

"That would be difficult," Angela told me. "Records from that far back, before they went to computers, are kept under lock in a basement storage area."

I told her there was no other way. She consented to do it, said she would go see her brother and the two of them would gather the records after everyone else had gone home. It was critical that I get them as soon as possible, that night or the next morning.

She offered to contact me as soon as she had the case records. I gave her the address and phone number of the City Lights Agency. There was relief and determination in her voice when she thanked me "for myself and a lot of other people." I returned the compliment.

After I thanked Franco for the use of his phone and bid his wife, mother, and two daughters a good day, I unchained the Norton and headed up Broadway to Gough Street, through the Fillmore District to the freeway heading south. The traffic was light and I cranked it, making Hillsborough in record time.

I pulled into Eileen Farragut's driveway, rang the musical chimes, and waited until the little peephole opened and the Oriental Cyclops appeared and examined me. I held up my ID and this time tried out a little of my tiny repertoire of Korean. I got a faster response than last time.

In a few minutes, I was shown into a greenhouse where Eileen was tending some African violets. I could have sworn I had seen this scene before. She was wearing a satiny peach dress and had a lot more color in her face than on our first visit. She either had high blood pressure or had taken up aerobics.

"What can I do for you, Mr. Fagen?"

"Were you serious when you offered to help, Mrs. Farragut?"

"I am not a frivolous woman. I'll do anything I can to assist Colleen. Have you found something?"

"I've found quite a bit. I'm convinced that there was a burglar in her house, and I now know where to look. But I'm running out of time and I need some help." I hesitated.

"Come, Francis, if it's money, that's the one thing I have in abundance right now. Time I'm a little short on."

The fact that she'd called me Francis made it a little easier to ask. "I want to offer a fifty-thousand-dollar reward to anyone who can identify the burglar or help me locate Ghiberti's silver plates. I'm certain the police kept the plates out of the paper to keep from setting up a flea market for crackpots. Now that I have a place to look, the reward might help."

There was more and she knew it. She waited patiently.

"I need a little money for extra surveillance and protection. I think Colleen's life might be in danger if it looks like we're going to win this thing."

Putting down her trowel, she started past me, nodding for me to follow. "Do you know who did it, who killed William?" she asked.

"No, but I think I'm heading in the right direction. It's been a long, difficult road." I felt another twinge of paranoia. How did I know she wasn't working with Calvin and had offered to help just to get close to me? What if they had all been on to me from the beginning and were just biding their time, waiting for the right moment to make a move?

She smiled. "Good," she said. "Keep at it, Francis. It's a terrifying situation she's in."

She showed me to an empty guest suite near the back of the house and had me lift up the carpet in the linen closet. Underneath was a floor safe as big around as a hubcap. Eileen gave me the combination and I opened it; it was full of stock and bond certificates and some personal papers. I removed them at her direction and found a tin box at the bottom. I handed it to Eileen.

"This is very trusting of you, Mrs. Farragut," I said.

"Are you untrustworthy, Francis?" She looked into my eyes and right through me, it seemed. I shook my head.

Smiling, she opened the box, counted out thirty-five thousand dollars into my hand. There must have been a hundred grand in there. Eileen's cookie jar.

"There's ten thousand for extra staff, twenty-five thousand as a down payment for information or return of the plates. I don't imagine you'd give it to them all at once. Not until you've coerced them into testifying for you." She was smart enough to be scary.

"I'll return this to you when I collect my bonus," I said.

"No, you won't. You'll have earned your bonus, whatever it is. This is my contribution. I'll give you the other twenty-five thousand when you find what you are after."

Returning the tin box to the safe, I put the certificates and other papers back, closed the door, and spun the dial.

"Just do me one favor, Francis," she said as I replaced the carpet. "Promise me that if all goes well you'll come back and give me the whole story, every smarmy little detail. All I get these days for entertainment is a bunch of old ladies complaining about their ailments and boring the piss out of me. Will you do that for me?"

"It'll be my pleasure, Mrs. Farragut."

When I'd asked her once more to keep our transaction to herself, I smiled, taking her hand, and caught the full effect of the blue eyes again. I practically bolted out the door. A little unnerved by my suspicion that Eileen might be involved with Sherenian—especially since she'd just handed me thirty-five thousand—I was suddenly overwhelmed with emotion, gratitude. Electric pinpricks of fatigue ran down both my arms, my hands shook, even my fingernails ached. My head was spinning, throbbing.

Struggling to concentrate, eyes not focusing properly. Long, boring, dangerous freeway run, keep the bike between the lines, too tired to sing goofy songs, back to North Beach, home.

Colleen was waiting when I arrived.

22

▼▼▼▼

COLLEEN DIDN'T SAY anything when I entered. She looked demure, drained, but very game, sporting the bravest, most convincing smile. I couldn't keep my arms from going around her. I could feel the shaking ease after a long minute.

"I'm starved, I need some energy." Nothing killed her appetite, a good sign. I called Irene at Caffè Roma and ordered a small feast, uncorked a Monte Falco Rosso, poured two glasses.

She got right to it, filling me in on the day's courtroom events. Ian Jeffries had recalled John Naftulin for the second part of his testimony. Naftulin reported that after twenty months of investigation, no sign of the burglars or the allegedly purloined silver plates had been found.

The food arrived, and the mood changed, temporarily.

"You're more than I bargained for," she said out of the clear blue. "Once in a while William would replay the tape of you attacking the verdict in Warren Dillon's trial, and while he was laughing and telling everyone how his biggest enemy had self-destructed, I just stared at the screen, fascinated. That took guts, Frank. Whatever happened to men with guts, with moral courage? I haven't asked much of you, have I? Be my lover, be my friend, save me from the worst fate imaginable. Oh, yeah, and I'll pay you later."

We both grinned.

"We'll make it, won't we, Frank? We're going to be all right, aren't we?"

She came around the table, put her arms around me, and squeezed. I could feel warm tears on my neck. "Thank you, Frank, for being more than I bargained for."

"We'll be all right, Colleen. I promise. We're getting close now. If I have to, I can buy you some time. That's all I can say. We'll make it, I promise you."

She straightened up, sniffled, sat on my lap. "Just do me one favor, please, Frank. Let me help if I can. I can't live in the dark. Not knowing where I stand is turning me into a mental case. Just tell me where we are, who we're looking for. If I have a chance, if I can help myself, keep busy, I can keep my spirits up, and that's getting tougher every day. That's all I ask."

I promised I would let her in. Half promised, actually, knowing that I would keep Calvin's betrayal secret until it was all over.

Colleen and I were clearing the table an hour later, after planning our lives post-acquittal, when the bell on the agency door rang. I called Martha to the kitchen, told her to stay with Colleen and take her down through the hidden door and out through the alley if there was any trouble. I took my .45 from the drawer, cocked it, stuck it in the waistband at the small of my back, and went downstairs to the office.

A man who introduced himself as Guillermo Estrella, Angela's brother, stood on the porch with a cardboard box in his arms. He was sweating despite the fact the temperature was in the upper forties.

"Angela asked me to deliver these things," he said, and I reached into the box and pulled out some files as he explained that they were the records of Tommy Rivera's former welfare cases. I took the box from him and he left, relieved.

In the box were over three hundred files of women who had once passed through Tommy Rivera's caseload. There were also confidential interdepartmental memos on Tommy's activities, a number of them charging him with sexual harassment of both coworkers and ADC recipients. A gutsy addition on Angela and Guillermo's part.

I went to my office and set the box down. When Colleen came in, I sat her down and looked for a good place to start. I was careful again to omit any reference to the Calvin hatchet job.

I told her I thought Tommy Rivera was responsible for the break-ins at the Schmidbaum, Castellano, and Rosenzweig houses and that the MOs of the burglars in the three cases made me think there might be a connection to the burglary of her own house.

"You think Tommy burglarized my house—Frank, do you think he shot William? Do you think that's why he's lying on the witness stand?"

"I don't think he shot William," I said, although the thought did not seem so ridiculous for a split second. Could Rivera have killed her husband out of jealousy and hit the daily double when she was charged with his murder? That would be a great incentive to commit perjury.

"I think he might have had something to do with the planning," I said. "I would be very surprised to find out he was actually there."

"But he knows," she said, "Tommy knows who did it."

"That's my theory. Tommy knows who did it because he sent them. Tommy organized the whole thing."

"But that would still make him William's killer. Whether Tommy did it himself or arranged for somebody to do it for him, he's lying to protect himself." She paced anxiously as she spoke.

"Yes. If he planned it and pulled it off, it doesn't matter where he was at the time. It's murder one."

"What are you going to do, Frank? How can you ever prove it?"

"I went to see a woman today. . . ." I hesitated, thought it over. This much I had to tell her. "Angela Estrella."

"Angela? I know Angela well, she's a great lady."

"She told me she hired Tommy at the Welfare Department, she was his supervisor. Do you know that he was almost fired because he exploited some of the woman he was supposed to be helping?

167

He gave them extra payments for sexual favors, and she says he even recruited some of them to commit burglaries for him."

"I've never heard that before. What scum, what . . . " She was at a loss for words to describe Tommy.

"Did he ever mention the names of any of the women in his caseload to you? Did he ever receive any phone calls from a woman? Did you ever see his phone book or any notes with women's names and numbers on them?"

She thought for a second. "No, never."

"What else do you know about Tommy?"

"Alice Stein, the journalist who caught William with the call girl? She investigated SOHO when it got pretty big, found out a lot of things but couldn't prove them. She couldn't get access to the files.

"But she was convinced that Tommy was tipping off my husband to which properties south of Market were going to go into foreclosure or were about to be condemned, so that William and his cronies could buy them before the city took them over. Helen Smidge would get them approved for demolition instead of renovation and give Willy and the boys big tax write-offs. He was getting them for nothing, just a promise to 'upgrade,' and getting tax credits to do it."

The last bit was a shocker. It raised the distinct possibility that William had known all along that his wife was having an affair with Tommy. And William could have set the whole thing up to discredit his wife in case she tried to take the matter to court and be released from her prenuptial agreement.

"I think I know how Tommy committed the burglaries." I started pulling the files from the box. "These are the files of Tommy's welfare clients," I said, putting a few in her arms. "They're in alphabetical order. My theory is he kept his connections with some of these women, women he'd used in the past." Just saying it again made it seem weak, desperate. It was the best shot I had. Where else would Tommy find these women?

"Look at every name in this file, see if any rings a bell, if by chance you remember any of them from the time you spent with Tommy."

Fatigue was playing with my mind. Doubtful I could make it even a few days more without getting caught, I suffered a wave of paranoia that I'd be discovered by Calvin. Every door I knocked on, every question I asked raised the level of fear.

I was starting to get my first touch of a familiar nightmare, a giant fist pounding on the door, a disembodied voice mumbling "The party's over."

23

▼▼▼▼

WITH HENRY STANDING by the monitors, armed to the nines, Colleen, Martha, Arnie, and I went through all three hundred files, organizing them into different groups. Martha and I took turns at the computer while Arnie and Colleen worked the Xerox machine, as we recorded and cross-referenced everything. This is the fun part of detective work you don't often see on network television.

After days of breakthroughs and revelations, burglaries, home-made bondage tapes, and people flying off bridges, the euphoric feeling of progress was dying out. Fear and a sense of impending doom kept our hearts pounding, our hands busy, our minds churning. You could feel the mood swinging back and forth in the room between desperation and hope that the answer was here at our fingertips, if we could just find it.

We made our lists: women who'd received the highest payments; women whose payments increased during their relationship with Tommy; the youngest women among his charges.

Seventeen women had filed one type of complaint or another against him, six of them charging sexual harassment. I put that list at the bottom of the pile, figuring that anyone who filed a complaint against him was not likely to turn around and commit crimes at his behest.

There were no pictures, or I would have arranged a list of the best-looking; I figured that would have been the most productive approach. It's easier to conspire with someone you're intimate with.

All through our search, I kept hoping that one of the names would jog Colleen's memory, that she had heard of one of the women. Nothing, not a ripple.

We were able to eliminate only fifty names, women who had moved to another state or died prior to the Farragut murder. That left us 250 women to track down and question.

I printed out the names and dates of birth and gave a copy to Arnie to drop off at Lloyd Dinkman's house so he could run a records check on them the next day. If any of them had any arrests or convictions for burglary, fencing, possession of stolen property they would go to the top of the list.

Tommy Rivera had probably done the same thing, looking through his caseload for women with priors, who perhaps were in danger of having their support payments cut off.

Near midnight Arnie's cousin Phil arrived to take over sentry duties from Henry Borowski. He donned his bulletproof vest, loaded his .12-gauge, and took his place near the monitors. Henry retired to the guest bedroom at the top of the steps, where he slept with the intercom on so Phil could wake him if he were needed.

I told Martha and Arnie to get a good night's sleep and to be back at seven to start the haystack phase of the investigation. Colleen and I went to bed, too edgy to sleep, emotional gravity killing any urge to make love. We lay there for a while, and then she said, "Do you want to tell me now?"

The question made my heart stop. Did she know about Calvin? How?

"I used the downstairs bathroom," she said, "I saw the photograph."

It was my turn to smile. The photograph was of me and a former porno star named Ginger Snapps standing in front of a poster for a movie called *Peek-a-boo*. On the poster, Ginger, in a black corselette and stockings, was surrounded by a large black keyhole.

It was the origin of my nickname, a story almost no one knew except Zane Neidlinger and my former cronies in the department.

"You really want to know?" I asked.

"I've been dying since day one."

It had been a rough day, a rough night, and I thought the story would at least get us off her worries and make it possible to sleep. With the city's lights streaming through the open window, I propped up a few pillows. She did the same, looking at me expectantly.

"When I was twenty-eight I got an early transfer to plainclothes during the last round of the Chinatown gang wars. I was only one of two officers on the force who spoke Chinese, and I'd gone to school with a lot of the older kids in the gangs.

"I gathered a lot of information and helped an Asian ATF agent—ATF is Alcohol, Tobacco and Firearms—infiltrate the Jake Howe gang. That resulted in the arrests for the Golden Dragon Massacre, when five Chinese kids went into a restaurant and mowed down about twenty people.

"As a reward, I got a permanent promotion to inspector."

"There had been a serial rapist working in Northern California for about two and a half years without anyone being able to grab him. They called the guy the C-Mart rapist because he grabbed his first victim in the parking lot of a huge C-Mart store in Daly City. That was his MO, grabbing women in parking lots, forcing them into a van, driving them into the woods, raping them and dumping them out.

"My first day, they assigned me to the C-Mart rapist case as a test. They figured after the publicity I got on the Chinatown massacre, they'd bring me back to earth.

"We knew the rapist was white, stocky, and drove several different vans. We also knew he was a porno nut. Some detectives up in Sonoma County got a tip that a weird guy in a van was staying at a local motel. When they got there, all they found were a few stolen credit cards, a stolen VCR, and a stack of porno videos."

"No fingerprints?" she asked.

I laughed. "Yeah, but they had no match anywhere."

"So the guy had never been arrested before."

"Right. And he'd never held a government job or been in the military. But his description was identical to the ones given by several of the victims. They also found a purse belonging to the most recent victim in the motel's dumpster.

"I got the stolen credit card numbers and I checked every charge the guy made. He bought or rented over a hundred porno videos. None of the store clerks remembered him, though.

"I borrowed copies of every one of the videos and fast-forwarded through most of them. There were two things that popped up in almost ninety percent. One was a voyeuristic theme: guys peeking through bushes, keyholes, watching women through binoculars, stuff like that. The other thing was a minor porno actress named Ginger Snapps. She'd made twenty-three films, and he bought every one of them on videocassette, including one the day it came out. I found out later she was the spitting image of his high school girlfriend.

"So, instead of chasing the perp—the perpetrator—I decided to bring him to me. I found Ginger Snapps living in Sunnyvale, retired from the business, married to an aerospace engineer. Great headline, huh? 'Porno Star Marries Rocket Scientist.' I talked her into posing for a poster for one last film."

"Peek-a-boo," Colleen said.

"That's right. The poster showed the peep-freak's delight, a woman undressing seen through a keyhole. I didn't see how our boy could resist. I leaned on all the porno stores in the Bay Area to have Ginger come and autograph pictures and sell her new video. All it was was a compilation of her previous films, which a lot of distributors do anyway.

"So, at the third signing the dumb son of a bitch shows up, stolen credit card in hand, and the motel owner from Sonoma and two victims ID him on the store's security camera. The guy had been on the loose for two and a half years, raped eleven women that we knew of. I nabbed him in a month."

"And the guys at the station started calling you Peekaboo Frankie Fagen."

"Cops are great ones for nicknames. But we never told the press how I got the name, in case we wanted to use the trick again on some other scumbag."

Colleen laughed, then was silent. Then she just stared at me, at my face, my eyes. I stared back, no fear, no embarrassment.

I had gotten to the point where I couldn't imagine what life would be like without her.

24

MARTHA WALLEY AND I were forty-eight stories above the ground, on the roof of the City Towers, an office and condominium complex just south of Market Street. A near arctic wind whistled through our ears, whipping fog around our faces and through our legs.

For five days we had knocked on every door, called on every friend and acquaintance of over two hundred women from Tommy Rivera's former welfare caseload. At every place, we stated our offer of fifty thousand dollars for any information leading to the burglars or the recovery of Ghiberti's silver plates. We promised immunity from prosecution—something we were in no position to offer, let alone guarantee. We left our business cards and told people to call us if they remembered anything. I had made the offer in five different languages.

I had hired extra surveillance people, PIs and off-duty cops, the latter from outside of the city, to conduct the twenty-four-hour watch on Bearden and Rivera. All they had learned was that Bearden was a workaholic and that Tommy's newfound wealth was swelling his manhood. He had already spent nearly ten thousand dollars buying six new suits, eight pairs of shoes, three leather jackets, two dozen pairs of silk boxer shorts, mostly black, and sending two dozen roses each to three women, none of whom was the woman he was living with. He paid cash for everything.

Two days after testifying, he rented a $950 suite at a Nob Hill hotel and treated himself to a ménage à trois with two different pairs of very expensive-looking call girls, running up a $1,143 room service tab and stiffing the waiters. Martha wanted to draw straws to see who would get to shoot the bastard if the opportunity presented itself, but I pulled rank on everyone.

I peered over the edge of the City Towers, the upper sixteen floors of which were condominiums, starting at a price of one million dollars. The fog was so thick that I could only see three floors down. Even at that the view was frightening, vertigo-inducing.

It had been built seven years earlier by Farragut Construction and had been the object of a vicious battle between the anti–high rise coalition and Farragut, whose case was argued by Sherenian before the board of supervisors. Helen Smidge had once again carried the day for her golden goose.

I rarely feared earthquakes, but I was reminded of Flynn Pooley's warning that if another 8.1 temblor hit the city, many tons of broken glass from buildings like the City Towers could shower the streets, cutting thousands of people to ribbons. I hoped the big one wouldn't hit for at least another few hours.

Sherenian owned the penthouse condominium one floor below us. Martha had spent parts of three different days doing reconnaissance on the place. She'd found a Vigilance Security Company sticker on the door to the penthouse, as well as on the doors of several other units in the building. She called the company and requested to meet the installer who had done such a wonderful job on the City Towers penthouse.

Using her biggest smile and shortest skirt, she got the hard-drinking bozo to tell her exactly what kind of detection devices were inside. Every security system in the world can be breached if you know what's waiting for you, and Sherenian's was not particularly difficult.

He had his front door wired, of course, and infrared devices installed in every room, so that if anyone walked through they would set off an alarm in the security office on the first floor, and in Vigilance Security's home office.

Calvin hadn't bothered to have his windows wired, probably on the assumption that the Flying Wallendas were not in the burglary business. It's doubtful anyone but us would be dumb or desperate enough to pull the stunt we were about to.

As Martha cinched a harness around me, she asked, "You sure you want to do this, Frank? We don't have to have the tape of Colleen and Tommy's rendezvous in Sausalito to get a mistrial; the photos of Tommy meeting Sherenian and Bearden should do it."

"Sherenian can always say he did it to try to help his client. He could even blame it on Colleen, make her look more guilty. Any kind of audio or videotape from that night in Sausalito will discredit Tommy and help prove that Sherenian is trying to get Colleen convicted by suppressing evidence. Besides, if he or Hayden Phillips did find the burglars, he might have evidence inside that would lead us to them. We have to try."

Martha looked at me skeptically. "You're not doing this because you still have some doubts about what'll be on a tape if we find one, are you?"

"Maybe I do. You with me?"

Martha nodded. We both figured that if Sherenian had a tape of Colleen and Rivera, it was either in his penthouse, his law office, or locked away in a safe-deposit box. That meant we should have better odds trying the penthouse than we'd had on anything since we started.

At 7:08 Arnie called on the cellular from his ground-level stakeout across from the City Towers lobby. Calvin Sherenian had emerged, climbed into his chauffeur-driven sedan and headed for the eightieth birthday celebration of one of his former law partners. Bruce Bearden would be joining him, as I had learned from Colleen only hours previously.

I dialed Sherenian's phone and got the answering machine. We were fairly certain there was no maid, butler, or, our worst night-mare, an armed security guard inside.

Checking my harness, Martha directed me to lean backwards and to walk my feet down the side of the building. I made the sign of the cross over my heart, kissed my Saint Christopher medal, and stepped back off the roof. She lowered me down the side, using a small hand winch we'd bolted to the ledge.

I couldn't see any of the neighboring buildings, thanks to the fog, but neither could anyone see me as I descended. I prayed it wouldn't lift until we finished. Martha eased the winch line out slowly. My heart was pumping double-time.

Two days earlier, Martha had rented a room on the top floor of a hotel a block away and used a thousand-millimeter lens to photograph the windows of Sherenian's penthouse. With the blow-ups mounted on the walls of the City Lights office, we figured out it would take only three things to break in.

When I reached the window of Sherenian's condo, I went to work.

I had ground down a one-inch wood chisel until the blade was half its normal thickness, and then coated it with vinylchloride plastic so as not to scratch the anodized aluminum window frame. I slipped the blade in between the window and the frame, with the wind howling in my ears and wisps of fog touching my face.

When I had wedged the window open far enough to slip a fishing line through it, I flipped a loop over the handle of the window. Sliding the chisel back to ease the pressure, I wrapped the fishing line around my gloved hand and jerked down hard. The handle popped and the window sprung open an inch, as far as the crank would let it.

I looked anxiously for anyone or anything moving inside—a guard, a dog—and saw nothing. I pulled out a rod with a ratchet wrench attached to the end of it, dropped it over the crank handle, and opened the window far enough to squeeze through. Then I signaled to Martha that I was going inside and pulled out my infrared goggles.

Peering through the window, I saw the first beam of infrared light a foot from the wall beneath the windows. I jumped over it, crouching in the darkness, my hand inside my jacket on my gun. Dead silence.

Relying on the goggles, I slid under or stepped over a half dozen of the red beams without tripping the alarm. Once into the massive living room, I removed the goggles and wandered freely about the warehouse-sized, single-floor condominium.

The entire place was stuffed with antiques; Persian rugs, Chinese armoires, a Louis XIV bedroom set.

In Calvin's office, I found a locked, four-drawer file. I called Martha on the walkie-talkie and had her lower down my burglar's kit, which included several sets of master keys. It took me forty keys to get into the filing cabinet.

Calvin must have had a thousand files in his home office, which would be not even a fraction of what he must have at his law offices. I looked under Farragut, Rivera, Hayden Phillips, Burglary, everything I could think of. It became apparent that all Calvin had in the home files were records of his real estate holdings and personal investments, insurance papers, and so on. Nothing.

I got down on my hands and knees and began feeling the carpet for a floor safe, a sizable chore considering the place had at least twenty rooms, several in which you could have played tackle football.

Then I remembered finding the floor safe at Bearden's house under a rollout section of the desk. Could the student have copied the master?

I tried desks in two rooms before I found a small laminated white component desk in an unused maid's quarters. I rolled it out, peeled back the pre-cut carpet, and found the safe. I pulled the stethoscope from my burglar's kit and went to work on the floor safe. Arnie could have done it in a third of the time it took me, but I wouldn't risk him being caught breaking and entering into Sherenian's place. After fifteen minutes, I heard the last tumbler fall into place. I wiped the sweat from my brow and opened the safe.

I carefully set aside a group of envelopes marked with the names of various real estate projects, assuming they might contain evidence of bribes or kickbacks. Beneath the papers I found a manilla envelope with the inscription *Sausalito Hotel July 7*. I could feel the cassette through the envelope. Bingo.

As I prepared to return things and close up, I noticed something that I had almost overlooked in my excitement. At the very bottom of the safe, wedged flat against one side, was an unmarked business envelope. Stuffed inside was a piece of white paper folded in four. It was headed FROM THE DESK OF HAYDEN PHILLIPS.

> Finally got C.A.C. to give me deathbed confess. Still wouldn't give me name of accomplice. She gave me hat from Schmidbaum burglary, described Farragut's clothing perfectly on night of murder. Admits Farragut burglary but denies shooting (naturally). Paid her in full. It's all on tape (enclosed). Be careful, this is the original. Make copy before playing for T.R., return original to me for safekeeping.

The P.S. was *Burn this note!* So much for honor among thieves. T.R. had to be Tommy Rivera. The note was handwritten, unsigned, and dated January 13, only a few months before the trial.

I had the strangest feeling of euphoria and dread. Phillips had found one of the burglars, identified only as C.A.C. and as "she." The bad news was she was dead.

The good news was that as of January 13, her accomplice was probably still alive and hadn't yet been found by Calvin. I had perhaps four or five days to find the accomplice, something Hayden Phillips hadn't done in the sixteen months between Farragut's death and January 13.

I prayed again that he hadn't found her since, that she wasn't dead, murdered like Simcic or McBain.

But where was the tape of C.A.C.'s confession? It was not in the safe.

I put everything but the Hayden Phillips memo and the tape from the Sausalito Hotel back where I'd found it. After spending another thirty minutes looking for the tape of C.A.C.'s confession, I became convinced it was in Sherenian's law office or in a safe-deposit box somewhere.

My terror of being caught in Calvin's place grew by the minute, and I feared that my fatigue and anxiety would cause me to make a mistake, leave some trace. I managed to convince myself that the tape was not important: it wouldn't lead me to C.A.C.'s partner, or the silver plates. The note, which I hoped proved to be in Hayden Phillip's handwriting, would be impressive enough all by itself when I handed it to Judge Walters with the rest of the evidence. I decided to take what I'd gotten and leave.

It took me fifteen minutes to get the window closed properly, dangling forty-seven stories up in the freezing wind. I was never so happy to see concrete as when I finally got back to the street below.

It took another hour and a half for my heartbeat to return to normal.

25

▼▼▼

COLLEEN WAS UPSTAIRS with Henry when Martha and I returned with the things from Sherenian's safe. I found an evidence file that Calvin had written on and compared the handwriting to the *Sausalito Hotel, July* 7 written on the manilla envelope. A perfect match.

Then I found copies of some reports signed by Hayden Phillips and compared the signature to the handwriting of the memo. It was Phillips's handwriting, without a doubt.

I removed the tape from the manilla envelope and put it in a large plastic bag to avoid smudging any fingerprints that might be on it.

Steeling myself to the thought of listening to Colleen and Tommy grunting and groaning together, I got my tape player out of the closet.

"Why don't you let me do this," Martha offered. "You check in with Colleen, see if anything happened today. If there's anything relevant at all on the tape, I'll call you." I knew she wanted to spare me having to listen to Colleen having sex with a man I hated. I accepted gratefully.

Colleen was sitting in my leather recliner, feet up, dressed in denims and a lacy white blouse, staring out my window at the bridge and Bay. She reacted with a start when I said her name.

I had a smile on my face. I could see the hope welling in her when she noticed it.

"Good news, Frank? Tell me some good news . . . please."

"Don't get your hopes too high, but we know there was a burglar in the house, we know her initials are C.A.C. We know she had an accomplice. Do you know anyone with those initials?"

She looked blank, the momentary burst of hope waning quickly. She shook her head.

"Think of only the first and last names; both of them begin with the letter 'C.'

Again, a blank.

"What about Consuela?"

"Her last name is Vasquez."

I felt foolish for a second, then told Colleen to ask Consuela if she had ever encountered anyone—a delivery person, a gardener—anyone with those initials. I had Colleen write out the names of everyone who had ever worked or done business at her house. I told her that C.A.C. was certainly dead, but learning her identity was crucial to finding her accomplice.

I did not tell her how I had found out, or that we had interviewed another forty women that day and found nothing.

I asked her how court went, something I always dreaded but was compelled to do.

"Calvin had my character witnesses take the stand, people who I'd worked with at various charity programs, telling the jury about my 'respect and reverence for human life,' how they found it impossible to believe I could kill anyone. It all seemed a little weak and phony."

That was just how Calvin wanted it to seem. Instead of hammering at the prosecution's case, Calvin was playing for sympathy, a tough sell for any lawyer. Most people have very little sympathy for women who marry rich. Calling character witnesses in a case like Colleen's usually did more harm than good. Calvin was building the perfect noose right down to the end.

"Calvin has decided not to call me," she said. I should have known. That was all he needed to do to convince the jury she was hiding something.

"I argued with him, but he said the trial had to be won on the facts, and the prosecution still hadn't satisfied the fundamental rules of evidence."

I just looked at her.

"I don't understand this, Frank. I thought the rule was, if you're innocent, take the stand. If you're guilty, don't."

"Calvin is a very smart attorney," I assured her, wishing I could tell her just how smart. "Do what he says." Then she dropped the really big one.

"They're starting closing arguments on Monday."

I told her everything would be okay, to trust me, and suggested we try to work. She was obviously anxious but agreed.

We spent hours going through the lists of women we'd already interviewed who claimed they knew nothing of the burglaries or Ghiberti's plates. I kept quizzing Colleen to see if any of the names jogged her memory. Nothing.

Throughout, I tried to keep her occupied, to keep her spirits up. Even though I'd told her earlier I could buy her some time, she had no comprehension of what that meant yet. It killed me to keep silent about Calvin and the potential mistrial when I knew what she was going through, but I was afraid that in her emotional state, any more hints or clues would change her demeanor enough that Calvin might suspect we were on to him. I decided she had lived with it for almost two years, she would have to bear it another few days.

I had difficulty concentrating. My mind kept drifting to Martha listening to the hotel tapes, thinking about Colleen with Tommy. I kept wondering if she'd told the truth, if she hadn't offered to pay Tommy to kill her husband. It seemed more improbable than ever now that I knew there'd been burglars in her home the night of the shooting, but I suffer from a perpetual case of mistrust.

I kept flashing back to Calvin's penthouse, reexamining my every move, wondering if I had made any discernible mistakes. I hoped that Calvin would not look in his safe before Monday and find the tape and the note missing.

At 11:22, with Colleen asleep in her chair, I looked at the five names I had culled from Tommy's welfare cases. Four women whose first and last names began with *C* and one with the initials C.A.C. All of them were still living and had already been interviewed by Frankie, Martha, or myself. I made a note to pay them another visit the following day.

Martha called me down to the office.

I went downstairs, my heart pounding. One more case like this and I wouldn't make it to forty-one.

"She never offered Tommy anything," Martha said when the door was closed. "He mentioned her husband several times, and there's not the slightest indication she harbored any kind of animosity toward him at all. Tommy lied."

I breathed a big, big sigh of relief, sinking into a chair. Then I looked at Martha, grateful for everything she'd done for me over the years. I was dead tired and sentimental.

"Colleen's not going to testify," I told her. "Closing arguments start on Monday."

There wasn't much to say after that.

26

▼▼▼▼

*T*HE NEXT DAY, Saturday, with Henry staying with Colleen on the top floor of the house and Arnie's cousin Phillip at the bank of monitors in the garage, I hopped on the Norton and rode to Lloyd Dinkman's house in Foster City. I'd called him a few hours earlier and gotten him to make a special trip to records. I was too paranoid to meet him anywhere in public or have him come to my office.

En route, I went over the few things we knew about the Farragut burglars. One of the burglars had the initials C.A.C., and barring some miracle cure, she had died shortly after January 13. The amateurish nature of the burglary spelled JUNKIE in flashing lights. The fact that they'd scaled the wall behind the Farragut home indicated that she and her partner were fairly young and semi-healthy.

After a relaxing ninety-mile-per-hour ride down the Bayshore Freeway, I arrived at Lloyd Dinkman's at nine, the approach of Monday's closing arguments weighing heavily on every part of me. My greatest fear was that C.A.C. might have been born and raised outside the city and gone home to die, and Phillips had managed to trace her to somewhere like Moose Dick, Montana.

But I got lucky. Lloyd Dinkman had found the death certificate I was looking for.

Candira Anne Chandler, Caucasian female, forty-four years old, born Parkersburg, West Virginia, died January 17 at San Francisco General Hospital. Cause of death was listed as "acute liver failure resulting from long-term heroin and alcohol abuse."

Her rap sheet listed six felony arrests, three convictions; one conviction each for burglary, possession of stolen property, and possession of a Class One substance, heroin. Probation reports also showed four trips to county detox.

Her name was not in the Rivera case files, but her death in S.F. General and the fact she'd gone to county detox instead of private facilities gave me a good place to start digging into her past.

I used Lloyd's phone to call Angela Estrella and convinced her to have brother Guillermo go back into Welfare Department records. Giving Lloyd Dinkman an envelope containing five hundred-dollar bills, I wished him a speedy recovery from the anxiety attack he was having over the volume of information he'd provided for me so far, then traveled back up the freeway at a sedate eighty miles an hour. When I arrived at Telegraph Hill, I went straight to my office and wore the carpet out waiting for Angela or Guillermo to call.

It was Angela who called. Guillermo had brought the records to her house this time, telling her he was afraid to be seen at the agency. I couldn't blame him. When I arrived at Angela's house, I parked, hit the buzzer and, once admitted, ran up the steps. She was waiting at the top to hand over the photocopied file.

Reading the file back in my office, I learned that Candira Anne Chandler had been on the welfare rolls with two children six years before Tommy Rivera started as a caseworker. But Candira's case had never been administered by Tommy Rivera, though her accomplice's case might have been.

I went straight to the evidence cart and found the burglary reports Lloyd had given me earlier, looking for the information on the cheese-eating burglar at the Schmidbaum house. The crime lab had made a plaster cast of the cheese, and there was a photo of it in the police reports.

I was giddy from fatigue, my expectations rising. Going back to Candira's welfare records, I found she had received emergency dental work on three occasions, all paid for by Medi-Cal.

Shortly after noon, I chained the Norton to a street sign in the Outer Mission District, across from Milton Goldblume, Quality Dentistry, credit plans, English, Spanish, and Vietnamese, Medi-Cal accepted. From the looks of the hallway and waiting room, quality dentistry probably meant Milton washed his hands every morning whether they needed it or not.

I flashed my ID and told him I needed the dental records of Candira Anne Chandler. A bored, puffy-eyed, gray-haired, stoop-shouldered Milton told me he was too busy to help me, but two hundred-dollar bills helped him find the time. When I told him Candira was dead, he threw the file at me and walked away.

I drove back to the office and compared the police file with Candira's dental records. The imprint of the burglar's teeth from the piece of cheese at the Schmidbaum house did not match Candira's dental X rays.

Candira had had a female accomplice in the Schmidbaum break-in; it was most likely she had the same partner in the Farragut burglary a few weeks later.

I was now one name, one face away from the person I was looking for.

27

▼▼▼▼

WHEN I RETURNED home a printout of two DMV photographs of Candira was waiting for me, compliments of a friend in Sacramento. The first, taken when she was twenty, showed a very attractive blonde. The second showed her at age thirty-two, bloated, with pasty white skin and baggy, swollen eyes. She looked closer to fifty than thirty. She must have been haunting houses just before she died.

There was also a message that Henry had taken from Lloyd Dinkman, who'd called with information on Candira's two children. The oldest, a son named Elvis, had been killed eight years earlier over a drug deal in the Western Addition. According to the records, he'd been born to Candira at a county hospital in Parkersburg, West Virginia, when she was fourteen years old.

Candira's daughter, Patsy, was born at San Francisco General when Candira was seventeen. Patsy, now in her early twenties, had given birth to a daughter at the same hospital eighteen years later and had named the baby Candira.

After hours of futile searching by my contacts at the telephone and utility companies in San Francisco, Alameda, Santa Clara and Marin counties, I got lucky with an old girlfriend who worked for the Forestville Water District in Sonoma County. Patsy Chandler was living in an apartment in Forestville, sixty minutes north for a normal driver. I made it in forty.

The apartment had to be the oldest and shabbiest in Forestville: overgrown lawn, overflowing dumpsters, dangling gutters, cracked trim, and enough holes in the faded stucco to pass for the Alamo's stunt double.

I knocked on the door of apartment 213 and got no answer. Newspapers from that day and the day before, Friday, were on the doorstep. I waited to see if any neighbors passed. When they didn't, I went to the manager's office.

An overweight woman of about thirty-five dressed in a quilted polyester robe, nursing a canned mai-tai, and smoking a menthol cigarette answered the bell. She'd probably been a knockout forty pounds ago. A loud announcer's voice babbled from the TV inside. She looked me over. I was still quite popular with the walking wounded.

"Excuse me, ma'am, have you seen Patsy? Up in two thirteen? I told her I was gonna stop by." I gave it my best smile, like I was delivering Patsy her winning lottery ticket and the orgasm of her life.

"You that guy she's been telling me about? What the hell name did she tell me, Slim? Or was it Slick?"

"Yeah, that's me."

"Well which is it, Slim or Slick?"

"Slim," I said.

"You sure? You ain't slim, you're kinda studly. I swear she said Slick. Yeah, that's right, Slick."

"Did she tell you where we met?" I asked, trying to cover my screwup.

"At the Sweetwater in Mill Valley," she said.

"That's right. You ladies must be purty good friends. I took one look at her and you know what I seen? Lust at first sight. Infinite lewd and lascivious possibilities. You seen Patsy today? I told her I might stop by, but when I knocked, I noticed there was two days newspapers by the door." My hillbilly was getting stronger by the second.

"Oh, hell, I better get them before the burglars notice. She didn't tell you she was going camping?"

"No. I didn't know she liked camping. Wait a minute, as a matter of fact, she did say something about Tahoe . . . or was it Yosemite?" I actually scratched my head. "I can't remember. I think I drank enough tequila that night to shave about fifty points off my IQ."

We had a good laugh.

"I don't think she even told me where she was going, to tell you the truth," the manager said.

"Damn, I'd love to surprise her. It wasn't over to Napa or Mount Tamalpais or anything?"

"Got no idea, sorry. You wanna come in for a while? ESPN's got Big Bob Bowser gettin' ready to drive over twenty-one cars in the Monster Mash. Biggest fuckin' truck I ever seen. I love that shit."

"Me too," I lied. "But I gotta find Patsy."

"Too bad," she said. "Sorry I can't help you."

"Did she say when she'd be back?"

"Yeah, as a matter of fact, she's gotta work tomorrow night. She's a waitress at some little dive down in town, the Silver Slipper."

"Thanks."

I went back to apartment 213 and got my lock picks out, happy that there was no dead bolt on the door. In less than a minute I had tripped the cheap lock.

Patsy Chandler was a card-carrying slob. Beer cans, pizza boxes, coffee cups transformed to fungi experiments, cheap posters of country-and-western stars half falling from the wall, a bathroom not quite as clean as the one at the county jail.

But she had a five-thousand-dollar giant-screen TV and a gaudy bedroom set that must have cost as much. Receipts in a shoe box on top of the television showed the stuff was only a few months old, and yet everything already had cigarette burns on it.

I found pay stubs from her job at the Silver Slipper Lounge, minimum wage for twenty-five hours work. I also found a receipt for a three-year-old Camaro for which she'd paid $8,500 cash three days after her mother died.

That's what Candira had done with the money Hayden Phillips gave her on her deathbed. She'd sold the truth, or part of it, to leave her daughter and grandchild some money. Given the choice between hiring a maid or saving for her daughter's education, Patsy had wisely bought a big-screen TV and a bedroom set from the Liberace collection.

I found a birth certificate for a second child, Tammy. The baby had been born three weeks after Farragut's murder. I figured it highly unlikely a woman eight months pregnant could scale the wall behind the Farragut place. Patsy Chandler was not her mother's accomplice.

Before I left, I took a picture of Patsy from a collection of vacation photos I found in a chest of drawers.

By the time I got back to the city, the sun was sinking behind the bridge. I was spent, queasy, with a headache that could have killed Superman.

I made a few phone calls to see if I could get back into any of the records at welfare, Pacific Bell, or the gas or electric companies. But it was Saturday night and everything was closed until Monday, inaccessible to any of my connections. The last part of my search would have to wait at least thirty-six hours.

I'd been brought to a screeching halt, not by the cops or Calvin, but by the weekend.

28

*T*HAT NIGHT, AS Martha, Arnie, Henry, Colleen, and I sat at my kitchen table eating Chinese food from Sam Wo's, I brought them up to date, plotting for the stretch drive.

"There were two burglars," I said, passing out copies of all the pertinent information—Candira's death certificate, dental records, and probation reports, the photo of the dental imprint from the Schmidbaum burglary, and my notes about Patsy Chandler's apartment. "Candira Anne Chandler was one of them. As you can see, she was a junkie who was on welfare the entire time she was in San Francisco, almost seventeen years."

"How did you find her?" Colleen asked, a look of relief and excitement on her face. "The cops couldn't find her, and they've been looking for almost two years."

"That I can't say. I can tell you what I know, but I can't betray my sources. Let's just be happy we're almost home." She accepted it. I sure wasn't about to say my information came from Calvin Sherenian's safe.

"I'm convinced that as of January seventeenth of this year, the date of Candira's death, her accomplice was still alive. This dental impression was made by Candira's partner when she bit into a piece of cheese during the Schmidbaum burglary. It's logical that she would have the same partner the night she broke into Colleen's house a few weeks later. I think the partner is still out there and she knows what happened to Ghiberti's silver plates."

As tired as we were, I could feel the excitement in the room. It added to the tension.

"Candira was not one of Tommy Rivera's welfare cases, but her partner may have been. Tommy could have recruited her partner, who told him about Candira. Candira's sheet verifies that she'd committed burglaries before the Pacific Heights and Presidio Heights break-ins. I want to stick close to the original theory, that Tommy recruited these women through his position at welfare."

"Where do we look for the other woman?" asked Arnie.

"I went to Forestville today, up in Sonoma County, to talk to Candira's daughter, Patsy. She was away on a camping trip, but I had a look around her apartment. There's . . . " I caught myself before I gave away the fact that Patsy had received the money Hayden Phillips had paid her mother. Everyone looked at me. I feigned fatigue.

"There are things in Patsy's apartment that made me believe she knew her mother was a burglar, or that perhaps Patsy herself was involved."

"You think she was the accomplice," Colleen jumped in.

"She was eight months pregnant with her second child the night your husband was shot. Since I'm convinced the burglars came over the back wall, it's highly unlikely that Patsy was the other burglar."

"But she might know who the other burglar is," Martha suggested.

"Right. Patsy might have received or sold some of the stolen property. Or she might be able to tell us who her mother's accomplice was. The welfare records don't give an address for Candira once she got off Aid to Dependent Children, when Patsy turned eighteen. If she doesn't know who her mother's accomplice was, maybe Patsy can tell us who her mother's friends were, where she hung out, where she lived at the time of the burglaries. People who commit crimes together usually hang together. And I'll wager her partner is also a junkie."

"We only have a few days," Colleen said. "I don't think they'll take more than a day or two for closing arguments. What happens if you don't find the woman you're looking for?"

"I don't want to waste time talking about what might happen," I said. "I told you I could buy some time if necessary. Right now, all I want to do is find the accomplice. I want to put an end to this nightmare. We've come a long way in a short time. We can find what we're looking for if we just don't make any mistakes. Tomorrow afternoon, Henry and I will be waiting for Patsy Chandler when she gets back from her camping trip.

"If Patsy doesn't know who the accomplice was, then Monday morning, we'll be rechecking any women from Rivera's caseload who lived in the same buildings as Candira, or nearby. We may have already interviewed her and she was just too scared to admit she was involved, even with the fifty-thousand-dollar reward. Or maybe someone we interviewed knew who it was and was afraid of reprisals. I just know we're close. Very, very close."

"You never told me anything about a reward," Colleen said when she and I were sitting up in my bed that night, with Henry at the monitors and Martha asleep in the bedroom down the hall. "Were you going to pay it out of your bonus?"

I'd misspoken, and it bothered me. "Eileen Farragut gave it to me."

"William's mother?" she asked, sounding shocked.

"Yes. Does that surprise you?"

"Only that you talked to her about it. It doesn't surprise me that she did it. She's about the only one who's believed me through this whole mess."

"She hates the things her son did," I offered.

"Yes. She hates everything every one of the Farraguts did, especially her late husband. She blames him for the way her son turned out. Eileen is one of those poor old women who woke up one day and decided everything she'd done was wrong. I feel sorry for her, living in that house all alone, feeling guilty about the man she married and the son she raised."

"She could have left her husband anytime."

"I guess she was just afraid. She was like me, born dirt poor, but in a time when it was a lot tougher for a woman to make a living."

We sat there silently, watching the lights on the bridge sparkling through my window.

"Frank, I want you to know something," Colleen began after a while.

I waited anxiously until she gathered the nerve. I'm always waiting for some kind of bombshell.

"No matter what happens, whether I'm found guilty or innocent, I just want you to know one thing. I've thought about this a lot. I keep asking myself if these feelings I have for you are those of a drowning woman clinging to her saviour."

She took a deep breath. "They're not. I've never met anyone so alive, so full of magic as you, Francis. I was infatuated with you before we met, and right now I'm more in love with you than I've ever been with anyone. I'll say this now and I'll say it after I'm free: I love you, Francis. You're the greatest man I've ever known. Do you know when I knew for sure that you were the one? The minute I saw you at the opera wearing that string tie with Trigger on it. How can you not love a man with guts enough to do something like that?

"In some weird way, if I survive this, I'll look back and see this whole thing as a blessing. I might never have known you otherwise."

She took my hand and a tear streamed down her cheek. She looked up, and sighed.

"I'll never forget you, Francis. Even if you say good-bye to me the day after the trial, I will never forget you, not until the day I die."

Then she just looked at me. I couldn't find anything to say for a few minutes. I'd never thought of that, our meeting a blessing disguised as a nightmare. I told her we'd make it.

We clung to each other until we fell asleep, the first real night's sleep either of us had had since we met.

29

▼▼▼▼

We slept until almost eight thirty Sunday morning, awoke fresh, starry-eyed, stupid with love.

For two hours, we got a respite from it all, a quiet before the climax of the storm. We made love with the room full of morning, my favorite way to do it, ate breakfast in bed, made love some more. The phone didn't ring, no one came to the door. The world didn't exist. It was a strange feeling.

For the first time since we met, we were cocooned by hope and optimism, a belief that somehow Colleen would soon be free and we'd be able to spend—that was the last scary part—a long time together.

It was the warmest, most wonderful morning I could ever remember. The city cooperated, glowing an incandescent blue outside the window, with warm, soft breezes filling the air.

At ten thirty I climbed out of bed, showered, dressed, and went to work. By midday, Henry Borowski was following me in his Rambler, honking and shaking his fist as he tried to keep up with the Norton. We were on Route 101 headed north, back to Forestville.

I had called the Silver Slipper the night before and learned that Patsy Chandler started her shift at six in the evening. I figured she'd at least come home a little early, shower, change, relax. I could have been wrong about the shower, judging by the condition of her apartment, but I didn't want to risk her getting back before we'd gotten there.

I brought Henry along for two reasons. That I'd been right on the first count became evident at 3:23 P.M., following two hours of life's most boring endeavor, the stakeout.

Patsy arrived in the passenger seat of a battered blue pickup with lumber racks and bald, oversize tires on pitted and rusting moon wheels. As she pulled her stuff out of the bed of the truck, Henry and I got a good look at Slick, the new boyfriend. Slim he wasn't. Slick he wasn't, either.

He was the size of a '59 Cadillac on its hind legs, with a beard like a half-eaten alpaca sweater. He was ruddy-faced, potbellied, with blacksmith shoulders and enough tattoos to look like he'd showered and dried off with the funny pages.

When Henry and I approached and I called out Patsy's name, he made a momentary effort to play hero.

"What the fuck do you want," he said, his head bobbing back and forth as he alternately attempted to intimidate Henry and me.

I flashed my ID. "We want to ask Patsy some questions about her mother."

"And what the fuck if she ain't answerin'?"

"Then we'll give the fifty grand to someone else."

He got real friendly after that. I peeled off a hundred-dollar bill and placed it in his paw, where it looked like a green Band-Aid. I told him to go have a few beers while Patsy and I talked. She nodded for him to go. He couldn't wait.

Henry and I lugged her suitcase and sleeping bag inside, where she turned on the lights, keeping the curtains and windows closed against the beautiful day, and lit up a cigarette. The place smelled like a nicotine factory.

Patsy was doing her part to make sure the nineties would be remembered as the decade of the bad haircut. She had stringy, chewed-up bangs and a mop of uneven shag-cut hair reaching the middle of her back, a good six inches of dark roots showing under the bleached blond frizz. She was hawk-nosed, beady-eyed, and wore a shapeless denim dress with polished aluminum stars and half moons sewn into it, topped off by enough felony blue eye shadow to alert the fashion police a mile away.

Her hands shook as she smoked with every other breath.

"We know most of the story, Patsy, but we're missing a piece or two. We know your mother was a burglar, we have her rap sheet, and we know that she burglarized at least two houses in Presidio Heights, including one in which a man named William Farragut was murdered. They're trying to pin it on Farragut's wife, and we're convinced she didn't do it.

"We know that your mother sold her confession, and possibly things from the burglary, to a man named Hayden Phillips. Then she gave the money to you. That's how you bought that big-screen TV and the bedroom set in there, and the Camaro you're driving."

She just sat there, stunned. I let it sink in, staring at her.

"Look, we're not cops," I said. "We're not here to arrest you. I know you couldn't have burglarized the place where the man was killed because you were eight months pregnant when it happened."

"How you know all this stuff?"

"I get paid to know it."

"Then why don't you give me some of that money?" I liked Patsy. She was too dumb to be dangerous.

I counted out five crisp, fresh hundred-dollar bills, real slow, watching Patsy's eyes grow larger, her breathing pick up noticeably. I made sure she saw the rest of the ten grand I was holding as I put the envelope back in my pocket and slowly handed over the five hundred. I hoped she wasn't going to have an orgasm on me.

"How's that for a down payment, Patsy?"

"That'll do just fine. Now, what can I do for you so's maybe you can do a little more for me?"

"Did your mother ever tell you about the burglaries she committed?"

"My mother was scum, Mr. Fagen, but she didn't tell nobody nothin'. Not me, anyway. I knew she ripped people off but she never told me no details. Nothin'." Her tone was soft, direct, disappointed. Fifty grand worth of disappointed.

"Do you know who your mother's burglary partner was?"

She shook her head. "No. I didn't see my mother for a couple of years, not very often, anyway. She'd just call once in a while, ask me for money, tell me where she was moving to. Just, you know. Stuff."

I looked at Henry, then at Patsy.

"Look, Patsy, I'm not interested in causing you any trouble, but there's a fifty-thousand-dollar reward, in cash, if you can help me find her accomplice. Do you know the names of any of her friends?"

"Believe me, if my mother was still alive I'd give her up for fifty grand, let alone one of her junkie friends. My mother give me twenty grand the day before she died, and I ain't got but eight hundred left. I don't know anybody she hung out with. Like I said, me and my mother didn't quite see eye to eye on a lot of stuff, and I hardly ever seen her. I been livin' up here in Sonoma now about five and a half years, and I ain't been to the city but two or three times to see a Grateful Dead concert. My ex–old man was a Deadhead, you know what I mean?"

I said I did and got her back on the subject.

"Did she ever mention the name Tommy Rivera to you?"

"My mother never dated no beaners, she was KKK all the way, know what I mean?"

"You said your mother called to tell you when she moved. Did you write down any of those addresses?"

"As a matter of fact, I did. I got 'em in my address book."

She went over to the table she'd dropped her purse on, opened the purse, and pulled out a ratty-ass old address book. My heart jumped.

"Here they are . . . shit, I never even crossed out the old ones,

I just wrote the new one under it. Must be five addresses, goin' back probably the last four, five years."

I held my hand out. Patsy got smart all of a sudden.

I reached in my pocket, counted out another thousand dollars. Her eyes were glued to the rest of my stash. I thumbed through it like I was going to give her more, changed my mind, held the thousand out toward her.

"That's fifteen hundred for your mother's old addresses, Patsy. You want any more than that, you gotta give me somethin' bigger."

She handed over the address book. I ripped the page out, ignoring her when she winced, folded it, and put it in my shirt pocket.

"Did your mother ever tell you about any silver plates, expensive silver plates she and her partner stole from the Farragut house?" I handed over the insurance photos.

"No. I never seen these before."

"Let me ask you one last thing, Patsy. If you hardly ever saw your mother and the two of you didn't see eye to eye, why'd she give you all that money just before she died?"

I'd saved the question to see if I could trip her. She barely blinked.

"Everybody gets sorrowful before they die, I guess. She was a shit mother and she give me the money hopin' it would make things right for me and my kids. Besides, there wudn't no pockets in the coffin, know what I mean?"

"Where are your kids?"

She didn't say anything, just put her head down. I'd noticed earlier there weren't any pictures of them. I waited, asked again.

"They're livin' with their grandparents, their daddy's ma and pa. They're in San Diego."

"You gave 'em up after your mother gave you all that money?"

"You're pretty smart for a private dick."

She belonged on the cover of White Trash Magazine. I walked over and handed her my business card.

"Keep this card, and keep our visit here to yourself. If you can think of anything—anything that leads me to your mother's accomplice in the burglary at the Farragut house—I'll give you the rest of the fifty grand, understand? But you got forty-eight hours to do it."

She looked at the card for a long moment. "The Farragut murder trial? I seen that on TV. Ain't that that rich bitch? I mean that bitch from Modesto or wherever that married that rich dude and shot him so's she could keep his money?"

I said nothing.

"Hope they fry the bitch," she said, "bitches like her get all the fuckin' breaks while the rest of us gotta bust our asses, and for what? Nothin'!"

I had to get out of there before I killed her.

The second reason I had brought Henry was so he could watch the apartment while I sped back to the city.

Patsy had no phone, so I knew that if she had to make a call to warn someone, she'd have to run out to do it. But I had a nasty hunch she was telling the truth: she really didn't know anything.

30

▼▼▼▼

*H*ENRY KEPT SURVEILLANCE on Patsy Chandler until 5:45 Sunday evening, knowing that Martha Walley was inside the Silver Slipper, waiting for Patsy to begin work.

An hour later he was back in the office. Patsy hadn't left the apartment to phone or visit anyone. She'd stayed inside until it was time to go to work, emerging in a wool skirt and frilly white blouse. She didn't seem anxious or in a hurry, according to Henry.

I had him and Arnie take Colleen back to her house that night instead of the next morning, in case Calvin or Bearden got suspicious and decided to check up on her. Henry would follow Colleen over the back wall and spend the night outside her bedroom door. When I kissed Colleen good-bye, she was smiling and full of hope. I was anxious and full of fear but did my best to hide it.

Once they'd left I went to my storage room and pulled out some city maps I'd had for years. They were detailed surveyor's maps of every real estate lot in the city, used by the building department and city utility companies to check property lines. Each one had the property address written next to the lot number.

When Arnie returned, he told me the media circus outside Colleen's house had grown to epic proportions. They were smelling the kill. I knew it would be too risky to sneak Colleen in and out over the next few days. I resigned myself to not seeing her until the trial was over.

We starting putting the last phase of the plan together. I was still convinced—partially convinced, but saying my Hail Marys—that Tommy had recruited a woman from his caseload, who then recruited Candira Chandler. Once again, I fought the feeling that it was ludicrous.

We marked all five of Candira Chandler's addresses from Patsy Chandler's address book. They were all within a two-block radius, ten blocks south of Mission Dolores and the park. Then we went through the records of every woman who'd been a welfare client of Tommy's, marking the locations of anyone who'd ever lived within five blocks of Candira.

There were twenty-seven women who had once been on Tommy's docket and had lived at some time in the same buildings as Candira Anne Chandler. We'd already spoken to twenty-one of them and gotten nothing.

I decided to expand the search. Not only would we concentrate on those twenty-seven women, but in all five buildings we would knock on every door and make our reward offer. And we still had almost forty women from the original list of 250 that we hadn't found.

I called Lloyd Dinkman and told him I needed any existing rap sheets on the twenty-seven women who had lived in Candira's buildings, adding I needed them by morning. I also asked for anything and everything on Patsy Chandler. She said she'd only been in the city two or three times in the past five and a half years, to see Grateful Dead concerts; I wanted to know if she'd gotten any parking tickets, if she'd bounced any checks, if she bailed anyone out of jail.

Lloyd was scared, reluctant. I offered him two thousand dollars. He didn't sound very happy about it, but he agreed to do it anyway. I wasn't too happy either—I worried that I might cost him his job, his pension. When I hung up, I put my head in my hands and prayed it would all be over soon.

Martha arrived at the City Lights offices shortly before two A.M. She had stayed at the Silver Slipper until a little before one, when things got so slow they closed. Patsy made no phone calls from the pay phone, nor had she huddled suspiciously with anyone in the bar. Just as I expected.

Arnie and I had already broken down the buildings and neighborhoods, drawing up assignments for each of us. I gave Martha her list. For our own safety, Martha and Arnie each slept in one of the empty bedrooms, guns under their pillows. If they slept at all. I didn't sleep a minute.

At five thirty I was up and making breakfast. Martha and Arnie appeared within minutes, dressed and ready to go. We talked, drinking coffee, fighting nerves, running things through our heads, looking for an angle, anything we had missed. Going back to some of the women we'd already interviewed made us uneasy. It made us wonder if we'd already missed the key clue or the prime suspect and were now staggering blindly toward oblivion.

I called Zane Neidlinger and asked for his read on the jury. "They seemed really torn until Tommy Rivera took the stand; that was the backbreaker. Sherenian's so weak, the jury believes that even he thinks she's guilty. You might get one or two of them to hold out for acquittal, get yourself a hung jury, but I doubt it. I think the ones who're strong for guilty will win out. Now, how are you doing?"

I told him he was either going to have the story of his life or a good friend who'd wasted a month of his own. All he said was, "You better hurry, Frank."

Henry returned at 7:45, following his all-night watch on Colleen. He announced he was fit enough to continue throughout the day. Because some of the neighborhoods were particularly rough and Henry's interview techniques were restricted by his English, I asked him to accompany Martha and keep records.

At eight, we left for our assignments.

I started in a five-story apartment house in the Mission District that hadn't been painted since the original Armistice Day, the place Candira was living when she died. I started on the top floor and worked my way down.

At 9:30, after eleven interviews with women who didn't know who killed Abe Lincoln, let alone William Farragut, I imagined the prosecutor, Ian Jeffries, was telling twelve ordinary citizens that the evidence of Colleen Farragut's guilt was undeniable and overwhelming.

The rest of the morning was no better. I knocked on doors and showed my credentials, starting out strong and ending every conversation with almost a plea for help. I emphasized the fifty thousand, told people that no one would be hurt, no one would get in trouble, and no one would be prosecuted. I sure didn't tell them they'd have to testify in court; I'd save that for later.

My eyes got red, my throat was parched, my feet turned numb as I moved from apartment to apartment, trying not to become so robotic that I failed to get my story across, missed something, failed to catch a guilty glitch somewhere.

And I watched the clock.

At noon, I stopped in a Latino bar filled with construction workers eating lunch and watching the news on Spanish language television. They reported that Ian Jeffries had methodically re-created the crime scene with large, posterboard drawings, demonstrating that Farragut was between the French doors and his assailant when shot, reiterating his claim that the shooter had come from inside the house, not outside.

After that, Jeffries emphasized that Colleen's fingerprints had been found on the murder weapon, and followed up by repeating the opinions of Inspector John Naftulin. Then they recesssed.

Jeffries would probably finish his summation during the afternoon session. No good prosecutor likes to lose a day between his evidence and his impassioned plea for conviction if he doesn't have to.

I called Martha and then Arnie on their beepers, had them call me on my portable. They'd gotten nothing, not a nibble. We agreed that they should expand the search: hit every bar, liquor store and shop in their areas, make their pitch quickly, leave their cards.

By day's end, I'd knocked on 134 doors and talked to over two hundred people, in several languages.

Nothing.

At six, I called my answering machine at the office for the fifth time that day and got a message from Colleen, in Italian. I could hear the sounds of people talking and feet scuffling around her and was certain she had called from the holding area of the courthouse.

She pretended to be an irate housewife whose plumbing hadn't been fixed properly. She wanted me to come by at *"mezzanotte"* and *"ricostruire corretto."* I smiled. Right about then, fixing her plumbing at midnight was about the only thing I felt I was good at.

I kept up the search, hit another seventy-five doors, shops, stores, and found nothing.

At ten thirty I gave up and crawled home. Martha, Henry, and Arnie had just come dragging in with food from Molinari's Deli. They looked worse than I did.

On my desk was a blank manilla envelope that someone had dropped through the mail slot. Inside was a typed note and information from Lloyd Dinkman.

Two of the twenty-seven women who'd lived in the same buildings as Candira and had once been on Tommy's welfare docket had records for burglary and possession of stolen property.

I hadn't been able to locate either of them, but both had rap sheets or had been suspects in burglaries outside of the Bay Area, which is why their records hadn't popped up earlier. Lloyd had done yeoman's work, finding information on one of them as far away as the Clark County Sheriff's Department in Las Vegas.

The first was Sharon Dean, Caucasian female, thirty-three years old and living on Waller Street in the Haight-Ashbury. According to the reports, she'd been arrested three times for residential burglaries in San Jose, San Diego, and Las Vegas. Never convicted.

She was a former prom queen from Mendocino County who'd wound up pregnant and strung out on drugs in San Francisco by the age of twenty. She'd also appeared in a few dozen porno loops and had once been a nude dancer at the Mitchell Brothers' O'Farrell Theater.

The second was Magdallena Mason, black, thirty-nine years old, a career junkie and burglar who'd also been arrested twice for selling stolen property at flea markets. One conviction in Monterey County, ninety days in jail.

In an early mug shot taken just about the time Magdallena first received ADC, she bore a striking resemblance to the pop singer Whitney Houston. Her caseworker had been Tommy Rivera. The years and the drugs had not been kind, however, and in recent photos she didn't even look like the same person.

Two prime targets.

I bolted down some cold pasta, grabbed the folder, and Martha and I went out to find Sharon Dean and Magdallena Mason.

We found both at home.

Both had been friends of Candira Anne Chandler.

Both denied any knowledge of anything even related to the Farragut burglary or murder. They both looked ill, strung out; the offer of fifty thousand should have been enough to make both of them want to confess to Kennedy's murder. But each shook her head and glumly admitted she knew nothing.

I was stuck, dead in the water, and the clock was not just ticking, it was pounding.

We went back to the office. After phoning in an order for sandwiches and drinks to a restaurant on Union Street that stayed open late I called Terry Brown, a boyhood friend who worked the late shift for City Cab.

Then I called Colleen on her private line. When Consuela answered, I told her in Spanish that "Frank from Firenze's Restaurant" would be there with their order at *"media noche."* She understood.

Forty-five minutes later, Terry's cab pulled up to the back gate of the Farragut mansion, where he rang the buzzer. While waiting for someone to answer, he was besieged by three dozen hysterical news hacks wanting to know what he was doing there.

"Delivering food," Terry told them. They wanted to know what kind, where it came from, who had called in the order: newsworthy stuff. Several offered him money to give them information on the way out about what she was wearing, who she was with, what her state of mind was like. Terry told them to go fuck themselves just as Consuela buzzed him in.

When the cab was near the garage area, out of sight of anyone on the street, Terry opened the trunk and I climbed out. I gave him a hundred dollars and arranged for him to pick me up on Lombard Street, half a mile away, before he ended his shift.

Consuela was waiting for me at the door.

She took me up in the elevator to where Colleen was waiting.

31
▼▼▼▼

COLLEEN WAS A VISION in a white teddy trimmed with ivory lace and a short satin robe that bared her strong, smooth legs. A fire filled the room with warmth and the red glow back-lit her as I went toward her.

She faked her best nothing-is-wrong smile, put her arms around my neck and squeezed. I felt like she was comforting me, encouraging me, instead of the other way around. I hugged her back.

She poured me a cup of tea, stirring in some honey, and asked how it was going. I was afraid to tell her that we'd interviewed several hundred people and gotten nowhere. I pulled out the file Lloyd Dinkman had sent over on the two women, Sharon Dean and Magdallena Mason, spread their photos and rap sheets out on the table, and asked if Colleen knew either one of them.

She looked at them long and hard, looked at my notes, scrutinizing them carefully.

"I've never seen or heard of these women. Tommy never mentioned their names. Why? Do you think one of them is the other burglar?"

"They both lived in the same building as Candira at the time your house was burglarized, and both had priors. Only Magdallena has ever been convicted, in Monterey, which is why their rap sheets didn't pop up right away. They're both junkies; I think

Magdallena has AIDS. And they were both real lookers when Tommy was their caseworker."

She studied the photos again. "I feel bad, Frank, I'm no help. For the life of me, I can't remember ever hearing these names or seeing these women before."

I asked her if Ian Jeffries had finished his closing arguments that day in court.

"Yes. The afternoon session went until almost five. He was pretty effective." She was silent a moment. "He was very effective. I don't see how a jury could vote anyone innocent after listening to the things he said today."

I couldn't think of anything to say. I pulled her into my lap and kissed her. I felt the pain an eighteen-year-old feels, kissing his first great love for the last time, before she moves a long way away, knowing that despite the phone calls and the letters and the I-love-you's they'll never see each other again.

At 4:45 A.M., with the media still entrenched out front, Colleen called City Cab and asked them to radio Terry and tell him he'd left his cap behind. That was his signal to meet me at the gas station on Lombard Street.

I got dressed and kissed a warm, half-naked Colleen good-bye. "Remember what I told you, Frank," she said. "Whatever happens, I love you."

Leaving by the back door, I went across the yard quickly and climbed the stone wall. Just before I dropped over, I looked up at Colleen's window and saw her watching, smiling at me in the moonlight. She stood there for a moment and let me look at her. Then she shivered, waved, and closed the shutters.

Once over the wall, I walked through the Presidio, smelling the eucalyptus, listening to the waves crashing near Fort Point in the distance. When Terry pulled up I climbed into the cab and rode home in silence.

The first cobalt patch of dawn appeared behind the Bay Bridge as we reached the top of Telegraph Hill. I stumbled upstairs, crawled between the cold sheets, and was asleep in seconds.

At 7:45 I awoke, groggy, sandy-eyed, and with a mouth like possum sweat. I forced myself to clean up and stumble downstairs, where Arnie had breakfast waiting for Henry, Martha, and myself. We were down to the last day of the trial.

32

▼▼▼▼

*A*FTER THE MORNING'S efforts we were no better off than we'd been the day before. While Martha, Henry, and Arnie worked our list of so-called leads, I concentrated on finding a hole in the stories of Sharon Dean and Magdallena Mason.

I checked with old landlords, neighbors, liquor store owners. I called three of the investigating officers on their previous arrests and told them I was investigating a new series of burglaries. None of them was able to tell me anything that wasn't in the old reports.

At noon I found another bar and waited for the midday report. The news came on and the female commentator said that Calvin had delivered an eloquent but fairly low-key summation. Calvin argued that the prosecution had failed to prove Colleen had been the murderer, referring often to Colleen's substantial humanitarian efforts. It sounded more like a plea for mercy than an assertion of her innocence.

After lunch, Judge Marilyn Walters would give the jury their instructions, then send them in to deliberate.

I was just about out of time.

For the next several hours, I knocked frantically on doors, hoping to find Candira's partner, praying that I wouldn't have to derail the process with a mistrial and force the court to retry Colleen a few weeks later.

I tried to ignore the agony Colleen was going through. I couldn't.

At five that evening, I sat in the El Nido Bar in the Mission District with my head in my hands, dead tired and defeated. I'd had dogs jump on me, a dozen people try to sell me dope, a few others threaten to kill me if I ever knocked on their doors again.

That's when I felt the tap on my shoulder.

"You look like a dude who could use some luck."

Even without turning around, I knew who it was.

Patsy Chandler. When I did turn around, she looked exactly as she had the day I met her; she was wearing the same things. Martha was standing next to her.

"I was just about to call you from a pay phone on the corner when I saw the Norton parked in front," Martha said. "You better come outside, Frank. Patsy has something to tell you."

A block away stood Mission Dolores. The door was open, the church nearly vacant. I said a brief hello to Father Joseph Guitterez, an old friend, as we entered.

We sat in a pew near the north side of the church. Several worshipers lit candles near the entrance or prayed at the altar. Patsy twisted the top of the plastic shopping bag she carried and looked about one *'boo!'* short of a coronary.

"You have something to tell me?" I asked her.

"I need that fifty thousand, Mr. Fagen. I want my kids back. I know I done wrong, but I need my kids again."

"No offense, Patsy, but I don't give a damn about your personal problems. I'm tired and pissed off and you got fifteen seconds to put up or get out of my face."

"I know who dunnit."

"How do you know?"

"After you left the other night, I started goin' through papers. I'm one of those people never throws nothin' away."

"Ten seconds, Patsy."

"All right, all right. Remember how I told you mom used to call and ask to borrow money sometimes? Well, one time she called and said she had this friend in jail, and if she didn't get her out, she was going to rat mom out for some stuff they stole."

I squirmed, got up, ready to leave. Martha put a hand on my arm. She nodded.

"I had a bitch of a time findin' her, but I did. About an hour ago. Her name's Magdallena Mason. She was mom's partner, she was in the house when that dude got killed."

Now she owned me.

"She said you come by a couple of times, said she knew you used to be a cop. She don't trust you."

"And I don't trust you. How do you know? Prove it to me."

"You give me fifty thousand if I prove to you she done it?"

"I give half to the person who gets up on that witness stand and says they were there that night. You get the other half. Twenty-five thousand each, that's the deal. You got five seconds left."

She reached in the plastic bag and pulled out one of Ghiberti's silver plates.

I slumped back down and just stared. I was so exhausted I wanted to weep. I took the photos out of my pocket, compared them to the plate. It looked like the real item.

"I give Magdallena five hundred just to let me show somebody that plate. I told her I had somebody who wants to buy it, but I didn't tell her it was you. She's expectin' him to come by tonight and give her the rest of the money. Mr. Fagen, I got to have some money." Patsy looked desperate, ready to cry.

I reached into my pocket and gave her a thousand. That helped her disposition immensely.

"Where's the other plate?"

"Magdallena said mom sold it to some pawnbroker in Oakland. She said she thinks the guy still has it, on account of a few days after the burglary the cops went by the pawnbroker's store looking for the plates and sayin' somebody got killed. The pawnbroker was too afraid to sell it, so he hung on to it. Magdallena wants to buy it back because she found out now it's worth a lot of money. She says the pawnbroker wants two thousand. I told her I could get it."

"Who did the shooting?"

"Magdallena says mom done it. She said when the dude showed up she ran, but mom didn't want to go away empty-handed."

"Did Magdallena see the shooting?"

"I don't know, she says she was outside but she could be lying."

"What else can you tell me about Magdallena?"

"She's a junkie. She's got AIDS. She's gonna die soon. She just didn't believe you were going to give her any money if she talked, and she was afraid of goin' cold turkey in jail. So I told her I could sell the plates for her, that I seen one of mom's old fences and he wanted to buy the plates."

My heart was pounding against my ribs. "Here's the deal," I said. "I'm gonna play a game on Magdalena, see if I can draw her out first, then offer her the reward money when it's over. But Magdallena has to take the witness stand, we have to have the other silver plate and the testimony of the pawnbroker, and Colleen Farragut has to be acquitted. Those are the rules. You in?"

"I'll do it, but I want my five hundred back that I give Magdallena for this plate."

I gave her another five hundred dollars. Then Martha escorted Patsy to return the silver plate to Magdallena. Without her testimony, the plate was meaningless. I followed a safe distance behind. By eight o'clock that night, I had the last step of the plan ready to go.

33

▼▼▼▼

ARNIE NUCKLES KNOCKED on Magdallena Mason's door at nine fifty that night. Across town, the jury was turning in for the night, sequestered after their first evening of deliberations.

In the Firenze Plumbing van across the street from Magdallena's apartment were Martha, Zane Neidlinger, Vincent Halloran, and myself. Vince was one of San Francisco's most feared and venerated attorneys, a long-time family consigliere who'd supported the Fagens throughout the war with the Farraguts.

Arnie was wearing a wire. Over the van's speakers, we heard his footsteps as he trudged up the wooden hallway, his knuckles rapping on the door.

After a few seconds of listening to Arnie's breathing, a door was unbolted.

"You Magdallena Mason?"

"Yeah, who you?"

"A friend of yours asked me to stop by. We got some business to discuss."

"Yeah? You bring the money?"

There was a short silence and then the sound of Arnie walking in, sitting on something squeaky, like a vinyl couch.

"I hear you got somethin' for sale?" he said.

"Yeah."

"Let me see it."

"Let me see the money."

Through the wire we could hear Arnie reaching in his coat, pulling out the leather pouch that held the money.

"Now let me see the silver plate."

Footsteps walked away, returned a few seconds later.

"You like that? Some famous Eye-talian done it, Michelangelo or one of them dudes."

"Where's the other one? Patsy said you had two of 'em."

"I ain't got it, but I can get it."

"How fast can you get it?"

"Tomorrow. But the dude wants two grand, and I got to have the money up front."

"We're talking about another silver plate here, the other one that you stole from that Farragut house."

"That's right. Just like that one, only different. Different pitcher carved in it, that's all."

"How do I know these are the real items, that they came from the Farragut house and you're not trying to palm some piece of junk off on me?"

" 'Cause I was there when they got took. There was two plates. Candira sold hers to the pawnbroker, and I hid mine on accounta the dude got murdered."

"You shot him?"

"I didn't shoot nobody," Magdallena snapped, getting a little riled.

"I can't use this shit," Arnie said. "I can't be buyin' shit with blood on it. I ain't doin' no time for no dumb bitches."

"I didn't kill him!" Magdallena practically screamed. "My partner Candira done it. I was outside. I heered two shots and Candira come runnin', laughin' like she was crazy or somethin'. She said the dude made a move toward her, she shot him with his own gun. It don' mean nothin'. They think the dude's old lady killed him, the bitch is on trial right now. I seen the papers, they're gonna fry the bitch, then it'll be okay. You can sell these plates, won't nobody say nothin'. I'm in a bad way, mister, I got AIDS and I gotta habit and I gotta have some money."

"There's five hundred down payment for this one. I'll give you two grand apiece . . . four thousand dollars, but I want 'em both, you understand? They're a set and they ain't worth shit unless I get both of 'em. You call the pawnbroker right now and set up a meeting for tomorrow at eight in the morning, tell him you'll have the cash in your hand."

"You wait here," she said. We could hear her voice, faintly, as she went into another room and talked on the phone. If necessary, I knew I could get the number she was calling from my friend at the phone company.

"He'll be waitin' for us at eight o'clock tomorrow mornin'," she said when she returned.

"You be ready at seven, and don't be so fucked up you can't talk, understand?" Arnie's heels clicked as he took a few steps across the bare floor. Then he stopped. "How'd a couple of horse players like you two case a place like the Farraguts'?" he asked. "You got a pimp?"

"I ain't got no pimp, I ain't no fuckin' 'ho. I just likes to get high."

"Then who was it? I know you and that other bitch ain't that smart, and I want to know in case some dude comes lookin' for his silver plates."

There was a long silence.

"Dude named Tommy Rivera. He was fuckin' that rich dude's wife, but she dumped his ass. He set it up, he set up a couple of other jobs we done. We ain't talked to him since Candira fucked up and shot the dude. You ain't got nothin' to worry about."

Then we listened as Arnie shut the door behind him and came back down the hall.

An hour later, Arnie, Martha, Zane Neidlinger, Vincent Halloran and I were in the living room of Judge Marilyn Walters's house. I didn't have any of the evidence I had of Calvin's betrayal of Colleen. The last thing I wanted now was a mistrial.

We sat and listened to the tape recording we'd just made.

Magdallena's story was every bit as dramatic the second time. Judge Walters sat in stunned disbelief. When the tape was finished I clicked off the recorder.

"That's incredible, gentlemen. But it's not admissible evidence. You had no court order to record her conversation. For all I know, you could have staged it."

I was ready for that. I pulled Ghiberti's silver plate out of my briefcase and handed it over with the copy of the police report and the insurance photographs.

"There's the plate that Magdallena sold Arnie. You'll see it matches the photo perfectly, and any art historian can verify its authenticity."

I waited as she made the comparison, fighting the fatigue, reminding myself to talk slowly, deliberately. "Your Honor, we're not asking you to use this tape as evidence against Magdallena Mason. As you heard, she has AIDS—and judging by the looks of her, not many months left. Prosecuting her might be useless; she'll be dead before a jury could ever be seated. But right now the jury is deliberating Colleen Farragut's fate, and Magdallena's statements and this evidence prove beyond any doubt that she's innocent.

"You heard what she said about Tommy Rivera. We believe Tommy Rivera lied in his testimony for two reasons: his vindictiveness toward the defendant, and his desire to have the case closed before the police found out he was responsible for setting up the burglary—which, as you know, makes him indictable for murder one." I waited for Walters to reply.

"If Mr. Rivera lied, Mr. Fagen, I could declare a mistrial."

"You can't declare Mr. Rivera's testimony as perjured until contrary evidence is entered into the record, Your Honor," Vincent put in. "And if he did perjure himself, the prosecution must be exculpated. To declare a mistrial after the two years of hell that Colleen Farragut has been through would be the ultimate travesty. She's innocent, Your Honor, and all of this proves it."

Juice; that's why we brought in Vince. Judge Walters thought for a minute.

"We know you can't authorize a wire to be worn by a private detective," I said before she could speak, "but you can send a cop with Mr. Nuckles tomorrow when he goes to find the other silver plate. I'd suggest a black female detective and that she go as Mr. Nuckles's wife. And that you call the chief of police and have it arranged tonight." I wasn't sure how Walters would respond to me telling her how to do her job.

Vince jumped in again. "If necessary, you may have to offer immunity on the burglary rap to Magdallena Mason in exchange for her testimony. The same for the pawnbroker, whoever he is. What's most important here, Your Honor, is that an innocent woman may be a day or two away from conviction for a crime she did not commit."

"Have you informed either the prosecution or the defense of any of this?" Walters asked.

"No, Your Honor," Vince replied. "We came only to you, as friends of the court."

Walters hesitated for a minute, gathering her thoughts. "I'll call the chief and I'll issue the warrant for a wire to be worn by the detective," she said. "If necessary, I will grant immunity to Magdallena and the pawnbroker, whoever he is, but on one condition.

"If there is evidence that Magdallena was inside the house at the time of the shooting, or that in fact it was she who pulled the trigger, I'll have her arraigned on murder charges. No immunity.

"And as for Mr. Rivera, if any of this proves valid, I'll issue a warrant for his arrest." She rose. "I'll call the bailiff to cease jury deliberations and have the jury returned to the courtroom tomorrow. I'll also have the defense and prosecution in my office tomorrow at ten. By that time, let's hope we know where we stand in regard to this missing silver plate.

"Thank you, everyone. You'll have to excuse me, I have a lot of work to do."

She showed us outside, where the starry, moonlit view of the city from Diamond Heights was spread out before us. Two blocks below was Bruce Bearden's house, where the story had first started to unravel. I couldn't wait to send him a thank-you card at Folsom.

I thanked Vince and Zane, arranging to meet them in court the following day. Arnie, Martha, and I climbed into the van.

"Are we going to tell Colleen?" Martha asked.

"Not yet. I'm afraid something might still come unglued. She's suffered this long, she'll just have to make it until tomorrow."

As we started to drive back to the office, I remembered Henry was still baby-sitting Patsy in the loft. I plugged in the cellular phone, called Henry and asked him to take her to a hotel, rent a suite and sleep in the outer room. I told him if she made any trouble to tell her she wouldn't get another dime.

When we got home, I staggered upstairs and collapsed on the bed with my clothes and shoes on. But exhausted as I was, sleep wouldn't come, and I lay staring up at the ceiling. Years of frustration welled up in me. My grandfather having to live with the memory of William Farragut II murdering a poor immigrant after his son had been crushed to death in a Farragut slum during the 1906 earthquake. My father never being able to pass a Farragut Construction sign without getting sullen. My own public humiliation after the verdict in the DiMarco murder case.

The curse was over, the incubus destroyed, a hundred years of horror and heartbreak skidding to a halt. I'd saved my client, my friend, a love I never expected to find. If history is the lie most commonly agreed upon, I was about to rewrite history, Farragut history, so that people would see them for the scum they really were. The diaries would prove that.

I could feel the tears running down the sides of my face, into my ears and onto the pillow. I squeezed my eyes shut in an attempt to stop them. It didn't work. I didn't care anymore. I just let them come.

I fell asleep.

34

▼▼▼▼

*A*T ONE THIRTY the next afternoon, two dozen deputies and courthouse security guards wrestled with a crowd of almost two hundred journalists, photographers, and television people in the hallway outside Judge Marilyn Walters's courtroom.

Walters informed the jury that new information had come to light which was significant to the case, and that they were to give the new evidence the same weight as all the evidence they had heard and seen earlier. The jury nodded their agreement.

Magdallena Mason was sworn in. A somber Calvin Sherenian approached.

For the first time, Colleen looked at me in court. She seemed frantic, almost terrified. I smiled a tiny victory smile. That did it. She breathed a long, slow, subtle sigh of relief.

"Miss Mason, you are testifying under a grant of immunity, isn't that correct?"

"Yes."

"Where were you on the night of September third two years ago?"

Magdallena looked blank. "I don't know. What was September third?"

My heart sank for a minute. A reluctant Calvin was forced to make it easier.

"A home belonging to William Farragut the Fourth was burglarized in Presidio Heights that night."

"I was there. Me and my partner, Candira."

"Do you know her full name?" This was killing Calvin.

"Candira Anne Chandler. She's dead. She died a couple a months ago."

"Did you burglarize the house?"

"We started to, but this dude showed up right after we walked in the back door."

"And who was this dude, do you know?"

"I seen his pitcher in the paper. It was that dude you said, Faggarut."

That got the courtroom laughing.

"You mean Farragut?"

"Yeah. The rich dude that owned the place. I seen his pitcher in the paper and on TV, like I said. It freaked me out."

Calvin showed her a photograph of Farragut.

"Is that the man?"

She answered yes and Calvin read into the record that Magdellena had identified William Farragut IV.

"Why did it freak you out?"

Magdallena seemed close to a coronary. She looked at the jury, her wide, sunken eyes pleading. Then she stared at the judge.

"We discussed the conditions of your immunity, Miss Mason. Please answer the question."

Magdallena looked away from Judge Walters, back at Calvin, the walking dead man.

" 'Cause Candira killed him. I told her let's just get out, put the gun down, but she had to stay behind and get somethin' for her troubles. She took them plates, and while she was takin' 'em, that dude Far'gut went for the gun. That's what she told me. It was his gun, we found it lyin' on the bar when we walked in."

"She told you but you didn't see it?" He was still working it, Calvin, trying to destroy his own witness.

"I didn't see it, but I heard it. Two shots. Then she come runnin' out with them silver plates. I wish I'd never seen them plates. Anyways, she was laughin' and all high and shit. . . ." She looked at the judge. "Sorry."

"And what did you do with the plates?"

"She took one and I took one. She sold hers to a pawnbroker she knew in Oakland. I kept mine 'cause I was afraid 'cause I seen on TV the next day that the dude was dead." Her hands shook so hard I thought her fingers might break.

"I never killed nobody, I never shot nobody. Tommy Rivera made us do it. We done other burglaries for him, he was pissed off"—Magdallena caught herself again—"he was mad, 'cause Faggarut's wife give him his walkin' papers. He said it would be a piece of cake, he said the maid was off on Monday nights, they all the time lef' the back door open. He said we could rob the place, and if her and her husband reported it, he'd tell the newspapers he was screwin' her and embarrass both of 'em. Shiiit."

That got the courtroom going. Walters banged for order. Calvin looked like he wanted to curl up and die. His brilliant little game was being destroyed by a raving, dying junkie.

Magdallena crossed her arms and stared sullenly at Calvin.

"No further questions, Your Honor," he said.

"Will the prosecution cross-examine at this time?"

"The prosecution will wait until after the next witness is called by the defense, then cross-examine both of them, Your Honor."

Calvin called Oscar Appell, a Berkeley pawnbroker who looked like he was down to his last forty breaths. His glasses were so thick his eyes seemed to be swimming at the bottom of an aquarium. He walked with an aluminum walker. I just hoped he didn't cash in his chips before he made it from his seat to the witness stand.

An electric buzz went through the courtroom as people twitched and whispered while Appell was seated. Judge Walters banged her gavel for silence. Appell took the oath in a clear, strong voice.

"State your name and occupation, please," said Calvin.

"Oscar Appell. I'm a retired pawnbroker. I live above my old shop on Shattuck Avenue in Berkeley."

"You are testifying under immunity from prosecution, isn't that true?"

"Yes. Judge Walters said if I told the truth, the police would leave me alone."

"Did you purchase a silver plate from Magdallena Mason shortly after September third, two years ago?"

"No. I purchased it from a woman named Candira Chandler. But Miss Mason was with her at the time."

"How much did you pay for the plate?"

"One hundred dollars."

"Do you have your receipt?" To most it appeared that Calvin was trying to preempt the prosecution's cross-examination; in reality he was slyly trying to destroy his own witness.

"No. I destroyed it several days after I bought the plate."

"And why did you do that?"

"The police came by and showed me pictures of two silver plates that were stolen during a burglary. I remember because Mr. Farragut had been murdered and his picture was on television and in all the papers."

"Did you know the plate was stolen when you bought it?"

"I wasn't sure, but I had a hunch. I bought it anyway. I could tell by the workmanship it was a very expensive piece. I had no idea it was as rare as it was, that it was a Renaissance treasure."

"Is this the plate?" Calvin handed it to Appell, who examined it cautiously.

"Yes, it is. The police confiscated it this morning. It isn't something you're likely to forget. I used to just stare at it sometimes."

Calvin had it tagged for evidence.

"Why didn't you come forward the first time the police came looking for it, after the murder of Mr. Farragut?"

"I was scared. I'm an old man, I didn't think my heart could stand even one night in jail. I had been in trouble once before—I bought some stolen items that I thought were legitimate—and I was certain they would send me to jail. My wife had been ill; I thought it might kill her as well."

"You knew Mr. Farragut's wife was standing trial for his murder?"

"Yes. But I didn't see how they could convict her. I read about all the good things she did, trying to help poor people and children. I just didn't believe she was guilty, or that they would convict her. I'm sorry . . . I was afraid."

"No more questions."

Ian Jeffries asked for a brief recess, and the courtroom exploded as soon as Walters banged the gavel.

A half hour later Jeffries, shaken, defeated, made a halfhearted attempt to discredit a sweating, trembling Magdallena Mason and a very poised Oscar Appell. By four o'clock Judge Walters was amending her instructions to the jury, and by four fifteen they were filing out.

Now came the hard part.

35

▼▼▼▼

*M*Y EUPHORIA OVER finding the plates, Magdallena Mason, and Oscar Appell died like a snowflake in the noonday sun the minute the jury filed out to deliberate for the second time.

For three days and three nights, Colleen and I stalked my house like zombies, unable to go anywhere for fear of her being recognized and mobbed. Even when we went up on the roof to escape the shrinking house, she wore a hat and a coat with a high collar.

We tried everything possible to keep ourselves occupied, to keep the spirit alive, except making love. There was too much fear this time for us to ignore. We spent hours just clinging to each other, talking about where we would go and what we would do with the rest of our lives.

We both agreed that it was Oscar's testimony, not Magdallena's, that had turned things around. I still hadn't told her about Calvin's treachery. I could get a conviction overturned on a mistrial, but I was too afraid to think about it. If a jury could convict her after Magdallena's confession and Oscar Appell's statements, after seeing Ghiberti's plates, a second jury might convict her all over again.

We slept fitfully. Colleen woke up with nightmares half a dozen times, crying and shaking in terror.

I had three armed guards working around the clock, two in the house, one watching the neighborhood. I was still afraid for Colleen, for myself. What was Calvin thinking, what were Bearden and Helen Smidge planning, what was John Naftulin up to? Would they try to kill her if she was acquitted, to keep her from getting the diaries?

We talked about how we'd get her out of the courtroom after the verdict—never mentioning the possibility that she'd be convicted. She would say nothing, would not acknowledge me in the courtroom at all. The minute it was over, she'd be hustled out the side door, where she would leave in the Firenze Plumbing van with Arnie, Martha, Henry, and Arnie's cousin Phillip. Once they were sure they weren't being followed, they'd take her to my house and stand guard until I arrived.

On Friday at 4:04 P.M. the phone rang. Zane told me the jury had come back. At five, with the ranks of the media swollen to moblike proportions and over forty harried officers and security guards struggling to maintain order, Zane Neidlinger, Vince Halloran, and I squeezed through a human tunnel formed by the deputies and found our seats in the front row.

The jury filed in. The judge and the bailiff did the formalities. The foreman handed over a slip of paper that was passed and read and then passed again to be read aloud.

The clerk cleared his throat. Colleen stood between Bearden and Sherenian. I could see that she was trembling.

"In the matter of the People versus Colleen Farragut, case number 687731-50, on the charge of murder in the first degree with special circumstances, we find the defendant not guilty."

Pandemonium. Shouts and screams of "Not guilty" echoing through the hallway. Colleen leaned forward, putting both hands on the table as her knees gave way and tears streamed down her face.

Calvin looked lost, Bruce Bearden positively terrified.

Walters banged the gavel. She thanked and dismissed the jury, who were only too happy to flee the scene, and told Colleen she was free to go.

Bailiffs hustled her out a side entrance, where Martha and Arnie were waiting to take her to the van.

"Your Honor," Vincent Halloran said as we both stood. "May we have permission to approach the bench?"

"Is it pertinent to this case?"

"Yes, it is."

Daggers from Sherenian, looks of horror from Bearden.

A few dozen people in the courtroom sensed something happening and stopped, waiting for the next move. I made a point of passing the defense table on my way to the bench. Stopping barely two feet away, I looked up at the clock, then looked first Bearden and then Sherenian straight in the eye.

"Remember the time and the date, gentlemen," I said, nodding toward the clock. "It's the exact moment when your bullshit came to an end."

Vince and I approached Judge Walters.

"Your Honor," Vince said to Walters, "I have a written motion requesting you to have two deputies accompany Mr. Fagen here to the following banks—there are eleven in all—for the purpose of removing the contents of certain safe-deposit boxes and returning them to Mrs. Farragut. I have Mrs. Farragut's signature on an affidavit and power of attorney to Mr. Fagen and myself."

"That's an unusual request, Mr. Halloran. Personal property is not usually the jurisdiction of the marshal's office, nor of the court, unless there's a legal matter involved. You better have some good grounds, Counselor."

"I do, Your Honor," Vincent continued. "We believe that Mr. Sherenian and Mr. Bearden conspired to convict their own client, that they met with and bribed Tommy Rivera to offer perjured testimony, in hopes that Mrs. Farragut would be sent to prison. Had that happened, Mr. Sherenian would have been executor of William Farragut's estate and would have destroyed the personal diaries that Mr. Farragut kept in those safe-deposit boxes listed in our request. There are a number of crimes, we believe, detailed in those diaries, and Mr. Sherenian wanted desperately to keep them from being made public."

Walters looked at Halloran with astonishment, then over at Bearden and Sherenian, who were already packing up and getting ready to run.

"Mr. Sherenian, Mr. Bearden. Please wait a moment," said Walters. I looked at them and winked.

"I've heard some outrageous charges in my brief time, Mr. Halloran, but you're bucking for the blue ribbon. Let's stick with the issue here: what proof do you have that Sherenian and Bearden bribed Mr. Rivera?"

I pulled out the photos of the meeting at the Woodside house and the hotel tape recording from Sherenian's safe, as Vincent explained that Sherenian knew all along that Colleen never offered Tommy money to kill her husband.

Walters really liked the photo of Bearden holding out the briefcase to Tommy while Sherenian shook Tommy's hand. I even gave her records of all the stuff Tommy bought with the money, the new suits and the silk boxer shorts and all.

"Bailiff, please take Mr. Sherenian and Mr. Bearden into custody."

That really started the place rocking again. Walters gave up trying to contain it.

"How long have you known about this, Mr. Fagen?" she asked.

"Mr. Fagen is not an officer of the court, Your Honor," Halloran answered for me. "He came to me this morning with this evidence, and I drafted these documents today." I just smiled sheepishly. Walters knew I'd gotten away with one.

"Any more surprises, gentlemen?"

I was on a roll. "Nothing big, Judge Walters, but we're looking into the possibility that Bearden and perhaps even Mr. Sherenian murdered a few people. At the request of Supervisor Helen Smidge."

"That's not funny, Mr. Fagen."

"I know, Your Honor. Especially when you see the evidence we're accumulating and you find out who else is involved."

"Humor me."

"Inspector John Naftulin, Assistant Coronor Michael Wentworth—"

"If you have any evidence to support these wild accusations I want it turned over to the district attorney's office immediately, or I'll hold you both in contempt."

"It'll be our pleasure, Judge Walters," Halloran told her, "but we need those diaries from the safe-deposit boxes to do it."

She speed-read the order and signed it.

36

▼▼▼▼

B Y CALLING THE banks from the courthouse and telling their officers we had a court order to remove the contents of certain safe-deposit boxes and an escort of two marshals, Vince Halloran, Zane Neidlinger, and I were able to collect 138 diaries bound in black, blue, and brown leather. The diaries went back to 1886, the year William Farragut I started the family tradition. Some years were so busy they needed more than one diary. They filled the entire trunk of Vince's Mercedes.

I pulled out the ones covering the years I was most interested in: 1906, to see if there was any mention of the incident involving my grandfather, and the five years preceding Warren Dillon's murder of Mayor DiMarco and the five years after, up until Dillon's parole and alleged suicide. I also took the diary for the last year of William Farragut IV's miserable life.

The remainder were locked into an antique four-ton Wells Fargo safe in the basement of Vince Halloran's house in Pacific Heights, where Zane Neidlinger would spend the weekend getting an eyeful and a bellyful.

Slipping Colleen past the media had been surprisingly easy for Martha, Arnie, Henry, and Phillip. When I returned home that evening, their shouts of congratulations rattled the windows, hitting a 9.1 on the We-Kicked-Their-Ass scale.

That evening, Colleen and I took my Corvette to Santa Cruz, escorted the entire way by Arnie and Henry in the Firenze Plumbing van.

Colleen had bribed Virginia Riley, her retired schoolteacher friend, to let us have her Victorian mansion in Capitola by buying her a plane ticket to Seattle so she could see her sons and her grandchildren. We spent the next two days, Saturday and Sunday, eating, falling in love, fucking, reading the Farragut diaries, falling in love, fucking, watching the news, fucking, planning our lives, falling in love, and fucking.

When I told Colleen about Calvin's plot, about his bribing Rivera to testify against her, the withholding of the Candira information, and the Sausalito hotel tapes, she sagged into a chair, speechless for almost an hour. Her dismay at my withholding the information from her vanished quickly. She was too happy to hate me.

We drank a toast to the news-at-eleven shot of Calvin and Bearden being taken from the courthouse in handcuffs, followed by a clip of two burly cops dragging a screaming Tommy Rivera up the steps of the city jail.

William II's 1906 diary provided a great deal of insight into my own grandfather, Byron "Bunky" Fagen. According to numerous entries, Byron had waged a two-decade clandestine battle to bring William to justice for murdering Armand Vahanian, the Armenian immigrant whose son was crushed in substandard Farragut housing during the quake. Byron had enlisted the support of sympathetic cops, honest judges, and muckraking journalists in his efforts, all of which were foiled by the devious old man.

Farragut's own handwritten boasting revealed a soul as twisted as any of his numerous progeny. One of his favorite pastimes was buying runaway teenage girls from a flock of kidnappers/procurers, keeping them in a Sausalito brothel and forcing them into sexual servitude when the urge overcame him. My grandfather tried in vain to put him away for that as well, and failed. No wonder Bunky Fagen never made detective.

As for my own war with William IV, it's too bad he died, because I might have gotten him thirty or forty thousand years in prison for the bribes, extortion, kickbacks, tax evasion, money laundering, and strong-arming that started when he was still in college.

Among the recipients of the felonious Farragut largess were more than a few cops, including my favorite—Inspector John Naftulin—two judges, a San Francisco assistant DA, Assistant Coroner Michael Wentworth, a former state attorney general, several California state senators, a U.S. senator, two congressmen, and, of course, the delightful supervisor for life, Miss Helen Smidge. No wonder Farragut worked so many hours; he had a lot of mouths to feed.

Willy IV and Smidge had also orchestrated the murder of Charles Simcic, after Simcic tried to extort money from Farragut in exchange for a promise to keep Farragut's affair with Lynne McBain a secret, as well as the murder of Flynn Pooley, who dared to tell San Franciscans that the sky as well as the earth would fall if they built high rises along the Market Street corridor.

Writing in the diaries, Farragut was lavish with detail, exorbitant in his praise for his own genius. I had to give him credit for the latter. Keeping it all a secret had been his family's twisted masterpiece.

The one thing I'd hoped to prove was that he and Smidge had been directly involved in the murder of Mayor DiMarco, but that turned out not to be the case. The key word being *directly*.

There were pages and pages, chronicling the long and frightening involvement of Farragut and Smidge with Warren Dillon.

It had taken considerable maneuvering by both Smidge and Farragut to get Dillon accepted into the police force, for several of his fellow officers knew of Dillon's high school propensity for getting drunk and bashing blacks and gays with baseball bats and five-irons.

"He was perfect," William IV stated in one entry, "and Helen recognized it when he was still in high school. Handsome, well-spoken, a sports hero, a poster boy for those old-fashioned yahoo values we can still market by the carload, regardless of what lurks beneath. We coached him endlessly, got him into the department, made him a spokesman for traditional mores, and only a few of us knew the unstable, hate-mongering psychopath that he really was."

From the moment that DiMarco was elected, they encouraged—and financed—Warren Dillon's campaign of hatred against him.

When Dillon was fired from the department for receiving bribes from several of Farragut's cronies to cover up everything from money laundering to hate crimes, Smidge, Sherenian, and Farragut negotiated his resignation, avoiding an embarrassing dismissal.

"We really worked on him after that," Farragut wrote. "We told him it was the mayor's fault, that the old queer hated him, that DiMarco alone could give him his pension and his shield back but was out to destroy him and his family."

An entry dated the day after the murder read, "I guess poor Warren just snapped. Today he crawled through a window at City Hall and put five shots in His Honor. My heart is broken, the champagne is chilling."

Another entry detailed the fix in his trial, the travesty of justice that allowed Dillon to serve only four years.

"We owned everything and everybody," Farragut stated. "We either bought them or convinced them that poor Warren was a victim, not a criminal. Just another Bible-quoting, tie-wearing, hardworking white heterosexual gone temporarily over the edge from junk food, job stress, and too much TV. It was our finest moment. Half the investigating team, the judge, an incompetent prosecutor—it was our tune they danced to. That's the secret to the family's hundred years of success: you deify the dishonest and then pander to the gullible. Progress is our biggest enemy."

He concluded with, "Even the jury was shocked when they heard the sentence that Dillon got. Had they known, every one of them would have voted for first-degree murder instead of manslaughter."

After parole, they went at Dillon relentlessly, telling him a "liberal hit squad" of "queers and Communists" had a contract on his life, until finally he committed suicide.

Neither Smidge nor Farragut had held the smoking gun; they had been too clever. All they were guilty of, as far as involvement in the murder, was a well-orchestrated campaign of feeding hope and hatred to a pinstripe suit with a white-hooded mind.

But the trial was different. Farragut's notes on the corroboration and co-opting of the trial were everything I'd hoped for. When the sections were published, everyone would know that I had been fired unjustly, that I was not a lunatic, that justice had been raped on that horrible day in San Francisco.

I went to bed that night and slept the sleep of vindication— Colleen and I were both too tired to do it again.

37
▼▼▼▼

*W*E RETURNED FROM Santa Cruz to San Francisco on Monday morning, driving at an almost leisurely pace north on Highway 1. We talked about our plans for leaving the city, for hiding out in the Italian Alps until the fury expired, which we reckoned would be ten years at least.

I turned Colleen over to Martha, Arnie, Henry, and Phil when we arrived in San Francisco. She had a lot of banks to visit, a lot of papers to sign to free up her property. She was making arrangements to sell everything, to give a tithe to a dozen charities, which would come to a good thirty million dollars. Later she planned to give a lot more. Christmas was coming early for a lot of people who needed it.

I sat in my house, alone for the first time in weeks, looking at it the way a college kid does when returning home for his first vacation. Everything seemed different, strange, as though I'd been gone a long time instead of a few days.

Somewhere in the late afternoon, I opened the diary covering William Farragut IV's last days on Earth, wondering what he'd been up to before he died.

It was then, while reading the pages of his last diary, that a tiny memo gave me my biggest shock.

At six thirty, Colleen arrived at the house, escorted by the City

Lights crew. She gave me a check for one million dollars. I handed pre-written checks to Arnie, Martha, and Henry for $166,666.66 each, thanking them for their help, and asked Arnie to wait downstairs for me.

I took Colleen upstairs and looked at her. She sensed trouble, but I could see she didn't want to speak if she didn't have to.

"I know," I said.

"What do you know?" she asked.

"About the plates."

She held her head down in shame. "How do you know about the plates?"

"Your husband was fanatical about his diaries. He recorded everything. One of the last notes he entered on the day he was murdered mentioned Consuela's brother driving from San Jose to pick up Consuela and take the plates back to his shop. Consuela's brother works for a silversmith, he's an expert on cleaning and restoration. William gave him five hundred dollars cash as a down payment. Candira Anne Chandler and Magdallena Mason never stole the plates, never sold one of them to Oscar Appell. You had them hidden after the murder. Tell me the story. Don't leave anything out."

It took her a few moments before she could speak. "William and I were arguing in his room, as I said. I found out that day that he had evicted some old man from an apartment he owned. The old man had lived there for thirty-five years and couldn't afford a forty-dollar rent increase. The old man hung himself in the apartment.

"William's words were, 'One less parasite on social security.' I screamed at him, and he screamed back. In the middle of the argument he went downstairs to get another drink. When he walked into the den, he surprised two burglars. When they ran he grabbed his gun and chased them through the back yard until they made it over the wall.

"I watched the whole thing from my window upstairs. He

looked up and saw me and he screamed, 'Get down here, you fucking bitch, you whore!'

"I went down. He was crazy, he thought I'd sent them. He thought they were the 'trash' that I was giving his money to, and this was how they wanted to pay him back. He threw the gun at me. I ducked—it just missed my head. Then he slapped me across the face, just like my stepfather did when he tried to rape me when I was fifteen.

"I went berserk. Somehow I got away from William. I grabbed the gun, pointed it at him, screaming I would kill him if he ever touched me again."

"He dared me to do it, he called me a gutless tramp, a whore, he started toward me.

"I shot him twice."

The tears were streaming. She looked at me like a child, totally lost and helpless.

"I was hysterical. I didn't think anyone could hear the shots. After a few minutes, I checked his pulse.... An hour later Consuela called. I asked her and her brother to come up, to help me. When they got there, they told me not to admit to anything. They said if the police caught the burglars, the burglars would deny it, and I would deny it, and maybe they wouldn't be able to pin it on anyone.

"But the burglars hadn't touched or taken anything. To make it look better, I did that lousy job faking the burglary—my heart almost stopped when Inspector Naftulin figured it out. Afterward, I took a shower for thirty minutes, I washed my clothes, I sent Consuela and her brother back to San Jose. They're the only ones who know the truth."

"And you kept the plates."

"I kept the plates in San Jose, in Consuela's brother's house. He adored me, I'd helped him and his family out a dozen times."

"And what about Magdallena, Candira, the pawnbroker? Or should I figure it out, and you stop me if I'm wrong?"

She nodded, unable to continue.

"You knew if the burglars were never found, you'd be dead meat. You knew the burglars were women, but you couldn't admit it because you'd have to admit having seen them, and if you saw them, you'd have to explain why you didn't call the cops or come down to check on your husband. You waited to call until the next morning because you were scared, because you had to think everything through.

"When Hayden Phillips and the cops couldn't find the burglars, you came to me. Did you suspect Calvin was doing a job on you?"

"I suspected the cops, the DA, everyone but him. He was so supportive, so helpful when I got arrested. I wouldn't have made it as far as I did without him. I still have a hard time believing it."

"So you hired me because you knew my desire to redeem myself would mean you could be sure I wouldn't be bought off by someone."

She nodded. I thought for a minute as she wept silently, taking a tissue from her purse, wiping her nose.

"When I told you I'd narrowed the hunt down to two friends of Candira's, I showed you their files, and you memorized the names and addresses. You went to Patsy's apartment, no . . . you had Consuela go." She nodded. "Consuela told Patsy about the two names, Sharon Dean and Magdallena Mason, and Patsy remembered Magdallena's name, right?"

She nodded again. "Yes. Patsy remembered her mother calling once, trying to borrow money to bail Magdallena out of jail. That's when she figured Magdallena must have been her mother's real partner. I offered Patsy money to cooperate."

"With Candira dead and Magdallena dying from AIDS," I continued, figuring it out as I went, "Patsy showed up at Magdallena's apartment, waving the promise of fifty grand, plus whatever you were offering, and convinced Magdallena to go along with it. She must have been the other burglar; her story was too convincing. All Magdallena had to do was add the part about Candira firing the two shots and laughing about it afterward. The stuff about Tommy was true; he did set it all up."

"I never suspected Tommy," she said.

"And finding Magdallena when I did couldn't have been better timing—I guess you just got lucky on that. If I'd found her sooner, they could have stopped the trial, they could have investigated further, maybe found a way to kick Magdallena's story, and the pawnbroker's. Now, even if the cops or the DA do find out, there's nothing they can do. Double jeopardy. You can't be retried." I shook my head.

"The only one I can't quite figure out is Oscar Appell. How did you find him?"

"I went to school in Berkeley. I rented an apartment that he owned years ago. He and his wife became like surrogate parents to me. He called me a few days after William's death, offering his help. I've had him lined up since a month after the burglary."

"How much did you pay for all this?"

"I promised them a hundred thousand apiece—Patsy, Magdallena, and Oscar."

"And they can't ever say anything about it or they'll go to jail for perjury and obstruction of justice."

She stood there a minute, sobbing.

"I have to go, I can't stay here with you knowing I betrayed you," she said when she could speak. "Please don't hate me, Francis, I was desperate and I was afraid."

"You could have told the truth, called it self-defense."

"Oh, yeah, they would have believed that in a New York minute." She cried some more. My heart was melting, and I didn't need that right now. "I'm going, Frank, but I love you," she said. "Call me when you decide what you want to do. Call me soon, please don't make me wait. I'll live by whatever you decide."

"I'll have Arnie drive you back to the house," I said. "I'll arrange for four guards around the clock, off-duty cops I'd trust with my own life."

She threw her arms around me, still sobbing, and kissed my neck. I held her tight. I didn't want to but I couldn't help myself. We went downstairs without speaking, where I turned her over to

Arnie after checking the street in all directions. It was dark and empty. I turned and walked back up the steps to call for security on the Farragut mansion.

I'd taken only five steps when I heard the shots. Five of them in quick succession. I grabbed the .380 from my ankle holster and leapt back down the five steps, hitting the bottom one awkwardly and twisting my ankle. Throwing open the door, I saw Tommy Rivera standing with his back to me, his arms stretched out toward Arnie, who stood facing him with his hands up.

Colleen was on the ground, her blood running down the steep hill in tiny rivulets.

Rivera was crazed, screaming. "I'll kill you, you bitch, for what you did to me, I'll kill you!"

I pointed my gun at the middle of his back, screaming, "Drop it, Rivera, or I'll kill you, so help me God I'll kill you."

He started to lower his gun. I was desperate to get to Colleen. Tommy lowered the gun to his side, then suddenly sprinted down Lombard Street. I couldn't shoot him in the back.

Arnie and I met at Colleen's side. By then people were screaming out of their windows, hysterical, calling for police. Several people had already stepped from doorways.

She wasn't breathing: he'd gotten all five shots in her chest. Her hair was soaked with her own blood. An old doctor who lived across the street came running with his bag.

I told Arnie to stay with her until the ambulance arrived, and then I went berserk.

I ran after Tommy Rivera.

He had almost a full-block lead on me when he turned left on Grant, heading toward Broadway. He looked over his shoulder and saw me, turned, pointed his gun. I ducked into a doorway, and he took off again.

His gun was a chrome-plated detective's special with the heavy magnum frame and a three-inch barrel. I knew he had only one bullet left.

My only thought was not to draw his fire and not to fire until

I had a clear, safe backdrop and wouldn't kill an innocent person.

Tommy ran like a crazy man, but I was crazier, and I had longer legs. I sprinted after him, ignoring the pain in my twisted ankle, and on every stride I must have gained six inches. When he turned right on Union Street, his lead was down to half a block. He turned left on Stockton, then left on Green Street.

He bumped two people on Green, sending one sprawling into the street, the other crashing into some trash cans. They both looked dazed but unhurt as I ran past, not that I would have stopped. But the impact slowed him down. By the time he turned right back onto Grant Avenue, I was only a hundred yards behind and gaining.

He ran into a small crowd of people, jumped up on the steps of the Coffee Gallery, aimed his gun. I didn't see him until just before he pulled the trigger. I threw myself to the ground. The bullet hit the wall of a bakery a block away, harming no one. A few dozen people ducked, screaming.

My hands and knees were banged and bleeding, and it took me a second to get going, but the adrenaline rush was even stronger.

Tommy zigzagged back and forth across the street but I was getting closer with every step. I suddenly realized he might have reloaded the gun while I was down. Twenty yards separated us when Tommy hopped the curb in front of the Caffè Trieste at the corner of Grant and Vallejo.

He turned and pointed his gun at me. Diving forward so I would have an upward angle and wouldn't hit anyone in the restaurant behind him, I fired three times before I hit the ground. The first two shots hit his chest; the third, as he was falling, entered under his chin and exploded through the top of his head.

He fell backward through the Trieste's picture window with a horrendous crash, landing on two female chess players, who screamed hysterically.

When I got to him there was pandemonium inside, people begging me not to kill them. I pocketed my gun and pulled out my ID.

Tommy was dead.

So was Colleen.

I identified her body at the morgue four hours later, after signing my statement at Central Station a block away.

38

▼▼▼▼

*T*HERE'S A PLACE I go when I need a little peace and quiet, a walking meditation, a chance to get away from myself. It's on a hill overlooking the Presidio, the Bay, and my bridge. It's hard to be selfish there, or to lie to yourself or to wallow in self-pity.

Sixty-two Fagens are laid out there, sort of a horizontal family tree going back to my great-grandparents, Arthur Fagen and Millicent DiPolito, and ending with my parents.

There is a church in the Mission that employs poor and homeless people by giving them flowers to sell. On the way I had stopped and bought sixty-two bouquets with the money I received from Colleen. I gave Father Ramirez fifty thousand, a tithe of my share of the one million, and asked him to split it among his poorest and hardest working. I lit a candle for Colleen Farragut before I left. Then I lit ten more.

I had to take my stakeout vehicle, the Firenze Plumbing van, to haul all the flowers. One by one, I laid each of the bouquets on a little granite headstone. I don't think I had ever felt so many conflicting emotions at one time. Not since the night I met Colleen.

Out there in the city, a firestorm was brewing such as they had not seen since April 18, 1906. Every day the *Clarion* was publishing excerpts from the Farragut diaries, edited and introduced by Zane, revealing greed and corruption dating back almost to the Civil War. That morning's edition had carried an account of a police hit squad carrying out the murder of a reformist police chief in 1905.

The DA's office might soon need an accountant to tally the indictments that were mounting up against Calvin Sherenian and Bruce Bearden. Bearden, Inspector John Naftulin, and Supervisor Helen Smidge had already been charged with murder one in the deaths of Andrew Simcic and Lynne McBain, with Assistant Coroner Michael Wentworth charged as an accessory. Thanks to another detailed Farragut entry, homicide inspectors were reexamining the alleged suicide of Flynn Pooley, and it was expected that it too would be added to the debit on the Smidge-Bearden-Naftulin balance sheet.

Smidge had been hauled out of City Hall in handcuffs, in front of the largest cheering crowd of her pathetic career. While pinning conspiracy to commit murder on her for the killing of Mayor DiMarco seemed impossible, blackmail, pandering, bribery, and extortion indictments were being added daily to the roster of charges against her. An imminent indictment against Smidge and Calvin for helping to rig the trial of Warren Dillon was the hottest topic of downtown gossip.

Helen Smidge was using the Nixon defense, screaming that she was the victim of political snipers from the jealous left. Smidge would inherit the cell at Frontera that had once awaited Colleen Farragut, unless they gassed her, which seemed unlikely.

In the middle of it all was Zane Neidlinger, a shoo-in for a Pulitzer, six-figure book contracts swirling around him. After thirty-one years of hard work, he deserved it.

For myself, relief and vindication had given way to an overwhelming sense of irony. When I was a good cop, I was run off the force; now that I had been duped by a client, I was the hero of the city. I had exonerated myself, reclaimed my honor by freeing the person who had actually killed William Farragut. Only Consuela, her brother, and I knew the real story. I couldn't even tell Zane.

The ultimate irony was that I didn't care. I didn't care that

Farragut was dead, I didn't care that Colleen had shot him. Greed and inhumanity had gotten their just rewards, finally. Colleen, perhaps thanks to some twisted poetic justice, had gotten hers.

If there was a hero in the whole sordid affair, it was the most unlikely one: Lynne McBain. An independent autopsy report showed blunt instrument trauma and rope burns on her wrists and ankles, indicating she had been tied in a chair and beaten. She had never given her final abusers my name, never tipped them off to my investigation. The entire story pivoted on her last, courageous act. Perhaps she had something to prove, as I did.

I wanted to tell Arthur and Bunky and Francis Paul and the eight other cops laid out at my feet that the war was over, that we had won, that we had been right all along. The Farraguts were as bad as we thought, and then some.

I'm not sure they would have accepted that. The price, they might have said, was too dear—justice betrayed, justice deceived. I could live with that. I had done my best and the bad guys were headed where they belonged. The crusade was over.

Someday I would take my place next to them, in a little plot already picked out and paid for by my parents, near a tall, thin redwood. I liked the view from my spot, I liked knowing that I could rest for eternity instead of haunting old lady Farragut or a drafty Tudor-style mansion moaning *Where're the diaries, where're the diaries?* We had come in together, the Fagens and Farraguts, and we would go out together.

With me a piece of the family history would end, the parade of cops, the line of city dwellers, a long line of people who had loved this city and were willing to pay almost any price to protect it.

I looked out over the mouth of the Bay to the Pacific beyond. In a will Colleen had written years earlier, she bequeathed half of her money to homeless and abused children, the other half to be split among her six sisters. I don't think she ever expected it to be three hundred million—at least, not until she put the two bullets into William.

She had also requested her body be cremated and scattered over the Pacific. I'd taken her sisters out in my boat to scatter her ashes, a tearful, solemn affair. Two of the women had gotten seasick on the way back.

Colleen's stepfather, sweetheart to the end, had filed suit against the Farragut estate from his cell at San Luis Obispo Men's Colony, claiming he was deprived of his lawful share. He was there doing two to ten for molesting a twelve-year-old girl. The judge would get a big laugh out of that one.

The hardest part was telling the story to Eileen Farragut, as I had promised, and having to leave out the truth about what really happened. I had not cried until then, but seeing Eileen's tears did me in.

When the coroner performed his autopsy on Colleen, he found out that she was three weeks pregnant. The media was having a field day; the father was Calvin, Bruce Bearden, Tommy Rivera, myself, or the ghost of her late husband, depending on which tabloid you read.

I missed Colleen. I don't know if I could have loved her and lived with her knowing what she'd done, but I would have tried. I had known her exactly one month to the day when Tommy Rivera killed her, and she had changed my life forever.

I wondered if the baby would have been a boy or a girl, if maybe, by some slim chance, the line of Fagen city dwellers and police officers died with her instead of with me.

For the first time in my life, I needed to leave the city. In a few hours, a moving truck would take all my belongings to storage. My sister in Mill Valley was renting the house to a friend at the University of California Medical School.

That evening I would be on a flight to Italy, en route to Valtournanche in the Italian Alps, near the Swiss and French borders. I would live in the small stone and timber house where my mother had been born. I'd always imagined living there someday, but never quite this early, never under circumstances like these.

On our last night together, Colleen and I made plans to live in that house after the trial. It would have been a wonderful place to raise a child, to sit on our front porch and watch the stella alpina bloom, the ibex grazing at the foot of Monte Cervino, the Italian side of the Matterhorn.

I had found the love of my life. But with every great love, there's always a hidden agenda, a chink in the *amore*. Either they leave the cat dish in the sink or they killed somebody. In every case, the crash is as painful as the ascent was delirious. The guy who said it was better to have loved and lost than never to have loved at all didn't say it the morning he got the news.

I knew one thing for sure, that I was finished being a private detective for a while, at least until the storm blew over. I'd fulfilled the Fagen agenda, the destiny I had dreamed of and abandoned until the night I met Colleen at the opera.

I didn't think it would be so hard to give it all up, to leave it behind for a while.

Colleen was going to be a tough act to follow.